CONTENTS

1. A Death   1

2. The Lodge   6

3. The Interview   11

4. The Old Rectory   17

5. Making A List   25

6. Muldoon   30

7. A Funeral   38

8. Cooperation   43

9. From The Pale To The West   51

10. The Vicarage   63

11. A Sad Encounter   74

12. The Dinner Party   83

13. Baroda (Newbridge)   91

14. A Phone Call   100

15. Enigmas   108

16. Briar's Cottage   115

17. The Spring Ball   125

18. A Recap   136

19.	A Lull In The Investigation	140
20.	Invitations	146
21.	A Second Death	156
22.	999 Call	163
23.	A Second Funeral	172
24.	A Strange Occorance	180
25.	Life Goes On?	184
26.	More Alibis	192
27.	An Epiphany	204
28.	An Arrest	210
29.	The Dog	221
30.	Loughfarraig House	231
31.	Deliverance	241
32.	A Wedding	250
33.	Accident or Attempted Murder?	259
34.	A Reassessment	269
35.	New Appeals	279
36.	"Keep The Faith!"	289
37.	The Missing Witness	296
38.	The Denouement	300

Chapter 1

A Death

On Tuesday morning there was a murder in the townland of Briarstown in North Kildare. Briarstown is a quiet country area with rolling green fields.

It is a mixed townland. There are big dairy farms and small cottages dotted on the landscape. On the surface, nothing much ever happens here. The inhabitants for the most part, go to church every Sunday. There are two churches, one for the Church of Ireland congregation and a larger, more ornate one for the Catholic congregation. Everyone seems to muddle along.

So, imagine the reaction, when the news filtered through the community, that there had been a violent death on one of the farms.

Jinny Galdstone had been found by her husband Adam at 8am, when he went to look for her. He had become worried as she hadn't returned from the milking parlour. He found her in a pool of blood, lying on her back, beside the cows who were lowing and agitated in their stalls.

Great commotion ensued. The police were informed. Adam had run back to the house in great distress, and dialled the nearest police station.

At around 9am sirens were heard in the townland. An ambulance and two garda cars were seen travelling at speed towards the Galdstone farm.

Inspector John Muldoon and his sidekick Sergeant Michael Dunne arrived at the farmhouse at 9.15 on the Tuesday morning.

The Inspector was a tall slender man with short brown hair and light blue eyes. His assistant was shorter and more rotund. John Muldoon drove into the yard. Adam was sitting with his head in his hands on the steps that led up to the parlour. There was a young male garda standing beside him who looked in complete shock. His face was as white as a sheet, and he looked like a rabbit in the headlights. When Muldoon approached him, he could smell vomit. The poor young garda had obviously been very ill, having viewed the scene.

"Good morning Liam, will you show me the scene please?" He turned to address Adam. "Mr. Galdstone, I assume? I know this is a dreadful time for you, and please accept my sincere condolences on the death of your wife."

"Thank you," Adam replied, and looked up at the two men.

He had obviously been crying as his eyes were red and swollen.

"I think it might be better if you were to return to the house, as we have to examine the scene, and once that's done we will call up to you. Are there other people in the house?"

"My daughter Clara is there with her son Jack, and my son John is on the way," he replied tearfully.

"Liam, will you ask Eoin to accompany Mr. Galdstone to the house."

Eoin was the other young garda, who was standing at the entrance to the hayshed. Eoin escorted the distraught Adam away from the parlour, and they headed towards the main house, which was a two minute walk from the farm yard. There was a laneway that led from the farm yard to the house.

When you entered the yard the milking parlour was straight ahead. On one side there was a hayshed, which held the feed for the winter. On the other side was a large barn where the cows spent the winter months. John Muldoon looked around him to take in his surrounds.

"Lead on Liam," he said.

Liam reluctantly led the way up the steps and into the parlour.

John Muldoon had never dealt with a violent death before. The scene before him looked surreal – like a vision from one of the murder programmes he had seen on the television. Of course, it was a lot worse in reality. The smell was strange. He wasn't a country boy, so wasn't used to the smell of cow dung. Immediately, he saw Jinny's body. She was lying on her back, her long blond hair, like Medusa's on the ground. Her eyes were wide open and lifeless, staring at the ceiling. Her arms and legs were splayed, and there seemed to be blood everywhere. She had been stabbed numerous times. He felt a bit dizzy and nauseous. He tried to compose himself. The cows were on either side of the body. They were moving restlessly. Their udders were attached to tubes, which fed the "cauldrons". There was no milk running through the tubes. The milking was finished, and the cows wanted to be released, and to escape back to the fields.

John Muldoon turned his attention back to the body. He counted five stab wounds in the chest. One struck the heart. There were a few defence wounds on her hands. There was no sign of a murder weapon.

"The coroner is here," said a voice from behind Muldoon.

"Good morning Doctor, it is a dreadful scene. I'll leave you to it. I'm going up to the house to see the husband."

Muldoon and his sidekick walked the short distance from the yard to the house.

The avenue led to a well maintained, fairly modern looking house. The gardens surrounding it were full of daffodils and other spring flowers. The hedges were box like, and there was an orchard to one side.

Muldoon knocked at the door. It was answered by a young woman in her early twenties. She looked very angry. She obviously hadn't been crying.

"Come in, I'm Clara, their daughter."

"Hello Clara, I'm so sorry for your troubles," said Muldoon.

The Inspector followed behind as she led him and Dunne into the kitchen. Adam was sitting at the kitchen table, with a cup of something in front of him, which was untouched, staring into space.

"Hello Mr. Galdstone, I'm sorry but I must ask you a few questions now while it is fresh in your head. I promise it won't take long."

"That's okay, go ahead," muttered Adam.

"Can you tell me when did you see your wife last?" asked Muldoon.

"I didn't see her at all this morning. She gets up around 6am to get the cows into the parlour for milking. She likes to do it on her own. She's normally back to get breakfast at around eight o'clock. When she didn't get back at the usual time, I went down to check on things, and I found her lying there. It was awful! I just stood there. I couldn't believe what I was seeing. I ran back up to the house and called the guards. Why would anyone do this to her? There's nothing to steal down there."

"It doesn't appear like a robbery," said Muldoon. "I'm sorry to ask this, but did your wife have any enemies, or did she have any rows or disputes with anyone recently?"

Adam and Clara looked at each other.

"Remember what that fecker down the road did? He really upset Mum about the land," muttered Clara.

"Who are you talking about?" asked Muldoon.

"Alexander de Bruin." whispered Adam.

Chapter 2

The Lodge

Alexander de Bruin, his wife Monique, and their three children lived in The Lodge, Briarstown, County Kildare. They were neighbours of the Galdstones – not immediate neighbours as there was another farm in between them. A lovely family called the Brownes lived here. They were mixed farmers on 50 acres, but it was just a hobby for them, as they were both solicitors. Alexander was a retired army officer, stationed for much of his service in the Curragh Camp. His wife was half Irish, half French. They had met when they were in UCG in the early 1970s. He was a cadet at the time, staying in barracks. They both studied business. Having finished his degree, Alexander was stationed in the Curragh Camp. Monique got a very good job with a large accounting firm in Dublin. They married in their early 20s and lived in army quarters in the camp. They spent 10 very happy years in quarters. Their two daughters were born there. It was a very close knit community. Most of their social life was spent in the messes. Army life was very happy. Alexander was transferred to Army Intelligence in latter years and had to commute to Dublin. Monique decided to become a consultant and so set up her own business, which meant she no longer had the long drive to Dublin.

They decided it was time to leave quarters, and buy their own place. They wanted to live in the country as they were both from farming backgrounds, and thought that it would be lovely for the children to be raised in the country, And also, Monique was pregnant with her third child.

And, so it was that they moved to The Lodge in Briarstown.

The Lodge had been, in times gone by, the manager's cottage of a large estate. The big house no longer existed and the land had been divided. The Lodge was large for a cottage, and the de Bruins did some renovations before they moved in. The house had walls of old stone, painted white. There was a short avenue that led up to the house, a yard to the right with some outhouses, a large barn, stables and a manege for the horses. The two girls, Alice and Maeve loved their ponies, and spent every spare minute riding them out. Young Max had absolutely no interest in them, but adored their two Bernese mountain dogs. He spent every spare moment at the local GAA club, playing hurling.

They had 40 acres with the house. They only needed 10 acres for their ponies and horses, so when asked by the Galdstones to lease it, they agreed that they would, but only as conacre as they just wanted to keep control of their own land, in case their situation changed. They also thought, there was something about the Galdstones that they didn't quite trust.

And so it came to pass that the de Bruins rented their land to the Galdstones on a year to year basis.

Two years before the murder, Alexander de Bruin had retired from the army and joined his wife's company as a director. They were very successful, and spent most of their time at their cottage, and devoted their time to rearing their children.

Both Alexander and Monique had heard the sirens on the Tuesday morning. They had hoped that no one was seriously ill or that there hadn't been a dreadful accident.

That day, Damien Browne knocked on the door, and gave them the horrifying news.

Everyone in the townland was shocked and frightened. There was a lunatic murderer at large. People's doors were locked for the first time.

Early the following morning, there was a great influx of young Gardai. There was an intense search ongoing. No one quite knew exactly what they were searching for. They were operating in lines with sticks, poking at the ground. There was a group on the road that led from the Browne's house to The Lodge. They were searching feverishly in the ditches. Suddenly a shout was heard.

"Found it." A young Garda was holding up what looked like a steak knife.

Monique de Bruin witnessed the find. She had been walking with the dogs in the field, which her daughters called the jumping field, as they had made some jumps from logs and tyres to practice jumping with their ponies. It was the same field where wild mushrooms flourish in October every year. Many hours of happy wild mushroom hunting had been spent here.

Monique walked back quickly to the house to tell her husband what had transpired. She went in through the courtyard behind the house, which led to the back door. The two dogs were jumping and panting, excited to get home. The two Bernese lay down in their beds in the kitchen, chewing on their treats, which Monique had given them. She then made her way into the sitting room, where she knew her husband would be working on a clients income tax returns.

Monique opened the door into a large room, with a floor to ceiling window, which looked out onto the field behind the house. There was an antique fireplace where an open fire made the room seem very cosy, despite it's size. Alexander was sitting at his desk, concentrating very hard on his work. The housekeeper was also there, busily dusting the books on the wooden bookcase, which filled one wall of the room. The bookcase was crammed full of books of every genre. There was a beautiful set of Henry James novels, which included The Bostonians, The Portrait of a Lady and several more, all with blue leather covers and gold lettering. French novels also adorned the shelves - Simenon, Moliere, Camus, together with poetry books, a whole set of Agatha Christie novels, history books and science tomes. It was a veritable library. The two bottom shelves held children's books, which included Roald Dahl, Beatrix Potter, Winnie the Pooh, and just about every Enid Blyton book available – The Secret Seven, Famous Five, and all the Mallory Towers novels. The children were obviously great fans of Enid Blyton.

"Good afternoon Mrs. Hannigan, how are you today? There is a lot of activity outside at the moment. It's a very sad situation and really frightening for everyone," said Monique.

Mrs. Joan Hannigan was a very petite lady with short brown hair. She abounded with energy and was always very keen to work. The de Bruins had known her since their time living in the Curragh Camp. She was married to Sergeant Liam Hannigan, who had served with Alexander, and even spent six months on a mission abroad with him. The Hannigans had lived in quarters in camp also, but in a two up two down red brick terraced house, which did not have an indoor toilet. The toilet was at the bottom of the back garden. They had two children, who were now grown-up and lived in London. Jean was a nurse and John a teacher. Mrs. Joan Hannigan was very proud of her two children. She had also minded the de Bruin children, when they were small. The two women were really friends, and their relationship was more than just one of a housekeeper and employer. There was an affection between them. That was obvious. The Hannigans had also moved out of quarters, when the sergeant retired, and now lived in a village, about 10 minutes drive from The Lodge.

Jean had a small red Fiat car that she loved driving to her various cleaning jobs. She worked at The Lodge on two mornings, and also cleaned for other families in the area, as she was a real workaholic, and also loved chatting and socialising.

" All fine, Mrs. de Bruin." replied Mrs. Hannigan. "It is indeed an awful business. I was up at the Galdstones only last Friday and they all seemed grand. I just can't believe that this could happen here, out in the middle of nowhere."

"I'm sure the guards will get to the bottom of it fairly quickly. There are an awful lot of them searching the whole area," answered Monique. "When I was out with the dogs, one of the young guards found what looked like a knife in our ditch between ourselves and the Brownes."

Alexander looked up from his work with a frown on his face.

"Strange place to hide a murder weapon, if it is indeed the murder weapon," he said.

Chapter 3

The Interview

At 10.30 the following morning there was a knock at the door of The Lodge. Monique answered the door and before her stood two men whom she hadn't seen before.

"Good morning, Mrs. de Bruin I presume. I am Inspector John Muldoon, and this is Sergeant Dunne. We are investigating the murder of your neighbour Jinny Gladstone. May we come in? We need to speak to both yourself and your husband. Is he available?"

"Yes indeed," replied Monique. "He is in the study. Please come through gentlemen."

The two men followed Monique into the large study, where Alexander was again at his desk, engrossed in his work.

"Alexander, these two gentlemen are from the police, Inspector Muldoon and Sergeant Dunne. They want to speak to us about the murder. Please sit down gentlemen. Would you like some refreshments, tea, coffee a mineral?"

"No thank you, Mrs. de Bruin," said Inspector Muldoon.

"How may we help you?" asked Alexander.

"Well, allow me to get straight to the point. We wish to interview all the Galdstones' neighbours, but particularly anyone who may not have been on good terms with the victim, Commandant."

Both Alexander and Monique were immediately aware of the formality of the interview, as Muldoon had used Alexander's army title.

"Please ask anything you wish," said Monique.

"While interviewing Adam Gladstone, he claimed that you had a serious altercation, a few weeks back with his wife. He insists that you really upset her and threatened her. Clara, her daughter said that she was a witness to this. You, Commandant de Bruin are the only person in the neighbourhood on bad terms with the victim, according to her husband and daughter. I wonder could you explain this to me. Could you also tell me if you have an alibi for yesterday morning, that is between 6am and 8am, when the body was found."

Alexander was somewhat taken aback by this line of questioning. Monique sat very quietly in her chair. There was, what seemed like a long silence before Alexander answered.

"I can assure you Inspector, that there was no altercation with Jinny Galdstone. I don't know whether you are aware of REPS schemes, where landowners take part in land preservation. Monique and I had decided to apply for such a scheme. In order to do this, our agricultural advisor asked us to check if the Galdstones had used our land maps for their scheme. I didn't believe they had, as we had not been asked about it or given our permission. While out for a walk, I saw Jinny in the yard and approached her. She looked a bit shocked at the question and said that she would check. Her daughter was also in the yard with her son. I received a phone call that evening, to state that they had used our maps without our permission. I certainly told her that I was not at all pleased that this should have been done behind our back, and that the land would no longer be available to them. I haven't spoken to them since. I don't understand what Clara thinks she witnessed, because, as far as I was concerned, the initial face-to-face conversation was extremely civil. I imagine Jinny may have been upset, following the conversation, as they had been caught out in what I would call underhand behaviour."

The inspector listened very carefully to this explanation and the sergeant took very detailed notes.

"And now, what about your alibi, Commandant de Bruin?"

Monique had been watching the inspector's face very intently, as Alexander gave his account of the meeting with Jinny Galdstone in the farm yard. She was convinced that Inspector John Muldoon did not believe her husband. She looked over at Alexander, and knew that the alibi explanation would certainly be suspect, in the eyes of the two policemen.

"So," began Alexander, "I don't have an alibi, as I was on my own. I usually get up at around 5.30 or 6 o'clock, as I did yesterday morning. I took the two dogs out to the field for a walk. I checked on the horses, making sure they had enough feed and water. One of the ponies is stabled, as she has a touch of laminitis. I cleaned out her stable and gave her some hay. They can't be out on grass when they have laminitis, as it's the rich grass that causes the swelling inside the hoof. They can become very lame, and it's very painful. I walked around, as I do most mornings, and checked the fencing. I came in for breakfast at around 7.30. I didn't see a soul."

Sergeant Dunne was still scribbling away. Inspector Muldoon was looking at Alexander with even more suspicion.

"Mrs. de Bruin, do you own a set of steak knives by any chance?" asked the inspector.

"Yes, indeed I do," she said. "Would you like to see them? They are in the kitchen – if you'd like to see them."

Monique led the way out of the parlour, down the hall, and into the kitchen, which looked out onto a small courtyard. She walked over to one of the counters and pointed to a set of six steak knives.

"There you are, Inspector, all present and correct."

Muldoon examined the set carefully.

Then he asked. "May I take them with me for further examination?"

"Of course, we have nothing to hide."

"I presume that Mrs Galdstone was murdered with a knife similar to those?" interrupted Alexander.

"We can't make any comments at the moment. It's an ongoing investigation."

The sergeant placed the set of knives and the holder into an evidence bag.

"That will be all for now, we'll be in touch again to be sure. Thank you for your cooperation."

Monique led the two men to the front door and showed them out.

"Good day, gentlemen."

"Goodbye, Mrs. de Bruin."

She then returned to her husband, who was standing looking out the window into the green luscious field. As Monique entered the room, he turned around to face her.

"Well, we know where this is going," he whispered.

"We do indeed," she replied, "those nincompoops think that you murdered Jinny Gladstone."

Alexander and Monique stood looking at each other in silence for a few moments. They both realised the gravity of the situation. Monique was worried, but knew her husband very well. He had had a very distinguished army career. He was not a man to panic under stress. Actually, she couldn't recall ever seeing him stressed.

He had weathered many a serious situation, both while serving abroad and at home. He had even been under fire on one of his peacekeeping missions to Africa.

Alexander had investigated several cases while in Army Intelligence. He was a very cool, calculating, methodical man. He had a wonderful mathematical brain with the ability to logically make deductions from the evidence before him. She was aware that he had been lead investigator in a number of cases, but knew nothing about them, as Alexander was not in a position to discuss them, as they were top-secret.

"You know what we'll have to do, sweetheart. We'll have to put everything on hold, and you'll have to investigate this. We can't leave it to those two nitwits or you'll end up in court or behind bars."

Alexander nodded and both he and Monique sat down at the desk.

"So, what do they think they have on me? Firstly, motive. The so called altercation, that wasn't an altercation. Muldoon and Dunne obviously believe Adam and Clara, that there was a row, and that I threatened Jinny. Adam did not witness anything, so they are taking Clara's word for this. As I told the guards there was not a row. I asked a simple question. Jinny answered that she would check, and I only said hello to Clara as she walked across the yard with her son."

"I don't understand why Clara would have made this up, unless Jinny became upset after you had left, since she realised that she had been caught out. Maybe because of the following phone call, and you taking the land back, that everything was conflated, and Clara ended up, exaggerating what had occurred in the yard. When she spoke to the guards, she was upset, and had to blame someone and that someone was you. Although, saying that you threatened her mother was a bit much."

"It's still a very weak motive. How on earth could Muldoon think that this was a sufficient reason for me to kill her, when, taking our own land back would make no difference whatsoever to our lives. It's a completely daft motive."

Alexander had written all this down in his neat hand.

"Next," he said. "Weapon. It would seem that Jinny was stabbed with a steak knife, that is either similar or identical to the ones we have. Otherwise, there was no need for the guards to take ours away as evidence."

"But ours are all accounted for," interjected Monique.

"I know," replied Alexander "but we could easily have had a second set and gotten rid of the other one or replaced the missing knife. The knife was obviously found in our ditch which you witnessed. They have stopped looking now, so they must have the murder weapon. Thirdly, opportunity. I certainly had opportunity, as I have no alibi for the time of the murder, and through my own admission, I was out and about with the dogs and walking the land at the time in question. I could easily have gone into the milking parlour and committed the murder. So, in the mind of Muldoon, I had means, motive and opportunity. Although he must realise that the motive is extremely weak."

"Well, where do you think we should begin?" asked Monique.

"I'm going to have a chat with Damien Browne."

The Browne family had been living in the area for generations. They would certainly know the history of family disputes et cetera. Damien was the solicitor for the de Bruin family, and also a close friend, since Monique, Alexander and family had moved into The Lodge.

"We can't be the only people who have had a disagreement with the Galdstones over the years," continued Monique.

"I agree," said Alexander. It's the Galdstones themselves who are pointing the finger at me. Perhaps, because this is the most recent argument. As far as we know there may have been many more in the past. I'll give Damien a ring, and arrange to pop over to see him."

CHAPTER 4

— ◆ —

THE OLD RECTORY

The following morning Alexander made his way to his neighbours' house. This was a five minute stroll. He passed the place where the murder weapon had been found. He reached the ornate wrought iron gates which had been left open, as he was expected. He walked along the winding avenue which was bordered by old majestic oak trees. In spring there always was a ribbon of yellow and white daffodils. During other seasons a splash of different coloured flowers adorned the avenue.

The avenue opened out onto manicured lawns and in the middle, a beautiful red bricked two storey house – dating back to the early 19th century. The Old Rectory, as it was always known, was one of the prettiest houses in the area. There are many period features to the property including sash windows with original shutters. On the left there is a grass tennis court and on the right a small walled garden. Alexander smiled as he looked at the walled garden where the Browne and de Bruin children spent hours playing when they were younger in their own "Secret Garden".

The house really reminded him of the army buildings in the Curragh Camp. This house was always called the Old Rectory although no one knew when the last rector had lived there, as the Browne family had inhabited the property and its surrounding lands for four generations. The old dark oak front door opened as he climbed the three steps. There stood his old friend Damien Browne. Damien is a tall well-built man with a shock of blond hair with a few grey streaks.

"Well hello there," he said. "Come on in."

Alexander followed him into the entrance hall with its red flagstones. It is an extremely beautiful hall, with an ornate staircase and pictures of old ancestors adorn the walls. They turned right into the drawing room with its recessed bookcases and log burner under a marble fireplace.

"This is an awful business," muttered Damien.

"It certainly is," returned Alexander.

"I suppose the guards have been down to question you both?"

"They were here yesterday. Don't think much of that Muldoon fellow. Can't really make him out. To tell you the truth Alex, he seemed very interested in you and your relationship with the Galdstones. I found it a bit strange really. Thought he would just ask us about ourselves and if we had seen anything out of the ordinary, but having done that, he turned his attention to you and some row that you were meant to have had with Jinny. I told him that I knew absolutely nothing about any row. He really seemed to be pointing the finger at you. He said that they had ruled out burglary as nothing had been stolen or disturbed. He was convinced that it was personal. She was stabbed about five times which showed a great deal of hatred. What kind of row was he talking about?"

Alexander explained about the events that had transpired and reiterated that he couldn't understand why Clara would have said that he had threatened her mother.

"It would appear from what Muldoon said that I'm the only one who ever had a disagreement with Jinny – certainly according to her family. I was hoping that you could give me a lowdown on anyone else who might have had a beef with them. I've decided that I'll have to investigate this myself, otherwise I fear that I'll be railroaded, and end up charged with something that I had absolutely nothing to do with."

"You're dead right, Alex. I'm not sure that Muldoon has ever investigated a murder before. He seems to be zoning in on you with no evidence. With your intelligence background you should be able to do a much better job. I'm sure you still have lots of contacts. I'll certainly help you in anyway I can as your friend and as your solicitor. I'm advising you to say very little to the guards from now on."

"I hadn't realised that Clara was back living at home again," muttered Alexander.

"Yes, seemingly all was forgiven. They were renovating an old barn at the bottom of the farm for herself and Jack. Dreadful that this should have happened after peace had broken out. Let's go into the kitchen and get a cup of coffee. We have a lot of things to discuss. All is not what it seems with Jinny Gladstone and her family."

The two men made their way down the hall to the kitchen.

"Is Lydia about?" asked Alex.

"No, she's in court today in Naas. Think she'll be late enough. A full day of cases. She's been very busy lately."

"Thought I heard a noise upstairs."

"Oh, that'll be Mrs. Hannigan. She comes here once a week. Lydia was delighted when Monique recommended her. She's really a godsend. Lydia is too busy these days to have the time for housework as well. It was great that she could fit us in as she cleans a good number of houses roundabout."

The two men sat down at the kitchen table and drank their coffee. Alexander took out his notebook and pen and took notes on everything that was said, as he knew how important a small detail could be, when investigating a case. He had investigated several cases before, during his intelligence days but never had he been the prime suspect.

Damien began to explain about the many disputes that the Galdstones had had with people down through the years. They were not known for being the most honest people. There had been a story told about buying in cattle and selling them on as their own. This is frowned upon among dairy farmers, in fact, all farmers, as diseased cattle could be brought into the herd. Damien was fairly sure that this wasn't the only time that this had happened, but wasn't aware of any repercussions. He said that he would ask around. He hadn't heard if they had used other people's land maps to claim fees from the department of agriculture as they had done with Alexander's maps, but again he stated that he would ask around. There was also the probability that the other landowners wouldn't have been aware of this. Both men agreed that this would not be a credible motive for murder, unless someone's herd had been infected with TB or some other disease.

"I really don't believe that anyone would stab a woman five times with a steak knife because of disputes over animals or land maps. This is a very personal murder. It must be something much more serious," muttered Alexander.

"There was the sad saga of young Mike Lavelle," continued Damien. "He was killed in a car accident on our road. This was before your time here. His mother blamed Jinny for his death."

"Was she directly involved with the accident?" asked Alexander.

"No, but Michael's mother believes that she is responsible. The family lives in one of the small cottages about a mile and a half down the back road. It's in a cul-de-sac. Every time the parents go into town shopping or the father goes to work or to the pub, they have to pass this way. It must be horrendous for them. A reminder of that horrible end every day of their lives."

"Why does Mrs. Lavelle hold Jinny responsible?"

"Well, we all know that Jinny used to move the cows for milking, from one side of the road to the other, at around 5.30 to 6am and back again. She put a rope from one side of the road to the other and just stopped whatever traffic was travelling down the road for 10 to 15 minutes. All of the people living around here know about this and do their best to avoid it. This happens four times a day.

Unfortunately, Mike was stopped for the cows for 15 minutes and was going to be late for his train from Sallins to college. He was driving his little Fiat car and had his friend Nick in the car with him. He took off quickly and skidded shortly afterwards. He hit a large tree on the driver side and was killed instantly. Mrs. Lavelle insisted that the car had skidded on cow shit. We all know that the Galdstones aren't very meticulous at cleaning up their shit off the road. You really need to have a chat with them. They have never recovered from their son's death."

"Oh!, that is such a sad tale," sighed Alexander.

"He was their only child. In fact they didn't have any children of their own. They fostered Mike when he was a little baby and he just stayed with them. He was the light of their lives, a wonderful young man."

The two men were silent for a couple of minutes. They refilled their coffee cups and sipped slowly.

"Well, there's certainly another side to Jinny and her family and not the one that they like to portray to the general public."

"That's not all," said Damien, "there is also the tale of Ena and Kitty's house and lands."

Ena and Kitty Hoban were two elderly ladies who had lived in a beautiful old stone house called Briar's Cottage about half a mile from The Lodge. Ivy and clematis hugged the walls of the house. Their home and lands bordered the back of the Galdstone farm.

As coincidence may have it, Monique and Alexander had met the two ladies at a friend's summer barbecue about a year before they moved into The Lodge. So, when the de Bruins moved into their new home in Briarstown, Monique became friends with Ena and Kitty.

There was a lovely quiet walk between The Lodge and Briar's cottage. Twice a week Monique visited the ladies. Ena and Kitty had a pretty cottage garden. There was a trellis of red and white roses over the front entrance. Monique always received a very warm welcome. Inside, the house was full of antique furniture, Lalique glass and dainty figurines. There was a ritual to the visit. They went into a warm sitting room with comfortable sofas and cushions. There was always a fire flickering in the hearth. Ena made the tea. The best crockery appeared on a silver tray and home-made scones or slices of Madeira cake were served. Monique and the two ladies enjoyed these pleasant, friendly chats. Unfortunately, Ena became ill and went downhill very quickly. She died within six months and Kitty was left bereft. Kitty seemed to lose the will to live. Only a year after Ena's death, she too passed away.

"It's common knowledge that the Galdstones had rented the land from Kitty and Ena," continued Damien. "There was one field that was reached by a right of way through one of the Galdstones' fields. We used to think it funny when the two ladies used to get into their car and drive through the field several times a year so that they could maintain their right of way. But maybe it wasn't that funny as they mustn't have trusted their neighbours. After Ena's death the land was sold very quickly to the Galdstones as you know. Everyone was surprised that it wasn't put up on the open market. If you remember there were no "for sale" signs on the house. Most of us thought that this whole business was very bizarre. Before we knew where we were, young John Gladstone, his wife and child were living in the house. There were rumours that Ena and Kitty's young cousin was not happy with the sale."

"What do you know about him?" asked Alexander.

"His name is Jerry Hoban and was their only relative – the only child of their first cousin. I know he lives somewhere near Newbridge with his wife and children. As a child, he used to spend summers with his cousins Ena and Kitty. To tell you the truth most of the old stock around here thought that he would come back to live in the old house, as he had been very close to the old dears. Something happened to his business during the early days of the recession, so it's said that he had to go to England to work on the buildings to make ends meet. Again, I think that with your connections, you should be able to find out where he lives. He was always a lovely young lad and I'm sure that he would be willing to have a chat with you. I really don't think that the Galdstones are flavour of the month as far as he's concerned."

And so it came to pass that Alexander had uncovered several new suspects after one conversation with his good friend Damien Browne. He wondered if Inspector Muldoon had done any investigative work to uncover any of the information that he had gleaned in half an hour. He really wasn't sure about Muldoon. He wasn't completely convinced that he was as clueless as he was pretending to be. Nevertheless, he was now more determined than ever that he would thoroughly investigate everything that he had learned today. He knew that Monique would be anxiously waiting for him at home. He gathered up his pen and notebook.

"Thanks so much for all your help Damien. Being a blow-in to the area, it would have been difficult for me to learn about all the history of this place. All that glistens isn't gold, it seems."

Alexander walked down the avenue and made his way home. He had a lot of news for Monique. No doubt she would be surprised at some of the things he had learned, and other things not so much.

CHAPTER 5

﹡

MAKING A LIST

"Well dear, how did you get on with Damien?" Monique greeted her husband as he entered the sitting room.

"Not bad at all," he replied.

Monique was sitting at the large oak table which was strewn with papers. She had been filling in entry forms for pony jumping competitions. Alexander saw two white booklets of Show Jumping Association of Ireland registration tickets, two pony passports and competition forms of various colours.

"I see you've been busy," he added.

"Yes, the girls have a competition this weekend in Mullingar. I don't know whether we should go or not with everything that's going on. They'll be home from school tomorrow."

Monique was sitting at the large oak table which was strewn with papers. She had been filling in entry forms for pony jumping competitions. Alexander saw two white booklets of Show Jumping Association of Ireland registration tickets, two pony passports and competition forms of various colours.

"I see you've been busy," he added.

"Yes, the girls have a competition this weekend in Mullingar. I don't know whether we should go or not with everything that's going on. They'll be home from school tomorrow."

Alice and Maeve attended a girls boarding school in Wicklow. They absolutely adored the school and their friends. It had always been their wish to go away to boarding school since reading the Mallory Towers books by Enid Blyton. Alexander was never too keen on their going away to school, as his own experiences at a Cork boy's boarding school had been far from pleasant. However the girls' wishes prevailed and off they went. Max followed suit two years later and he had nothing but praise for his school either.

"Maybe it would be good for them to get away to a show. I don't think I really want them around here, especially if we have any more visits from the guards."

"You're probably right," returned Alexander. "As long as you can manage the horsebox. Between the kids and yourself I'm sure everything will work out. Certainly I can't go, as I have a number of phone calls to make and I will probably have to visit a few people who, according to Damien, could be suspects in the murder."

"Tell me more," insisted Monique. Alexander sat down beside her and showed her the notes that he had taken at the Browne's.

"Well, that's all very telling," she said. "We all knew that Ena and Kitty's land sale was strange. So, you're going to have to locate their cousin Jerry Hoban in Newbridge and get to the bottom of it. That's a very sad story about Mike Lavelle. Presumably you'll be able to question the parents and get hold of the coroner's report. Maybe Damien will be able to find out the name of the farmer who bought the suspect calves. That would save a lot of work."

"I certainly have enough to be getting on with," observed Alexander.

"Don't forget the husband – never forget the husband. I'm sure even Inspector Muldoon suspects Adam."

"They always came across as a united couple," returned Alexander.

"Mrs. Hannigan has had a thing or two to say about that. She is convinced that Adam did it."

"And what has drawn her to that conclusion?" asked Alexander.

"Seemingly, there have been vicious rows in the house. They go back years to when Clara became pregnant."

Clara was 18 when she became pregnant. She had been at UCD studying architecture. She was a very clever young woman but became involved with a fellow student. When she informed her parents that she was expecting, they disowned her and threw her out of the home. They no longer gave her financial help and so she had to leave college. None of the neighbours knew anything about her predicament until several months later when they learned that she was living in a small bed-sit in Naas. Her boyfriend didn't want to know, and so she was on her own, living off the pittance she got from the state. When Jinny ever spoke of her it was with distain.

"She's out, she broke the rules," was all that she said.

Clara had her son Jack and then got a job in one of the supermarkets in Naas.

"According to Mrs. Hannigan, Adam had been less forthright and more forgiving and wanted to heal the relationship with Clara. He also wanted to spend time with his grandson. These rows went on for several years."

"Well," said Alexander, "according to Damien, all is now forgiven. Clara and Jack have returned home and they were even going to renovate an old outhouse at the bottom of the farm for them. Clara and Jack, as you know were in the yard when I spoke to Jinny about the land."

"That's not the only thing that they were rowing about, it seems. According to Mrs. Hannigan, there was another bone of contention. Adam had accused Jinny of having some sort of a relationship with the new vicar, Jonathan Edwards, or at best of spending too much time in his company."

Jonathan Edwards and his wife Mary had arrived in the parish about 18 months ago. They had lived in North Cork before they moved to the village. Mary had been a nurse in Cork where Jonathan was curate. It was an unusual marriage, as Mary was a catholic and there weren't many mixed marriages among the clergy. They had three children within five years and then Jonathan was offered the vicarage in the village of Clonee in North Kildare when the old vicar died. The Edwards family were very popular from the offset. They both threw themselves into parish life with gusto and Mary was always a great help to her husband in his parish duties. They lived in the vicarage which was situated near the grounds of the church of Ireland in Clonee. Mary organised after-school activities for the children and on occasion, there were very pleasant ladies lunches at the vicarage.

Sunday school had always been the responsibility of the mothers of the parish, under the leadership of the vicar. Jinny Galdstone had been a leading light in the Sunday school brigade for years but her enthusiasm for volunteering for such events increased exponentially after the arrival of Jonathan Edwards.

"That sounds like a lot of gossip," said Alexander, "but of course we know nothing about the goings on among the church of Ireland members."

"I don't like gossip either Alexander, but Mrs. Hannigan was very adamant that there were dreadful rows between Adam and Jinny and that she overheard his accusations on several occasions. Adam and

Clara are pointing the finger squarely at you for the murder. I think it's absolutely ridiculous, and if there were rows and arguments and distrust in that family, if Adam and Jinny's marriage was in trouble, well then, he had a much greater motive for killing his wife than you had. Muldoon hasn't questioned Mrs. Hannigan as yet, so I've advised her that when that time comes, that she must tell him everything that she has told me."

"Of course you're right," said Alexander. "I'm sure that Muldoon will question anyone who spent time in that house including Mrs. Hannigan. There seems to be a dreadful web of deceit in that family. Now we will have to try to unravel all the intricate secrets. Jinny appears to have caused a great deal of hurt to many people."

Alexander and Monique sat quietly at the table, looking at the ever-growing list of suspects.

CHAPTER 6

—— • ——

MULDOON

Inspector John Muldoon sat alone in his office at Naas Garda station. The office was sparsely furnished. There was a cheap table with a black phone sitting atop. Folders were neatly piled on the right hand side. A plastic jar held numerous pens and pencils. He sat very quietly, gazing at a red folder which held the autopsy report on Jinny Galdstone. On his desk was also a photo of his wife and daughter. His wife, Lucy, was about the same age as Jinny. She too had long blond hair. His stomach was not well. He hadn't been able to eat or sleep properly since he had seen the body. When he had fallen asleep there had been nightmares. Jinny's long blond, bloodied hair moving about like snakes. Big cows, heads moving and lowing. Tubes with milk floating above his head. Then he would wake up in a sweat and found it easier just to stay awake. He knew if he fell back to sleep, that there would be more horrors.

His police life up to now had not been filled with death and horror. He had investigated three other murders during his career but none had been as bloody as this. They also had been quite straightforward. Two were gang related in Dublin and one was a row between brothers in Meath. The culprits had been caught, questioned and charged in short order and that was that. Even giving evidence in court had not been difficult.

This was very different. All those stab wounds, all that blood, the whole horrible scene, the smells, the nightmares. John Muldoon took a deep breath, gathered himself together and made himself open the folder. There, before him were the photos from all angles. Then the diagrams with arrows pointing to the wounds. Then the details, the weight of all the organs. Where the blade penetrated. The size of the blade and on and on and on. He felt sick again. He took a sip of water. "Pull yourself together," he whispers to himself.

Sergeant Michael Dunne entered the room with another folder under his arm, this time a blue one.

"Good morning Sir, I have the forensic results on the set of steak knives, taken from the de Bruin house and the forensics on the knife found in the ditch. The one found in the ditch is the murder weapon. The blood found on the blade is that of Jinny Galdstone. Unfortunately, the handle has been wiped clean so there are no fingerprints. The murder weapon is identical in size and make to the set taken from the de Bruin's. I made a few phone calls to various shops and these sets of steak knives are quite common. Many of them have been sold in the region.

"Thank you, Michael. I suppose, no surprise there."

John Muldoon looked back down at the folder. Five deeply penetrating stab wounds with a steak knife. One to the stomach at a perpendicular angle. The coroner believed that the assailant was standing in front of the victim when the first blow was inflicted. It looked like the victim staggered back and placed her hands on the wound, before hitting the ground. Both lungs were punctured and her heart was gouged. It appeared that when the heart was stabbed, the assailant moved the blade from side to side as if to obliterate the heart.

This was a crime of absolute hatred. Whoever did this wanted to inflict as much suffering as possible. This was a crime of rage, hate, emotion, revenge. This was really personal and up close, whoever did this looked into her eyes as he or she stabbed her in the stomach. Then, finished the job with conviction, continuing to look into her eyes as he or she struck downwards four more times and moved the blade around when it entered the heart.

"I've made a mistake," thought Muldoon. "This is a hatred that has been seething and brewing for months or even years. This has nothing to do with a dispute over a land map that has recently come to light. This has nothing to do with Alexander de Bruin. I've been misdirected either by chance or by design."

When John Muldoon looked up from the report, Michael Dunne was still standing there, waiting for his orders.

"We'll have to start again. I know we've interviewed some of the neighbours, but we are going back to the beginning. Everyone is to be re-interviewed. Send the men into the village to do a house to house. Prepare a form that each witness is to fill in. I no longer believe that Alexander de Bruin is a suspect. The murder is too personal."

Michael Dunne left the room to prepare his work and left Inspector John Muldoon alone with his thoughts.

He sat there for several minutes, just quietly mulling over the events. He took out his notebook and pen, and the first name he wrote down was Adam Galdstone. He knew that this should have been his modus operandi from the beginning. When the wife is murdered, the first suspect is always the husband, then the immediate family, then the extended family and then you work out like a spiral and somewhere along the way all the clues will make sense.

John Muldoon soon realised that he knew very little about Briarstown

and it's inhabitants. There had been no reason for his involvement
with the community as there was rarely any crime in the area. The next
village Clonee was also a very sleepy, quiet place where nothing much
ever happened. How on earth was he going to find out about their
secrets?

John Muldoon decided that he needed help from someone who knew
the area and the people better than he. His wife's brother was in the
army, so perhaps a phone call to him might be helpful, for, although
he had thought that Alexander de Bruin was originally a suspect, he
now had reservations about his earlier suspicions.

John Muldoon received a phone call that afternoon from Colonel
Brian Mangan, stationed at the Curragh Camp.

"Good afternoon Inspector Muldoon, my name is Brian Mangan.
I am your brother-in-law's commanding officer. I have been told that
you are making enquiries about Alexander de Bruin, retired."

"Yes indeed I am. We have a very complicated murder case on our
hands, and I have decided that I need some help from someone who
lives in the area. I came across de Bruin during my initial investigation,
as he is a near neighbour of the deceased woman."

"Well, I can assure you, Inspector, there would be no better man
for the job. He was an excellent officer throughout. During his final
years in the army, he was in Intelligence and solved many mysteries for
us. Obviously, I can't go into any of this, but I can assure you that he
would be of great assistance to you. He still helps us out on occasion
when we are stumped by some complicated problem. Alexander has
also been of help to the guards themselves in a few cases in the past.
Obviously, this wasn't broadcast and only those directly involved were
in the know. You will probably have to communicate with Superin-
tendent McEvoy at Garda Headquarters to get permission for Alexan-

der's involvement. I'm sure you'll both prevail"

John Muldoon hung up the receiver and thought carefully about what the Colonel had said. He felt extremely foolish, having initially suspected de Bruin of being a murderer.

"The man must think I'm a complete eejit to have pounced on that theory," he mused.

"Anyway, onwards and upwards. But how on earth am I going to approach the man and ask him for his help, having treated him so badly at our initial meeting.

Inspector John Muldoon need not have worried about Alexander's reaction. He had faced many more serious events during his life in the army. Phone calls were made between the higher-ups in the Army and in Garda Headquarters and the way was smoothed out for the cooperation which would ensue between the two men.

Sergeant Dunne had prepared the questionnaire which he would hand out to the young Garda officers, who would go house to house. He came back into Muldoon's office to pass it by him.

"That's perfect Michael, get it out as soon as possible. We should have done this a few days ago. People's memory fades very quickly. They may have been talking to each other and sometimes what they remember is actually what someone else has told them they remember. The sooner this is done, the more accurate the information we get. The coroner has put time of death between 5.30am and 8am. We knew this already because of the information the husband has given us. Although he doesn't have a time for his wife leaving the house, as he didn't wake up. We knew she moved the cattle from one side of the road to the other, as she did every morning and led them to the parlour, attached the machines to the udders and started the milking machines. We need to find out, who drove down that road between those two times. There are certain people who have to pass that way to get to the main road to Naas. There are people who are on shift work in Naas and Newbridge who have an early start. Alexander de Bruin had been out on his land with his dogs, checking the horses et cetera. He hadn't seen anything or anyone out of the ordinary. Of course he was a fair bit in from the road and a good five minute walk from the Galdstone farm."

"Does this mean that we've now ruled him out as a suspect?" asked Sergeant Dunne.

"I believe so," answered Muldoon. "Having read the autopsy report, I'm convinced that it was a personal, frenzied attack by someone who had great animosity towards the victim. There was such hatred and malice in the attack, Michael. I've also received information about Alexander de Bruin which paints him in a different light. I'm just sorry that I didn't have this information before I initially questioned him. I am also convinced that the murder weapon was placed in that particular ditch to point the finger at de Bruin. It looks as if I'm going to be working the case with the Commandant. It appears that he was a member of Army Intelligence and has worked cases already with Garda Headquarters. He is held in the highest esteem by all who know him and is the least likely person to have committed any crime, never mind this dreadful murder."

The sergeant stood looking at his superior. There was a quizzical look on his face.

"So, does that mean that I won't be accompanying you on the job, Sir?" he asked.

"I'm not sure yet how this will all work. I need to travel to Briarstown and have a chat with de Bruin. I will probably get a better idea from him about the goings on in that particular townland. It may be that he and I will question the suspects together or that we do it individually. It depends on the people involved and whether they would be more forthcoming with information, if questioned by a police officer or a neighbour. I might just need you to hold down the fort here. All the young officers have to be given their orders and all the statements they take must be checked and collated. I will need you to look out for consistencies and inconsistencies in the witness statements. The smallest detail could be of the utmost importance."

The sergeant was very disappointed, although he didn't want to show it, as he loved being Inspector Muldoon's sidekick. He really enjoyed being out and about meeting people, watching the inspector at work, asking his questions, taking notes and then coming back to the office to discuss their day's work. They had worked together for five years and he really liked and admired his boss. He found that people in general, tended to underestimate Inspector Muldoon. They did not really believe that he was clever enough for the job. He had a way of asking questions that made the suspect feel at ease and even superior. In actual fact he was a clever, thorough man with a keen mind for detection. Although thinking back on his questioning of the de Bruins, it had been somewhat different. He seemed to show his hand too quickly and made it obvious that he suspected the commandant. This was a mistake that the sergeant has not seen previously. Of course this was a particularly distressing case, one that neither he nor his boss had experienced before. The vision of horror in the milking parlour will never be forgotten. It would have been easy to have felt overwhelmed and out of one's depth on that morning. Adam Galdstone had been so distressed and his daughter so angry, it had been very difficult to take control of the situation. Not only had one to take care of the Galdstones, but there were also the young officers who had been so shocked, that they had been physically sick.

The sergeant looked at his boss, sitting behind his desk with his folders, papers and pens in front of him. He felt a sense of relief. Muldoon looked calm, collected and organised. He did not look as exhausted and strained as he had that morning when he had first entered his office. It looked as if a great burden had been lifted from his shoulders.

"Well, I'll get on with organising the lads so, Sir," said Michael Dunne.

"Yes indeed, thanks Michael," returned Muldoon.

The sergeant walked out of the office. "He's back," he thought to himself.

CHAPTER 7

— • —

A FUNERAL

Ten days after her murder, Jinny Galdstone's funeral took place.

The night before, Jonathan Edwards was preparing his sermon for the following day. He was sitting in his office in the rectory, looking down at his sheet of paper, pen in hand. But, he was having great difficulty organising his thoughts. He was usually very good at putting pen to paper – not so tonight. His wife Mary came in to check on him and bring him a cup of tea and a delicious scone with butter and jam, just the way he liked it.

"How is it coming along, darling?" she asked.

"I can't get my thoughts straight," he answered.

"That's not like you," Mary added. "You've usually no problem at all preparing your sermons and you are particularly good at funerals. There is something wrong Jonathan, what is it?"

Mary looked down at her husband and could see a frown on his forehead. He looked anxious and puzzled.

"You know that I've been up to the Galdstones on three occasions since Jinny's murder. The first time was that evening and I didn't stay long – just to give my condolences and say that I would do anything I could to help. The second time I was just really delivering some literature so that they could discuss readings and hymns and thirdly was yesterday, so that we could decide on the ceremony, readings, hymns et cetera. Well, the visit yesterday was very strange. Adam, Clara and John were there. John hardly spoke at all, said that he would prefer just to leave all the reading et cetera to me, as it was my job. Clara was very matter of fact and she chose the reading and the three hymns "Abide with me", "How great thou art" and "Precious Lord take my hand." I thought they might have chosen something more uplifting, but anyway, it was up to them. But Adam was behaving very strangely towards me. I know the man has had a dreadful shock and is grieving but he just sat there, glaring at me. When I asked him a question there was a monosyllabic answer. It seemed that it was much more than grief. I felt like he hated and despised me. I wish you had been there Mary, you might have been able to suss out what was going on with him."

"Oh dear! Jonathan, you're such an innocent abroad. I know what's bothering him. The whole parish knows what's bothering him, except you."

Jonathan gazed at his wife in astonishment.

"Pray explain," he whispered.

"From the first moment that Jinny laid eyes on you, she fancied the pants off you. Whenever you organised a meeting she was there. Any committees you were on – she was on them too. Wherever you were, she turned up. Her hair became blonder, her make up more evident and her clothes more revealing. She even volunteered to go on the scouting weekend. If you remember I had to organise my mother to mind the kids, so that I could go with you as well. It certainly wasn't my love of camping that inspired that. It was my urge to protect you. You are so naive, my darling, when it comes to some women. You are young, good looking, charming and so so kind, that this can be misinterpreted by women who aren't happy in their own lives. I would say that everyone in the parish could see what she was up to. She would have willingly taken you away from us."

"But, you know that's crazy. First of all, I hadn't a clue what was going on, and secondly I would never do anything to hurt you and the kids. Mary, you're the only girl I've ever loved, and ever will love, you're my whole life."

"I know that, my darling. At first, I thought that she would just get over her crush on you and that she would realise that feelings were not reciprocated, but then it went on and on. It became really annoying and I had made up my mind to have a chat with her and explain to her, that she was just making a fool of herself. Fortunately or unfortunately, whichever way you want to look at it, I never got round to it."

"Do you think that Adam believed that there was something going on between us?" asked Jonathan.

"It's hard to know, but it doesn't really matter, because he probably hates you, since he knows that his wife was in love with you."

"This is a right turn up for the books. How in God's name am I going to be able to face the whole parish, and get through the funeral tomorrow?" he implored.

"We are going to put one foot in front of the other and carry on. You will write a beautiful sermon, singing her praises. I will help you. You will prepare "a face to meet the faces that you meet" as J. Alfred Prufrock would say."

Mary and Jonathan sat at the table in his office, every so often looking out the window, from where they could see the small church and graveyard.

"This time tomorrow it will be all over," thought Mary.

The next morning, Jonathan, donning his funeral attire, stood in solemnity and sorrow with his congregation, awaiting the arrival of the hearse. The only attendees were relatives of the deceased. As it happened, all of the church of Ireland parishioners were there, as they were all related to each other, either by blood or marriage. Jonathan led the cortège into the church and the ceremony began.

It was a sad affair. Adam, Clara, John and Frank – the son who lived in California – were in the first pew. Adam looked like a broken man. His eyes were swollen and his face was gaunt. John and Frank showed very little emotion. A lady in the congregation commented how stoical Clara was and how she resembled her dead mother with her long blond hair.

"She is so like her mother was, when she was her age," she whispered to her neighbour.

Jonathan's sermon was well received. Mary listened in admiration, as her husband delivered his words with such sincerity and with a straight face. He said all the right things – what a wonderful wife and mother she had been – what an inspiring member of the church and parish – how helpful she was – what a wonderful worker and businesswoman – how much she will be missed – it will be so hard to replace her – her enthusiasm and love for her animals et cetera et cetera. Jonathan concluded his sermon "Death leaves a heartache no one can heal, love leaves a memory no one can steal." Mary wondered would she soon be beatified, as she sat in front of the organ and played "Precious Lord take my hand". The congregation sang with enthusiasm.

"And now let us conclude with Nunc Dimitis," said Jonathan, and led the congregation out into the graveyard where Jinny Galdstone was laid to rest.

Inspector Muldoon and Sergeant Dunne were leaning against the old stone wall of the cemetery as the congregation emerged from the church, led by the vicar. They gathered around the graveside. The two men couldn't hear what was being said but they presumed that last prayers were being read. They watched all the mourners carefully. They knew that attending the funeral had been by invitation only, so they knew that their suspect pool was restricted to the Church of Ireland members only. They recognised of course Adam, Clara and John. They presumed that the other young man, standing beside John, was the son Frank, who lives in California. The three children showed very little emotion as the coffin was lowered into the ground. Adam was distraught and was shaking slightly as he said goodbye to his wife. Mourners gathered to shake hands with the family. Clara looked impatient and obviously keen to get away.

"I don't think there is anything else to be learned here," said Muldoon, and the two men walked back to their car.

The two grave diggers had been standing at a discrete distance, virtually hidden behind an old tombstone. When the crowd had dispersed, they moved towards the grave with their shovels and began the grim task of covering the coffin with clay. Jonathan had returned into the church where Mary was tidying up after the service. She had collected all the hymn books.

"Well done, Jonathan, I knew you could do it," said Mary.

Jonathan was silent and just went over to his wife and hugged her. He held onto her closely for about two minutes.

"Let's go home," he whispered. "I'm absolutely shattered. I think that was the most stressful service I've ever done."

They walked out the door of the church, closed it behind them, and walked arm in arm back to the rectory.

CHAPTER 8

—— ◆ ——

COOPERATION

The day after the funeral, Inspector John Muldoon arrived at The Lodge to make peace with Commandant Alexander de Bruin. He walked up to the beautiful wooden door, took hold of the brass horse shaped door knocker and knocked three times. Less than a minute later, he heard footsteps inside and the door was opened.

"Good morning, Inspector, please come in."

"Thank you," answered Muldoon and walked over the threshold.

"We'll go into the kitchen first. Monique has prepared a light lunch for us. I received a phone call from Garda Headquarters yesterday, and they brought me up to speed. It looks like we'll be working together on this case."

"Yes, indeed, I hope that we will be able to cooperate. I have been informed that you have some experience in investigating difficult cases and that you have worked with the Gardaí before. We did get off on the wrong foot and I apologise for that," said Muldoon.

"Not to worry about that, we are starting anew, let's have lunch."

The two men strolled into the kitchen where Monique had laid out quite a spread. There were meat cuts, a quiche, several salads and two types of bread. John and Alexander had a very convivial lunch. They chatted about family and hobbies, avoiding the case at hand until after lunch.

Alexander cleared away the dishes.

"Let's take our coffee into the office and get on with the job."

John Muldoon took his briefcase, followed Alexander down the hall and into his office. The two men sat down at the large oak desk. Alexander already had his notes neatly stacked on the right hand side of the table.

John opened his briefcase and took out the folder which held the autopsy report. Alexander took the folder from him. He perused the photos, the diagrams and the written report from the medical examiner. He wasn't quite as shocked as John had been, as he had seen similar photos before. Of course he hadn't witnessed the awful scene in person, as John had done, and which had caused him to have sleepless nights and nightmares.

"Oh my," said Alexander. "What a dreadful end. I presume that you have come to the conclusion that this is very personal. This wasn't a burglar who happened upon her."

"Absolutely right," answered John. "There are five stab wounds. The one to the stomach which would have incapacitated her, but not killed her, then the other four, any one of which, would have been fatal. The one to the heart is particularly vicious, as the killer moved the knife around after its insertion. It was a frenzied attack with complete overkill."

The two men sat silently for a few moments, as if once again, taking in the gravity of the situation.

"I presume you went to the funeral yesterday, John?"

"Well, Sergeant Dunne and I stood in the cemetery. We didn't go into the church. We really didn't learn very much. Our suspect pool was very limited as the only people invited were relatives. When there's an open funeral we can look out for other suspects besides the husband

and family. As you probably know, murderers, for whatever reason, tend to make an appearance at the funeral of their victims. So we were a bit stymied here."

"Let's begin so, with the immediate family," suggested Alexander." I presume I'm off the list," he smiled.

"I am really relying on you for local information. On the face of things, Adam and Jinny appeared to be a very happy couple and upstanding members of the community," added John.

"As you probably know John, I'm what's regarded in these parts, as a blow-in, although we've lived here for over 10 years, but I am very friendly with our next door neighbour Damien Browne, who incidentally is also my solicitor and has advised me not to speak to the police without his being present,"

A smile sneaked across his face.

"Fortunately, the Brownes have been living here for generations and I've been able to get the lowdown on all that's been happening over the years in Briarstown. We also have a housekeeper, Mrs. Hannigan, who works for the Galdstones and a number of other families in the area. She was able to give Monique some insight into the state of the Galdstone marriage. To be absolutely fair to Mrs. Hannigan, she was never a gossip and would usually not say anything negative about other people. However, when she learned that I was the prime suspect in the case, she felt she had to speak up on the matter."

Alexander related the story that had been told to Monique about the rows in the house. John Muldoon listened carefully to the sad tale of Clara's banishment from the house following her unplanned, out of wedlock pregnancy. He found the story of Jinny's infatuation with the young vicar extremely interesting. This certainly puts Adam in the frame, plus the vicar and his wife.

"What about the other family members?" asked John.

"Well, Frank lives in California and only arrived home for his mother's funeral. John, his wife and family now live in Briar's Cottage. He just seems like a very hard-working young man. I believe that he got on well with his mother. There doesn't seem to be any story at all there."

"So, our main family suspects are Adam and maybe Clara," continued John.

"Yes, but according to the Brownes, Clara has now moved home and they have begun renovation on an outbuilding for her and her son Jack."

"So, have you come up with any non-family suspects, apart from the vicar and his wife?" asked John.

"There are a number of interesting possibilities," mused Alexander. "As you are aware, I found that the Galdstones had been less than honest in their dealings with us regarding the renting of our land, which led to my no longer allowing them onto our property. I did this as a matter of principle. While Adam and Clara have claimed that I was aggressive and bullied Jinny, this is utterly untrue and I believe that this is what led you to see me as a viable suspect, together with the finding of the murder weapon in my ditch. According to my good friend Damien, this sort of underhand behaviour was not a one off."

Alexander told the inspector about the selling of calves, that were not their own, to an unsuspecting farmer, which may or may not have had serious consequences for said farmer. Damien Browne was trying to locate the name and address of the man in question. Secondly, there was Ena and Kitty's house and lands at Briar's Cottage, which was now inhabited by the son John and his family. He told Inspector Muldoon that he would leave finding the address of their cousin, Jerry Hoban, who had inherited the property, to him. There was certainly some sort of shenanigans going on there. Finally, John Muldoon heard about the death of Mike Lavelle, and about the blame that his parents laid at the feet of Jinny Galdstone.

As the two men were contemplating the list of suspects, the phone rang on Alexander's desk. He picked up the receiver.

"Hello, Alexander de Bruin speaking. Yes, indeed, that's very interesting."

He listened to the speaker on the other end of the line for a few minutes.

"Thanks so much for that. We'll chat soon."

He returned the receiver.

"That was Damien Browne. He found out the name of the man who purchased the calves from the Galdstones. He is a farmer from Roscommon, called James Healey. Seemingly, this gentleman had met Adam Galdstone at one of the marts. He had liked the look of his cattle and made an agreement to buy five female calves from Adam the following spring. This happened before our time here. According to the grapevine, the Galdstones purchased cheap calves from a dodgy source, changed the tags and sold them on as their own, at quite a high price. There was a rumour – tuberculosis was found in this man's herd about two months later. Damien said that his source did not know the consequences for James Healey and his herd, but he didn't think that it was good. To tell you the truth, John, it could have been disastrous for him as all the tuberculosis reactors would have to be culled."

John Muldoon, not being of farming stock himself, did not fully comprehend the machinations of country life, and was very glad that he was able to call on the expertise of both Alexander and Damien.

"That sounds extremely dishonest and underhanded," said John. "There seems to be a Machiavellian quality to this family. Although it sounds a bit far-fetched that twelve years after the event, this man would drive to North Kildare, from Roscommon at all hours of the morning, and stab Jinny Galdstone in her own milking parlour."

"I agree with you, to a certain extent," returned Alexander. "However, we don't know what has happened because of the Galdstones' actions in the intervening years. There may have been a long lasting effect to this man's herd and/or family. I think one or both of us will have to take a trip to Roscommon and either rule him in, or out. We have to start somewhere. Being a dairy man himself James Healey would be aware of early morning milking, but as to how he timed it – that's another question. We know she was killed between about 6am and 8am, but we need to try to be more exact," continued Alexander.

"I have my men going door-to-door with questionnaires," replied John. "Because of the importance of this road in getting to the main route to Naas, Dublin, et cetera, there must have been several cars passing here early that morning, with people on their way to work. Perhaps someone was stopped on the road as she moved the cows across for milking."

"All the people in the know, try to avoid this road at around 6am and then at around 8am, but Jinny would change her timing and could be either 15 minutes earlier or 15 minutes later. She really never gave a thought about inconveniencing other people," Alexander muttered.

"So," continued John, "we'll leave the gathering of questionnaires and trying to pinpoint when the cows were moved to the parlour, in the capable hands of Sergeant Dunne. I think both of us should travel to Roscommon tomorrow, if that suits you. I need to be there as the Inspector in charge and you need to be there to decipher what may have been the consequences for James Healey."

The two men decided that Alexander would collect John at the Garda station in Naas at 9am the following morning. In the meantime John would telephone the Healeys to make an appointment for 11.30am.

Inspector John Muldoon gathered up all his folders and papers and placed them in his leather briefcase. Alexander showed him out and closed the oak door behind him. As he made his way back to the kitchen he heard the back door opening.

"Darling, I'm back," said Monique.

She had decided to visit her friend Lydia Browne so as to give Alexander privacy to talk to Inspector Muldoon.

"I'm in the kitchen," replied Alexander.

Monique strolled into the kitchen.

"Put on the kettle Alex and tell me all about it. I presume you're no longer the prime suspect."

"It all went extremely well really. It turns out that we may have underestimated Inspector Muldoon. He's actually quite a bright fellow. I believe he felt a little out of his depth initially. The dreadful sight of the body hit him for six. He's also not a country boy, so our lives are a bit alien to him. I could see that he was slightly annoyed at himself for having jumped to the conclusion that I was a suspect. He realises that he was manipulated towards this opinion by what the Galdstones had said about me. Of course he has also had conversations with people higher up the ladder, in both Army and Garda Headquarters, and is now aware of who I am and what I'm capable of. He brought the medical examiner's report and the autopsy folder with him. It was a dreadful, frenzied killing. Whoever did this seemed to have gone mad, because there was complete overkill."

"So have you put a plan in place?" asked Monique.

"Yes dear, we are off to Roscommon to visit a poor farmer who was duped by the Galdstones. I think we'll just be ruling him out as I believe it's a longshot. But you never know, it's a start anyway. Well, how was your visit to Lydia? Any news there?"

"To tell you the truth Alex, most of the talk was about the murder and who could have done it. It's really amazing how we could have been living here for 10 years and not known people. We had no idea about the skulduggery that that family were up to over the years. If we had known, we would never have given them the land. I realise we were somewhat suspicious about them, but that was all. Of course, Lydia and Damien were very worried about you. Damien was still very adamant that you should not be talking to the guards without his presence. He calmed down a bit when I explained that Muldoon was ruling you out, and that you were now going to be assisting them."

"They are very good friends and neighbours to us," said Alexander. "We have been so busy that you never got to tell me about the horse show at the weekend," smiled Alexander. "I really haven't been able to spend time with the kids, but I will make up for it when all this is resolved."

"The kids are fine Alex. They were as happy as Larry when I dropped them back to school. Maeve was still giving out about her pony having eight faults. The show was fantastic..."

CHAPTER 9

FROM THE PALE TO THE WEST

At 8.30am the following morning, Alexander de Bruin waved goodbye to his wife and started out on the 15 minute drive to Naas to pick up Inspector Muldoon. He drove past the Brownes and the Galdstones and onto the main road. There was no traffic on his road as everyone had already gone to work and everyone's cows had already been milked and back in the fields to spend hours chewing the cud. The hedges and trees were green and lush. The odd rabbit scurried across the road. Alexander drove in silence until he reached the garda station. Inspector Muldoon was waiting on the kerb for him, carrying his usual briefcase.

John Muldoon opened the passenger door and jumped in. He laid his briefcase at his feet and slipped on his seatbelt.

"Good morning Alexander, how is everything?"

"All fine," answered Alexander. "Is everything in place for us to visit James Healey?"

"Sergeant Dunne made contact with them. James Healey Senior is dead, but his son James Healey Junior is very willing to talk to us. I have the address. It's 2 miles outside Castlerea. Do you need directions?" asked John.

"Not at all, I'm very familiar with that road. Monique and I know the west of Ireland very well," answered Alexander.

"It should take us about 2 1/2 hours. He is expecting us at around 11 .30. Do you mind if I do some work? I have an awful lot of paperwork to catch up on."

"Not at all, go ahead. I don't mind the silence at all."

Alexander put the car in gear and they headed towards Newbridge. As they drove into the town, Alexander thought that it was a shame that the town hadn't taken off. It had great potential with the river Liffey running through it. On the left-hand side there was the Holy Family secondary school, beside the convent and a very beautiful church. You could get a glimpse of the roof and playing fields of Newbridge College. Some members of his cadet class had gone to Newbridge College. As they drove up through the town it seemed very quiet. Between Newbridge and Kildare town there was the Curragh Camp and the Curragh Plains. The land here was very rich. There were several stud farms on the outskirts. As he looked left he could see some of the towers of the army buildings. He couldn't help reminiscing about the wonderful years he spent living in quarters as a young married officer. Monique and he had been so happy there. Their children had been born there. He recalled the Sunday afternoons playing rugby, and later all the players and families going to the club for drinks and refreshments. He remembered the Christmas dinners with all the ladies in their long evening dresses and the officers in their dress uniforms. Monique would always straighten his bow tie and make sure the gold cord lanyard on his shoulder was just right. The kids loved the Curragh Camp. There were lots of children their own age living in quarters. Nearly every Saturday morning, Monique and he would take the children to the swimming pool for lessons. All the children followed the orders of Sergeant Long. He took no prisoners but all the kids ended up being very proficient in the water. Above all, the children really loved running and playing in Donnelly's Hollow. Families would meet up there for picnics when the weather permitted. Donnelly's Hollow was famous for the boxing match that took place between Dan Donnelly and George Cooper in 1814. Dan Donnelly won and he became a hero. The hollow is a naturally perfect amphitheatre at the Athgarvan end of the Curragh. The parents could sit at the top and watch the children run around for hours. And so, they made their way through Kildare town, into Monasterevan and then turned right towards Portarlington.

The land became boggier as they drove through Offaly and into Westmeath. They had left the rich pastures of Kildare and were heading mile by mile into the poorer lands of the west of Ireland. No wonder Cromwell said "To hell or to Connaught".

Having passed through Athlone and Roscommon they reached Castlerea. There was a certain beauty to the wild countryside in the west. Although the land wasn't rich, there was a wild ruggedness about it. The stone walls dividing up the fields were magnificent. Alexander's mother always called them "the famine walls". He always thought about the manual labour that went into building those walls.

"Right John, where to from here?" he asked as they reached the outskirts of Castlerea.

John looked up from his papers and answered, "take the second right after the bridge, down the road for a mile and a half. Then second left for another half mile and the house is on our right."

Alexander followed the instructions and reached the destination in less than 10 minutes.

In off the road, they saw a small white cottage with a path leading to the front door. On either side of the path there was a lawn with no flowers. To the right of the house as they looked at it, there was a large driveway which led into the farm yard. All the walls of the house and the outbuildings were whitewashed. As they sat there, a man beckoned them to drive into the driveway which led to an opening in another whitewashed wall with a blue gate. They went in through the gate which led to a small courtyard. A man in his late 30s came towards them, hand held out.

"Hello, I'm James Healey, come on inside and meet the wife and child."

The two men introduced themselves and followed James into a back scullery, where they noticed an old fashioned butter churner and butter shapers. The walls in here were white as well. This led into an old fashioned kitchen with a green Aga cooker, a dresser with a glass cover through which one could see all the crockery. There was a linen tablecloth on the table and it was set for tea.

"Please take a seat," said James. "This is my wife Lily. Our baby is asleep in the bedroom."

Lily was only about 30 years old but was dressed in a very old-fashioned manner and wore a full apron, decorated in roses.

"Please have something to eat and a cup of tea."

She poured the tea and they partook of scones and fruitcake which were delicious. They all made small talk for about 20 minutes as they imbibed. Finally, John Muldoon said "We need to talk to you about your interactions with the Galdstones of Briarstown in County Kildare. As my sergeant has informed you, Jinny Galdstone was murdered last Tuesday week, and we are making enquiries and speaking to anyone who may have had dealings with her or her family, especially if there was negativity involved."

"I never had much to do with them. I Just met them once. It was my

father, God rest his soul, who met them at a mart. It was a bad day that
he did business with that lot. It destroyed him and just about ruined
us all."

"Please take it from the beginning and tell us your story," said Alexander.

Alexander always liked to get a complete history of a suspect's life. He
believed that insights could be gleaned from a person's life story and
background.

"Don't leave anything out. Has your family been living long in this
area?"

"My grandparents moved here in 1941," he began. "They used to
live near Westport in Mayo, where they had two smallholdings. The
land commission gave us this holding with 50 acres. I still have the
document in my files. It was, what was called, an exchange of hold-
ings, carried out under section 23 of the Irish land act 1909. It was
a condition of the exchange that the land commission would erect a
new dwelling house and out offices on the land in Castlerea.

They had a mixed farm. Some dry cattle, some sheep. They always kept
a few cows for milking. My grandmother made butter and sold the
excess in the village. They also kept geese, ducks and hens. They were
very hard-working people. It was hard enough to make a good living.
My father decided when he took over, that it might be a better idea
to go into dairying. They seemed to be doing a bit better than other
farmers. So he started expanding the herd, to see how things would go.
We had a very small milking parlour which only held eight cows at a
time, and we used to milk them by hand. Nevertheless we managed.
We all mucked in as such, and we also employed two young lads from
the parish who were a great help. Dad always had a look to the future.
He was always on the lookout for good stock to add to our herd. By
this time we had about 30 cows. He had also managed to get a loan

from the bank to expand and modernise the milking parlour. He went around the mart looking for new female calves to introduce to our herd.

So it was that he met Adam Galdstone at the Mullingar Mart. Dad thought that the heifers that Galdstone had for sale were beautiful animals. He approached him and asked him if he would sell five female calves to him the following spring. In the meantime my mother became very ill. She had been in remission but unfortunately, her illness came back. That was a very difficult time for the three of us. Lily and I decided to get married while Mam was well enough to attend the wedding. Lily and I had been sweethearts since she was 15 and I was 18. So, the three of us looked after Mam here. In the spring, Adam Gladstone arrived with the five calves in a truck one afternoon. Dad had said to me that they weren't quite what he had expected, but he had paid a hefty price for them and he had a lot on his mind, as Mam's health had worsened. Mam passed away three weeks later. We just did the work on the farm like robots. I don't think that any of us were paying enough attention to the cows and calves. They had been getting sick. About eight weeks after the calves had arrived, a good few of the animals were looking bad. There was weight loss, a hacking cough, a lot of diarrhoea. We called the vet who immediately suspected TB. Our own cows had been tested six months earlier for the disease and all had been well. We had 20 reactors, including the five calves we had bought from the Galdstones. They had to be slaughtered and destroyed. Everything had to come to a standstill. Several more interval tests had to be carried out, before we got the all clear. My father really fell into a depression. We were both convinced that Adam Galdstone had sold us five reactors. My father just couldn't believe that one farmer could do this to another. Not alone had we lost half our herd but my father had a lot of debt to pay off. We decided to travel to Briarstown to confront the Galdstones. Perhaps, they would be reasonable and either compensate us for our loss or replace the slaughtered animals with healthy ones, with clear TB tests. My poor father had looked somewhat hopeful as we started our journey to Kildare.

When we arrived at the Galdstones we were shown into the kitchen. Both Adam and Jinny Galdstone were there. Dad explained our predicament and our hope that they would help us out. Adam said nothing but just stood there looking down at the floor. Jinny did all the talking. She was insistent that our problems had nothing to do with them. There was absolutely no TB in their herd. Her voice was slightly raised and dictatorial. She reiterated that it was a problem of our own making. We had either given the animals bad feed or badgers had infected the herd. As you know a lot of farmers believe that badgers should be culled and are a major problem in the spread of the disease. She offered to show us her own cows which we took her up on. We saw the cows and heifers. Dad and I both thought that the calves they had sold to us bore very little resemblance to the ones in the Galdstones' fields. We were later convinced that the five calves that we had been sold, had never been on this farm. Adam probably bought them from some dodgy person and just sold them to us at a great profit. Jinny also insisted on showing us their TB testing results – all clear of course.

My father asked her if they were going to help us at all. She answered with an emphatic no. I looked at this tall woman with long blond tresses and icy, cold, blue eyes and thought I was staring into the eyes of evil. I then glanced at my poor father. Life had gone out of his eyes as if she had taken a blade and plunged it into his heart.

To cut a long, sorry story short, three weeks later, my poor Lily went out to the hayshed to collect some eggs for breakfast and found my dad hanging from a beam. I will never forget the howling and screaming that I heard from the barn, nor the sight that awaited me as I ran into the barn. My poor dad could take no more.

The years have passed and we have managed. We still have a few cows but it's mostly sheep now. We have been blessed with a beautiful baby. I work in a sawmill a few miles away, which is a great help to us. I don't know if the Galdstones know about our tragedy. I don't believe that woman would have cared. Our own neighbours here have been wonderful to us. Bit by bit I'm paying off the farm debts. So I suppose you want to know if I killed her. Well, I didn't, not because I wouldn't have liked to, but because I have too much to lose."

Alexander and John had sat very quietly and had listened very intently to James' account. John had taken notes.

John looked up from his notepad "I still need to ask you if you have an alibi for the time of death, that is between 6am and 8am of the Tuesday morning. "

"I did some work on the farm and then I was at work in the sawmills from 8,30am."

"What about you Mrs. Healey, where were you?"

"Oh I was here with Rose," answered Lily.

"Lily doesn't drive," added her husband James.

"No, I never learned," said Lily. "James drives me everywhere."

She looked across at her husband lovingly.

"Well James," said Muldoon. "If you could just give me the details and phone number of the sawmills where you work, we still have to check everythingout."

James wrote the information down on a sheet of paper and handed it to inspector Muldoon.

"Thank you both so much for your cooperation," added Alexander, as both men stood up to leave.

They all shook hands and the two men walked out to the car as the young couple stood at the door and waved them goodbye.

Inspector Muldoon and Alexander de Bruin began their journey back to Kildare. They drove along the country roads lined with beech and hawthorn hedges which led into Castlerea. They were silent for a while, both pondering what they had heard. John Muldoon spoke first.

"What did you think of that?" he asked.

"That poor couple have had a very hard time. I am inclined to believe that they were sold reactor calves. We may feel very sorry for them, but we must still check out their alibis," returned Alexander.

"Did you find it strange that neither of them asked how she died, Alex?"

"Perhaps, but not everyone asks that question. Some people don't ask it out of respect for the dead, or because they don't want to appear overly interested," answered Alexander. "What I did find interesting, was the comparison "as if she had plunged a knife into his chest," he continued.

"I wonder would James have said that if he had plunged a knife into Mrs. Galdstone's heart," returned John.

John Muldoon looked through his notes as Alexander de Bruin drove along the winding, country roads back towards Athlone.

"By the way, I will return your steak knives when I'm in Briarstown next. Did you see any steak knives in the Healey's kitchen? I didn't. Of course you wouldn't leave a set out that was missing the murder weapon. So, did you notice any problems or inconsistencies in their statements?"

Alexander thought carefully for a moment.

"First of all, James claims that he was at work in the sawmill at 8.

30am. You have his employer's phone number, so that can easily be verified. That being true, doesn't mean that he hadn't time to drive to Briarstown, murder Jinny Galdstone and be back in Castlerea for 8.30am. Being a dairy farmer himself, he would know about early milking. He also admitted that he had visited the Galdstone farm with his father, so he would have known the layout of the place. Secondly, the couple were very insistent that Lily didn't drive. We can get Sergeant Dunne to check with the Department of Transport, if she is in possession of a driving license, as she herself could have driven to Briarstown, murdered Jinny Galdstone and returned home, believing that her husband would have an alibi at work and she would have a great alibi because she doesn't drive."

John Muldoon sat quietly in the passenger seat and thought about James' description of Jinny Galdstone with her long blond tresses and icy cold blue eyes, and remembered the horrible vision he had encountered in the milking parlour that morning, which had reminded him of the Greek legend of the monster Medusa. He thought about the amount of hardship that had been caused to that poor family by the selfishness and apathy of the Galdstones. The desperation that had led to James senior's suicide and the resilience of the young James and his wife Lily.

John was jolted out of his reverie by a bump on the road and looked down at his notes again and then over at Alexander who was concentrating on the road. They were about halfway through their journey home. They had left the poor soil of Connaught and were entering Westmeath. Both men were very relieved when they finally reached the flat plains of the Curragh and headed towards Naas.

"I intend calling into Adam Galdstone tomorrow morning to inform him that you are no longer a suspect and explain to him that you will be assisting me with the investigation, and accompanying me during my interviews with relevant people. I don't know how he will react, as he and his daughter had been so keen to point the finger at you. I'll let you know how I get on."

John Muldoon alighted from the car and walked slowly towards the Garda station entrance, carrying his trusty briefcase. Alexander de Bruin put the car in gear and headed out of Naas and towards Briarstown. Ten minutes later he drove into the rear entrance of The Lodge. He sat in the car for a couple of minutes, just resting. He walked under the archway, at the back of the house, and made his way in through the back door, down the hallway towards his office.

"Monique, I'm home," he called out.

Monique appeared from the kitchen and walked towards him. He gave her a big hug and held her closely for a moment.

"Is everything okay?" she asked. "How did your interview in Castlerea go?"

Monique listened intently as her husband recounted his day. Monique was sad and angry but mostly shocked, as she took in the enormity of the catastrophe that had befallen the Healeys.

"That makes the Galdstones completely amoral," she ventured.

"As you know," continued Alexander. "I've come across these types before who care little about anyone else. They are not as rare as you might hope. I suppose it's unfortunate that they are our neighbours. But it's not my job to judge. John and I must solve the murder, gather the facts, interview any suspects and witnesses and draw our conclusions."

"How did you get on with John Muldoon?" asked Monique.

"Extremely well," answered Alexander. "He is a very thorough man, he is clever and diligent. I think we make a very good team. We seem to know already what each other is thinking. I'm very optimistic that we will solve this murder. Enough of that now, how was your day?"

"Well, I was chatting with Alison and we decided to take Mrs. Hannigan out for our usual lunch next week."

Alison and Robert King were great friends of the de Bruins. Robert was in Alexander's cadet class. Both couples had lived in quarters in the Curragh Camp and had children of the same age. Alison was a secondary school teacher. The two ladies were firm friends and both couples socialised together a lot, mainly in the messes. Mrs. Hannigan had been most helpful through the years looking after both sets of children, when required. Monique and Alison were very fond of Mrs. Hannigan and the three ladies went to lunch about four times a year and always had great chats about everything.

"Where are you going to lunch?" asked Alexander.

"Probably the Keadeen Hotel. It's very handy for everyone. I can pick up Mrs. Hannigan from the village and Alison just has to drive from Naas to Newbridge."

Alexander and Monique sat down at the kitchen table and continued to chat over coffee and biscuits. Alexander knew that there was most certainly another difficult interview tomorrow.

CHAPTER 10

———— ❦ ————

THE VICARAGE

I nspector Muldoon arrived at The Lodge at 11 o'clock the following morning. Alexander met him at the front door and they went
into the kitchen for morning coffee and a chat.

"Well, I called up to the Galdstones and I've just left them. Adam
and Clara were there. John, the son was working on the farm and
Frank is staying with a friend in the village. I explained the situation
to them and neither of them was best pleased. I told them that you
were ruled out and that you've had experience investigating such cases
in the past. I added that all the necessary checks had been done on
you and that an Garda Siochana were very pleased to have your help
in the matter. Adam seemed to finally accept the situation reluctantly
but there was no moving Clara. She was extremely angry. She insisted
that you were the only one with any bad feeling towards her mother
and she reminded me that the murder weapon had been found in
your ditch. I did my best to reassure her and eventually I had to tell
them that there were other viable suspects that we were investigating.
Clara was somewhat taken back by this and was insisting that I tell
her who they were. I told her that the case was ongoing and that I
wasn't in a position to divulge any information on the other suspects.
She accepted this, but stated that none of the family wanted you on

their property, questioning them. I agreed to this for the moment, but explained to them that you were officially part of the investigation team and may have to be involved with them at a later date. I made an appointment for us at the vicarage for 12 o'clock. Both Jonathan and Mary Edwards will be present."

"Well, we have a few minutes before we have to be on our way, let's have a coffee and prepare a few questions," said Alexander.

The two men sat at the table and discussed how they would manage the interview. It was difficult to know exactly how suspects would react to certain questions, and sometimes, one just had to go with the flow. Alexander and John left the house at 11.50 and arrived just on time outside the vicarage.

The trees and shrubs around the vicarage were very lush and green, intermingled with red and pink foliage. The men looked across at the graveyard where Jinny Galdstone had her last resting place. They made their way to the door and knocked. Mary Edwards answered the door with a smile.

"Good afternoon, I'm Mary Edwards," she introduced herself.

"Inspector John Muldoon, and I think you know Alexander de Bruin," said Muldoon.

"Yes indeed, please follow me, my husband Jonathan is in the sitting room. He is expecting you."

John and Alexander followed Mary into a cosy warm room, with a log fire. Jonathan was sitting on the settee beside the fire. There were two armchairs across from the settee. He rose when the three entered the room. Mary introduced them and they shook hands.

"Please sit down gentlemen," Jonathan said, pointing to the two armchairs.

Mary took her seat beside her husband. Jonathan looked very nervous and clasped his hands together tightly on his lap. Mary seemed more relaxed and composed. There were knitting needles and lemon coloured wool with a half knitted baby's cardigan on an occasional table beside where Mary was sitting. John wondered if she were expecting another baby or was it a present for a friend. There was a lovely smell of baking, wafting from the kitchen.

"May I offer you some tea or coffee and cake?" Mary asked.

"No thank you," answered Alexander. "We've just had some refreshments a short time ago."

"May we begin?" said John. "We have some questions regarding the death of Jinny Galdstone. We are trying to paint a picture of her life here. What were your dealings with her?"

Mary answered first.

"She was a member of the church community and was very involved in all aspects of the parish. She was a very helpful person, isn't that right, Jonathan?"

"Yes indeed dear, she helped us out a lot with the church preparations, flower arrangements in the chapel, any baking that had to be done, the ladies lunches. She was a very good Sunday school teacher – seemed to know her Bible very well. She even volunteered to supervise on the camping trip with the scouts. Very helpful all around."

Mary seemed to move closer to her husband on the couch, as if to support him. Jonathan was finding it hard to make eye contact with either man.

"So, she was an extremely helpful person all around," added John.

"Yes, we would certainly say that," returned Mary.

Jonathan nodded.

"Did either of you have any ill feeling towards her at all?" interjected Alexander.

The couple looked at each other and Mary answered, "No, not that I can think of. Everything we did together had to do with parish work, so we've never had a row or anything like that with her."

"Are you not aware at all, of the rumour that is circulating about a very close relationship between you, Jonathan, and Jinny Galdstone? It's a very small parish here," John said.

Jonathan Edwards blushed and his face went a very deep red colour. He looked down at his shoes and then looked beseechingly at his wife. Mary took his hand and looked lovingly at him. Mary's eyes flashed at them and she straightened up in her seat. She still kept a firm grasp of her husband's hand.

"OK," she said. "I'll tell you about her. Let me assure you that Jonathan had no idea whatsoever that Jinny had feelings for him. It was only when he had gotten the cold shoulder from Adam Galdstone and felt really confused as to why, that we discussed it and this was the night before the funeral. Jonathan had been with the Galdstones preparing the reading and hymns for Jinny's funeral. Adam was downright rude and nasty to him. It was while Jonathan was trying to prepare his sermon and was having great difficulty with it that I had to tell him what I knew, or at least suspected. This isn't the first time that this has happened to Jonathan. He is a kind, gentle, thoughtful man, who always has time for all his flock. There have been women in the past who have had a crush on him, but these were decent women who avoided him for awhile, until their feelings had passed. Jinny was different. She took a look at him and wanted him. She was so persistent. She was everywhere, inveigling herself into our home. She got involved in every aspect of parish life. Everywhere Jonathan went, she was there. I even had to go on the camping trip with the scouts as I had to protect Jonathan from her. Of course, my poor, dear, innocent husband saw none of this. Everyone else recognised what was going on, including Adam, I suppose. I must tell you, I detest camping. I was hoping that her feelings for him would subside, and that she might even move on to some other poor, unsuspecting male. But, no such luck. She became more determined. I had made up my mind shortly before her death, that I would have to tell Jonathan and confront Jinny. But she died before I could get around to it. Poor Jonathan was so shocked when I told him about it, that night, before the funeral. It took all the courage he could muster to write the sermon and deliver it the following day, and to complete the whole ceremony and burial, knowing that everyone present was watching, listening and wondering. But we did it together. I played the organ in the church. And, here we are, getting on with our lives and work," concluded Mary.

"Thank you for your honesty, both of you. I know that this can't have been easy for either of you," Alexander said.

"I have just one more question before we leave you both in peace," said John. "Have you both got alibis for the morning in question, that is between 6am and 8am of the Tuesday?"

"We were here together," insisted Mary. "We usually get up at 7.30, have breakfast, get the kids ready for school and start our day. It's the same every weekday morning and we certainly remember that Tuesday morning with all the commotion that ensued."

The two men stood up to leave, Mary and Jonathan Edwards led them towards the front door and showed them out.

"Thanks again for all your help. We will probably be in touch again," said John, as they walked towards the car.

Alexander and John drove back up to The Lodge. They repaired to the sitting room for a chat and to compare notes.

"Well, they've given each other alibis," began Alexander.

"They have indeed and spousal alibis as we know, aren't always very reliable."

"I'm not sure that Jonathan Edwards is capable of murder, never mind such a violent, bloody killing like this. He just comes across as a very gentle, soft person who wouldn't hurt a fly. I'm also convinced that he was oblivious to Jinny Galdstone's feelings for him. He appears to adore his wife and relies a great deal on her support," continued Alexander.

"Mary is much stronger than he is. She's the rock in that family. She holds it all together. I wonder how far she'd go to protect her husband and her children. She's no shrinking violet, despite appearances. There is nothing more awe inspiring than a wife and mother protecting her own. I wonder though, would Mary have used such violent methods?" John pondered.

"It's very unusual to see a woman murder in such a fashion. Mary Edwards is a very calm, intelligent woman. I don't believe that she is prone to tantrums or bouts of rage. I think that if she had murdered Jinny Galdstone, it would've been with a calmer method such as poison. Poison is the most popular method of disposal among female killers," added Alexander.

"I wonder did Mary ever confront Jinny? She claims that she had never gotten around to it" John muttered.

"Well, I'm sure she wouldn't have confronted her at 6 o'clock in the morning, with the steak knife, in the milking parlour. I don't see how we can refute her statement, that she had never discussed Jonathan with Jinny," continued Alexander.

"I'm of the opinion that we remove Jonathan from the suspect list. I just don't see him wielding a knife like that. He really doesn't seem to have any rage in him at all. While I wouldn't completely rule Mary out, I think we can place her on the "maybe" list. I feel that she is capable of doing anything to protect her family. Jonathan is her alibi. They got up at 7.30, which leaves time very tight indeed," John observed.

"Whoever committed this crime must have been completely covered in blood. He or she had to have disposed of the clothes and shoes that they were wearing, showered, unless they were covered from head to toe in protective clothing of some sort, changed into their normal clothes and got on with their day. And of course, wiped the handle of the murder weapon and deposited it in my ditch. I'm beginning to think that this was very carefully planned, indeed," added Alexander.

"I need to ring Sergeant Dunne at the station," said John. "May I use your phone in the office?"

"Yes of course, go ahead."

A few moments later John re-entered the room.

"I was just checking about James Healey's work alibi. He did arrive at work at 8.30 on the Tuesday morning, which I suppose only proves that he couldn't have murdered Jinny after about 6.20am. That leaves his window of opportunity at less than 15 minutes. The Department of Transport has not yet returned with their answer about Lily Healey's driving licence. I fear this may take some time. If Lily Healey drove to Briarstown, her husband must know that she was missing. The only way either of them could have committed this murder is if both of them were in on it," concluded John.

The two men sat down at the table and made some changes to their notes.

"Have you the photos of the crime scene there?" asked Alexander.

John handed the photos to Alexander who looked at them intently.

"There's blood all over and all around Jinny Galdstone. The blood is matted in her hair, yet there are no footprints in the blood, no fingerprints that shouldn't be in the parlour. The murderer made sure that his or her shoes did not make contact with the blood, even as he or she was standing or crouching over her for four stab thrusts. The only footprints that are in the parlour are those of the family's Wellington boots. Of course, many people have wellingtons with the same sole thread. So, the killer could have worn Wellington boots with the same sole thread. There's a woman's size 6 and size 7 and a man's size 11 and 12 which all correspond to the sizes worn by Jinny, Clara, Adam and John. The sole threads also correspond to the Wellington Boots taken from them for examination. Unfortunately they are very common sizes. We need to get your men to examine the soles of any Wellington boots owned by the other suspects. We can do our own comparisons as we proceed with questioning the next group of suspects."

"So, it was either by luck or design that the killer wore boots that are the same size and have the same sole thread as members of the Galdstone family," returned John.

"I see that Jinny had no defence wounds and no skin or hair under her nails. She must have been taken completely by surprise with the first stab wound to the stomach, and lay there incapacitated, while the other four wounds were inflicted. There was a gash to the back of her head, where she hit the ground hard, when she fell. Her skull was cracked which led to more bleeding. The medical examiner still thinks that she was conscious when she received the four wounds to her chest and heart. Death would have come very quickly after the stabbing to the heart, which was vicious. He thinks that might have been the last one. So I think we have made some progress in our investigation," concluded Alexander.

The two men returned the photos and other documents to the folders. John Muldoon put them into his briefcase. Alexander left his notebook on the oak table. They returned to the kitchen to have a cup of coffee and take a break from their investigation.

"Is Monique about?" asked John.

"No, she and her friend Alison have taken Mrs. Hannigan for lunch in Newbridge. She thought today might be a good day for it, as she knew you and I would be busy and might need the office here to discuss our findings. I don't expect her back before 4 o'clock, as when the three ladies get chatting, they can go on for hours. They really are great pals and especially enjoy their lunches. You'd never know, John, but Monique might return home with some more useful information. You recall that Mrs. Hannigan cleans a lot of the houses around here. Remember, she was the person who informed Monique about the troubles in the Galdstone marriage. It's these small titbits of information that might break the case. I'm quite sure that the three ladies will be chatting about this investigation. I'll be very interested to learn about their insights into it. They will probably come up with some very interesting theories," smiled Alexander.

That afternoon, Monique did not return home until after 5 o'clock. She had spent a lovely afternoon with her two good friends. They had laughed and chatted about everything. Mrs. Hannigan loved to tell stories about her two adored children. Mrs. Hannigan was a great chatterbox. She was also a wonderful student of human character. She was able to read a person very quickly. As a matter of fact, she disliked very few people she worked for, which was a good sign. However, she appeared to have very little time for the Galdstones. And of course, on that afternoon at lunch, the Galdstones were one of the topics of conversation. Monique and Alison listened very attentively to her opinions on the family. She found Adam Galdstone to be a very weak man, who just went along with whatever his wife said. He was downtrodden and sometimes seemed as if he had lost the will to live. There had been rows in the house. Several years back the dispute started over Clara, and Jinny's insistence that they would cut her off. She was a very hard, cruel woman, according to Mrs. Hannigan. Adam had argued Clara's case, but to no avail. He really had no backbone and Clara was out, with no financial help at all, or no emotional support.

There had also been the suspicion over the years that Frank was gay. This would have been anathema to Jinny. She had no tolerance for anyone who broke the rules in her house – except for herself of course. So, after his leaving cert , Frank took himself off to California and no one had seen him again until his mother's funeral. The rows had started up again about six months ago. Adam was very annoyed that Jinny was spending so much time with the new vicar. Mrs. Hannigan overheard the rows, as she cleaned the upstairs bedrooms. Mrs. Hannigan didn't know John very well, except that she was aware that he was the golden boy, who got everything. He never visited the house while she was there, but worked long hours on the farm with both parents. Clara had been welcomed back into the fold about a year ago. She moved back into the house with her son, Jack. She came across as an angry, bitter, sad young woman and who would blame her! She seemed to just tolerate both her parents. The Galdstones had begun renovations on an old outhouse for herself and her son. Clara still did shifts in a supermarket in either Naas or Newbridge. The poor girl was not very happy.

Monique recounted her afternoon with her two friends to Alexander, on her return to The Lodge .

"That's new information about Frank," said Monique.

"It is indeed," replied Alexander, "but he couldn't have murdered his mother, as he only came home from California for the funeral. Although I'll have to get John to check out the flight manifest, to make sure he arrived in Ireland when he said he did."

CHAPTER 11

— ⁂ —

A SAD ENCOUNTER

M r. and Mrs. Lavelle lived in a three bedroomed cottage in the cul-de-sac not far from The Lodge. They were both local people and their families had lived in this area for generations. Inspector Muldoon had made an appointment to meet them on Thursday morning at eleven o'clock. Mr. Lavelle had taken a day's leave from work to facilitate the meeting.

John Muldoon collected Alexander de Bruin on his way to the Lavelle's. On the short drive from The Lodge to the Lavelle's, Alexander explained what he had found out about Frank and asked John to check the passenger list for Frank's flight into Ireland for his mother's funeral.

They arrived at two minutes to eleven at the front of the cottage. The two men alighted from the car and walked towards the house. There was a small iron gate, which opened onto a short path that led up to the house. On either side of the path was a well maintained lawn but there were no flowers. All around the boundary of the property was a box hedge, neatly trimmed. John knocked at the door. They heard footsteps inside before the door was opened by a very slender woman in her mid to late 50s.

"Good morning Mrs. Lavelle, I'm Alexander de Bruin – you probably know me from The Lodge."

The de Bruins had never had a conversation with the Lavelles in all the time they had lived in Briarstown, as the Lavelles were not very active in the community. The Lavelles kept themselves very much to themselves.

"This is Inspector Muldoon from Naas Garda station."

"Please come in, Jimmy is in the sitting room waiting for you."

The two men entered the hallway. The walls were beige and the carpet, a plain brownish colour. The house did not have the feeling of being lived in. It was a very sad house. Mrs. Lavelle herself was dressed in a cream blouse, beige cardigan and brown skirt. Her short brown hair was neat and she wore no makeup. They walked into the the sitting room which had a similar decor. Everything was very clean but looked worn just like the couple who lived there.

"This is Jimmy," said Mrs. Lavelle.

A gaunt thin man, also in his mid to late fifties stood up from his armchair and shook hands with Alexander and John. Although there were a few logs burning in the grate, the room still felt chilly and dark.

"Take a seat," said Jimmy. There was a two seater couch facing the fireplace. John and Alexander sat on this, as Jimmy had sat down in his armchair and Mrs. Lavelle sat in hers, at the other side of the fireplace. They must have spent many an evening, sitting here contemplating their sad lives.

"Can I get you a cup-a-tea?" asked Mrs. Lavelle.

"No we're fine, thank you very much, mam," answered Alexander.

"As you know," continued John, "we are investigating the murder of Jinny Galdstone. We are trying to get as much background about her and her family and we are talking to all the neighbours, together with anyone who had any dealings with the Galdstone family. We know that you have both lived here all your lives, so your insights may be very helpful to us."

"Yea, we've lived here all our lives," answered Jimmy Lavelle. "What do you need to know?"

As they all sat there, Mrs. Lavelle's eyes welled up with tears.

"Don't upset yourself Dora love," whispered her husband.

"We are so sorry if we are causing you both any upset," intervened Alexander. "We certainly don't mean to. We know about your dreadful loss and that you blame Jinny Galdstone for your son Mike's death. Perhaps if you just told us your story from the beginning it might be easier and that way we can get a full picture of what went on."

"You know I'm glad she's dead," said Dora Lavelle. "She was nothing more than a witch."

Jimmy leaned across and patted her on the hand.

"Now, now, I know love." The couple looked sadly at each other and Jimmy sat back into his armchair.

"Tell us about your life here and Mike," suggested Alexander.

Jimmy Lavelle began. "We've lived here all our lives since we got married. We were very young you know, only 18. We were always very happy. I got a job in Irish Ropes in Newbridge. I used to cycle eight miles to the bus stop in Naas and then get a bus into Newbridge. I still work there you know. They are great employers. Dora always stayed at home and kept house. She's a great cook you know. When I used to come home of an evening there'd be a lovely stew and some cake afterwards. She loved knitting and sewing. She made all the curtains and cushions and bedspreads for the house. They were so pretty, just like Dora. When I saved up enough I was able to get carpets at a reduced rate from Irish Ropes. We had a lovely house, if I say so myself. We were very proud of our little house. The years passed but no child arrived. Dora went to the doctors loads of times but they couldn't help. One of Dora's aunts, Joan, said to us one day that there were kids that needed fostering and if Dora could be minding a child she wouldn't be thinking so much about our own troubles. Me and Dora went to the parish priest, Fr. Kelly to ask his advice. Low and behold, it wasn't long before this woman arrived out to the house from the Health Board with a tiny little baby boy. She says to us, this little fella needs a good loving home. Fr. Kelly had put in a good word for us. His name was Mike and his mother wasn't able to look after him. She had taken off to England and her family didn't want anything to do with the baby and the father was nowhere to be seen.

The three of us were a right little family. We were so happy. I'd never seen Dora so content. She looked after Mike so well. She knitted little outfits for him. I always looked forward to getting home from work. Sometimes when I was late and Mike would be in bed, I'd sneak into his room and look down at him sleepin'. The years just passed so quickly. Mike went to the local national school. When he was old enough he became an altar boy. Fr. Kelly was always very kind to him. Mike's mam never came back. The Health Board got a letter from her when Mike was ten, tellin' them that she had married an English man, that he knew nothin' about Mike and she wanted to keep it that way. To tell ye the truth, we were very relieved. Mike was a very good, kind little fella. He'd always help his mam in the house and in the garden. You could hear the two-a-them laughin' outside havin' great fun together. Our Mike was a very clever fella. The teachers always told us so. He was top of his class all the time. He'd come home to us with his report card. Always As and Bs. He was as proud a punch and me and Dora couldn't be prouder. The teachers used to say to us that boy will be able to go to university. Me and Dora left school after the Inter Cert, so we were very happy for Mike. I used to say to Dora that we'll have to save like mad to be able to send him up to Dublin or down to Galway to university. We had a good bit saved by the time he'd finished school. Our Mike did very well in his leaving cert and got a place in Trinity College. Imagine our boy going to Trinity College, the best university in Ireland. We were a bit worried because we didn't know how he'd fit in there – not being from a well to do family and bein' a simple lad from the country. Anyway Fr. Kelly helped us with the grant application and he organised everything. Mike was a great young lad and always had a summer job since he was 14. He saved a lot of money, and managed to buy himself a small car the summer after his leaving cert. Fr. Kelly was trying to organise somewhere for him to stay in Dublin. In fact he had found digs for him with a woman who would look after him. Mike didn't want to leave home. You know there's a train from Sallins early in the morning. So Mike made up his mind that he would stay at home and travel up and down everyday. Fr. Kelly was very kind and he said that the woman in Dublin would give him a bed anytime he needed to stay over. So our Mike used to drive to Sallins station early every morning and take the train to Dublin. Sometimes he'd give his friend Nick a lift. Nick was his best friend all his life."

Jimmy Lavelle took a deep breath and sighed. He slumped further back into his armchair and stared into nothingness.

"Would you like to take a break Mr. Lavelle?" asked John.

"Just give us a minute," he answered.

The four of them sat silently for a few minutes. Inspector Muldoon looked down at his notes. Alexander looked around the room and thought that he had never been in such a melancholy house, full of memories, but overwhelmed by grief and sadness. He noticed all the photos of young Mike on the walls and on the mantlepiece. There was a beautiful wedding photo of a very young smiling bride and groom among the photos of their beloved son.

Jimmy Lavelle took a deep breath and straightened himself in his armchair, as if he were facing a firing squad.

"I'm okay now," he said, "just needed a break, its coming to the hard part. Everyone down this road has to pass by the Galdstone's farm when we want to get to the main road to anywhere. It was the same for poor Mike. We all know that that awful woman would stop all the traffic with her cord across the road so she could move her cattle from one side of the road to the other. I used to tell Mike, give yourself enough time lad, don't be rushin' and speedin on them roads. He was such a good lad, he always listened to us. But if anyone got caught, you could be there for ten or fifteen minutes. If Mike was delayed that much he'd miss his train. You could never be sure what time Jinny Galdstone would decide to move the cows. It was anytime between 5.45 and 6.15. So Mike tried to be past their house before 5.45. He'd be in plenty of time then. He picked his friend Nick up at 5.35. He only lives down the road and they headed for the main road. They would have had plenty of time to get by the Galdstone's farm, only for that dreadful woman had the cord across the road at 5.40. Nick, thank God wasn't injured in the crash, so he was able to tell us everything that happened. They got to the Galdstones at 5.40 as usual but, there she was, with the cord across the road letting the cows move across. Nick said that Mike rolled down the window and asked if she could stop for a minute and let them pass by. He explained that he had to get to Sallins to catch their train. Seemingly, she just ignored him and stuck her nose in the air and pretended that she had heard nothing. He called her name and asked her a second time, but again the witch turned her back on them and continued moving the cows. The two lads were stuck there for over 15 minutes. Nick said that it seemed like she was really taking her time and getting some sort of pleasure out of delaying them. When she removed the cord Mike revved up the car and sped off. He drove over a load of cow manure on the road – that lot were never good at cleaning up the mess after the cows – and the car skidded and the drivers side of the car slid into a tree. Our poor Mike suffered head injuries and died instantly. That was the worst day of our lives.

Mike's funeral was huge. Everyone who knew us and Mike came – everyone except the Galdstones. Not one of them called to the house to sympathise, not one of them came to the wake, not one of them came to the funeral. They didn't care a damn about our poor boy. There was a Coroner's inquest a year later. We tried to tell them that it was her fault. We both stood up and told the story. Mike wouldn't have skidded if they had cleaned the road. She shouldn't be allowed stop people on a public road to suit herself. The Coroner was very kind but ruled death by accident. I don't know why these people can do what they want on our public road and cause an accident that kills our boy and get away with it."

Jimmy Lavelle sat forward in his chair and put his head in his hands. His wife sat with tears in her eyes and her hands clasped as if in prayer.

"We are so sorry for all your suffering and loss," said Alexander.

"I wouldn't mind," said Dora Lavelle, "but Frank Galdstone was at school with our Mike. They used to hang out together and were friends."

"Yes, they were," continued Jimmy Lavelle. "They were very interested in cars. When Jinny Galdstone bought her MGBGT, Mike was fascinated by it. He spent a few hours up at the farm with Frank lookin' at it. I remember when he came home he was so excited and kept talkin' about it. "Dad," he said, "it's a blue MGBGT, 1.8 coupe with two doors. It's a petrol convertible with a black interior. You can pull the roof back. It's a black, cloth, fold down roof." "Imagine," he said, "it has alloy wheels."

"She was still driving it around with the roof down like lady muck," interjected Dora Lavelle, "looking down her nose at everyone. She never looked at us again. It was as if we didn't exist. She'd fly by in the car every summer and expect the rest of us to get out of the way."

Dora Lavelle was now shaking slightly and the tears ran down her cheeks. She took a hanky from her sleeve and blew her nose and wiped her tears away. Her husband stood up and walked over to her chair, stood behind it and put his hand on her shoulder.

"As you can see, we have never recovered. The day our dear boy left us our lives changed. The light just went out. When I drive to work every morning, I have to pass that farm and the place where our dear boy was killed. Every time Dora has to go into the village or to church or shopping she has to do the same. Our whole life is a nightmare caused by that witch. We're not sorry she is dead. We're glad she's dead," concluded Jimmy Lavelle, with a long sigh.

"Once again we are so sorry that we have put you through this, but we are very grateful to you for having told us your story," said John Muldoon. "Once again, please forgive us but we have to ask certain questions. We need to check where everyone was between 6am and 8am on the day of the murder," said Alexander.

"Well," answered Jimmy, "I leave here every morning at 7am to get to the "Irish Ropes" in Newbridge for my shift at half seven. When I passed by the Galdstones, there was no one around. I saw your big black dogs in the field as I passed your place," he indicated to Alexander.

"And what about you Mrs. Lavelle?" asked John.

"I always get up with Jimmy and get him his breakfast and have a cup-a-tea with him. I don't sleep well anyway."

"I have just one more question before we leave," said John. "Do you have Wellington boots and may we see them please?"

Jimmy Lavelle led the two men to the scullery where two pairs of Wellington boots stood guard. John picked up each pair and looked at the soles. He replaced them in their original position.

"Thank you for all your assistance," said Alexander.

John and Alexander walked back into the sitting room where Mrs. Lavelle was still sitting on her chair looking out the window.

"Goodbye and thank you Mrs. Lavelle," said John.. "Please don't get up. We'll be on our way now."

Jimmy Lavelle showed the two men out. They walked back to the car in sombre mood and drove back up to The Lodge.

They spent about an hour discussing the case and planning their next moves.

"The thread of the soles on the wellingtons are different," said John. "Jimmy definitely passed by your place when you had the dogs out for a walk that morning. I'll have to check his time of arrival at the Irish Ropes in Newbridge. By the way, the Department of Transport got back to Sergeant Dunne, and Lilly Healey has never had a driving licence. He also checked with a local guard in Castlerea and she has never been seen behind the wheel. He also checked the passenger list for Frank's flight to Dublin and he was on it alright, so that's another thing cleared up."

"Jinny Galdstone has caused a lot of people a great deal of hardship. The story that the family tells us about a loving wife and mother, beloved by all who knew her is far from the truth. The more we get to learn about her, the more convinced I am that she had many enemies. We have yet to meet anyone apart from Adam and Clara who are mourning her death," concluded Alexander.

Chapter 12

The Dinner Party

The next afternoon Monique went into Alexander's study and greeted him with, "We've been invited to an impromptu soiree, at the Browne's tonight. Although there's never anything impromptu about Lydia's dinner parties. She always has everything so perfect, and she is such a good cook. They've also invited Alison and Robert so I've decided to ask them to spend the weekend here."

Over the years the Brownes had become good friends, not only with Alexander and Monique but also with their army friends Alison and Robert King who visited Briarstown quite often.

"Thought we'd make a weekend of it as all the children are away at school this weekend."

Alexander smiled and replied, "you know that Damien has set this up so that he can interrogate me about the case."

"Of course he has," said Monique, "but there's no harm in that, as you never know what other local information Damien has lurking in his brain. It will also be very interesting to get the Kings' take on everything. They are a fresh pair of eyes on this and Alison may have caught some titbits from Mrs. Hannigan during our lunch chat that I may have missed."

The Kings arrived at the Lodge at 6 o' clock that evening laden down with wine and chocolates.

"I brought a nice red Bordeaux for the men," said Alison, "and a bottle of Mateus Rose for the ladies."

"Many thanks," said Monique and smiled as she welcomed her friends to her home and showed them to their bedroom. Monique always found the shape of the Mateus Rose bottle fascinating. She had found out that the iconic flask shaped bottle had been inspired by flasks used by soldiers in World War 1.

Two hours later the four friends were dressed in their finery and making the short walk from The Lodge to the Old Rectory. Damien greeted them at the front door.

"Welcome," he said, and led them through to the large sitting room.

"Hello there," greeted Lydia, "It's so lovely to see you all. I see you've brought my favourite wine. It certainly is "le vin du jour," she laughed.

The three couples sat down in front of the log fire and sipped their cocktails, which had been proffered by Damien. Half an hour later they were sitting at the large dining table eating a sumptuous meal and drinking delicious wine. Damien had managed not to mention the case until dinner was over and they were once again back in the sitting room sipping a digestif. Eventually Damien asked.

"Well, Alexander tell all, how is the case coming along?"

Alexander did not at all feel that it was inappropriate to discuss the investigation with his friends. After all, it had been Damien's local information that had been so helpful in pointing the finger at several suspects. Between Mrs. Hannigan's information and Damien's insight, Muldoon and Alexander were well on their way to solving the murder.

"There are an awful lot of suspects in this case," answered Alexander. "Thanks to you we know about James Healey, the farmer from

Castlerea who bought what we believe were TB infected calves from the Galdstone farm. The consequences for them were horrendous. Quite a number of the rest of the herd became infected and had to be destroyed. Financially they were in debt and James Senior could take no more and hanged himself from a rafter in one of the outhouses. We were chatting to the son James and his wife. They now have a child and on the face of it, seem to be getting along with life. The only way that either of them could have murdered Jinny Galdstone was if they were both in it together and if they were, they had means, motive and opportunity. Although John Muldoon and I had wondered about the steak knife. We thought it was a strange murder weapon to bring all the way from Roscommon and then for some unknown reason to throw it into our ditch. So, while not ruling the Healeys out, they are not top of our list. We haven't as yet visited Gerry Hoban, the cousin of Ena and Kitty Hoban from Briar's cottage. However John and I called to the Lavelles. Their tale is so very sad and I have no doubt that neither Mr. nor Mrs. Lavelle is sorry that Jinny Gladstone has met a sticky end. She was very cruel to them, and showed neither of them, nor their boy Mike any respect. Mr. Lavelle has to pass the Galdstone farm every morning to get to work. They both hated Jinny Galdstone. They believe that their whole lives have been ruined by her selfishness. They are still very strong suspects as they know the routine at the dairy. They certainly have a very strong motive. Neither of the Lavelles even tried to hide their feelings towards the Galdstones, Jimmy in particular. I believe that if any of the Galdstones had gone to Mike's funeral and even called to the house to offer condolences that the Lavelles might have accepted it as an accident, but Jinny Galdstone didn't even look at them or show them any respect. As it turns out Mike had been quite friendly with Frank and had spent time at the Galdstones. Seemingly he had a great interest in Jinny's MGBGT as he was really into classic cars. I thought it was particularly bad form that not even Frank went to the funeral."

"I don't remember if I told you about Frank's trouble with his family," interjected Damien. " We all had a fairly good idea that Frank was gay. That certainly was not accepted by his family, particularly his mother. That's why he went off to California. I presume you noticed that he wasn't staying at the farm during the funeral. He stayed with a friend at the village. I know that he wouldn't have felt welcome at home."

"Yes, John Muldoon looked into his alibi," answered Alexander. "He checked the passenger list on the plane. Frank was not in Ireland when Jinny died so he can be positively ruled out as a suspect. The rest of the Galdstone family are most certainly still in the frame for the murder."

"Oh my! This is turning out to be a very complicated case," said Monique. "At least Alexander has been ruled out."

The three couples sat quietly by the fire for a few moments digesting all the information that had been, so far, imparted. They were all looking at the flames dancing in the fireplace. Damien added another two logs and embers jumped in the hearth. He refilled their glasses. The three men swirled the brandy in their balloon glasses and the ladies sipped their port.

"Jinny Galdstone really seemed a bit of a psychopath or sociopath," whispered Alison. "I know that I shouldn't speak ill of the dead but she seemed to have run roughshod over everyone who got in her way."

Both Alexander and Robert knew all about psychopaths and so-ciopaths. They had met their fair share of them during their army careers. They had had to deal with both homegrown terrorists, and those abroad during their missions. Robert had always taken a great interest in what makes a terrorist, psychopath or sociopath. He had studied the subject at length.

"It's really difficult to differentiate between a psychopath and a sociopath. Psychiatrists are generally of the consensus that psychopaths are more likely to be violent and go on a murderous rampage. So, I am more of the opinion that Jinny Galdstone tended more towards sociopathy. People who are sociopaths know the difference between right and wrong. We can only presume that she knew the difference but how can we be sure?"

"What are the main symptoms of being a sociopath?" asked Monique.

"Well according to what I've studied," continued Robert, "there are seven main symptoms.

Number one being a lack of empathy and remorse.

(2) Disregard for the feelings of others.

(3) Manipulation with charm.

(4) Poor interpersonal skills.

(5) Unstable relationships.

(6) Hostility, aggression or irritability.

(7) Lack of morals or conscience."

"How does she fit into this list?" Monique continued.

"I believe she fits into all the symptoms mentioned," insisted Damien. "I've known her since she married Adam and moved into the farm as a very young woman. She always believed herself to be a great beauty and had an exaggerated sense of her self worth. I suppose she was an attractive enough woman with a slim, tall figure and long blond hair, but to be quite candid I thought her facial features were sort of horse like."

"Don't be cruel Damien," interjected Lydia. "She always made the best of her appearance."

"She appeared to have charm but I always found her to be insincere and false," continued Damien.

"I wonder, how discussing her sociopathy helps us find the murderer?" asked Monique.

"In most murders, the victim knows the perpetrator," said Alexander. "So, understanding the victim's relationships with the others should help us with our viable suspect list. If a victim has enemies, ergo they are our suspects. All the victim's enemies have motive so then we have to find means and opportunity, and so narrow it down."

"So, what conclusions have you come to so far?" asked Alison.

"Well, everyone whom we've interviewed has motive, the Healeys and Lavelles as I've said."

"But what about the vicar and his wife?" asked Lydia.

"I don't believe the vicar himself is a suspect. When we interviewed him, it was obvious that he had been oblivious to the way Jinny Galdstone had been chasing him, until his wife told him the night before the funeral. He had suspected that there was something amiss when he visited the Galdstones to prepare the funeral rites with the family. He could feel a dreadful coldness from Adam and could not understand it. I think we can rule him out, but his wife Mary was protecting her marriage and family, so she certainly had motive, but we don't really see how she could have been missing from the house to commit the murder without her husband noticing her absence."

"The way she chased after that young vicar was really a disgrace. She didn't care if she destroyed his family. That certainly shows a disregard for the feelings of others and a total lack of morals or conscience," added Damien.

"She really reminds me of some sort of a mythical monster wreaking havoc on all those around her. How horrible," whispered Alison.

Alison sat very still staring into her glass.

"All of the family, apart from Frank are still in the mix, of course," added Robert.

"Yes indeed," returned Alexander. "Adam has most to gain financially. We are not yet sure about her relationship with the eldest son John. We know that there was a breakdown in the relationship with Clara over her pregnancy, but there seems to have been a rapprochement recently."

"I know it's an awful thing to say, but if anyone deserved a violent end, it is she," said Lydia. "She was a dreadful, evil witch who caused an enormous amount of suffering to those whom she encountered."

The mood of the room had become quite sombre. They all stared into the fireplace. It had become very dark outside. Lydia stood up to pull the large drapes.

"Lets change the subject," suggested Monique.

"Yes indeed," agreed Alison.

And so they began to chat about their children and their ponies. They described the horse shows that they had attended. Damien spoke about the hopes he had for a wonderful young filly that was grazing in the front paddock. The three couples began to chatter and laugh and forgot for a little while about the murder and the people who were suffering because Jinny Galdstone had been in the world.

At eleven thirty the dinner party ended. They all hugged each other. The two couples returning to The Lodge wrapped up warmly, as the night had turned quite cool. There was a beautiful full moon and the stars glistened and danced in the night sky. They walked slowly along the path back to The Lodge.

They reached the front door. As they entered the hallway the two couples began to chat again with enthusiasm. They all agreed that they had a wonderful evening and that Lydia and Damien were fantastic hosts. The four friends retired to the drawing room and decided on a nightcap. The two men as usual talked about army life. They discussed, at length, the different missions abroad. Monique and Lydia sat together on one of the sofas. They too reminisced about their wonderful life in the Curragh Camp, and about all the fun and laughter they had enjoyed through the years, and the part Mrs. Hannigan had played in it.

CHAPTER 13

❖

BARODA (NEWBRIDGE)

A t ten thirty a.m. on the Tuesday morning following the dinner party, Alexander drove to Naas Garda station to pick up John Muldoon. Inspector Muldoon had made an appointment to interview Gerry Hoban, the cousin of Ena and Kitty Hoban, who had lived in Briar's Cottage. John Muldoon was standing on the footpath outside the Garda station when Alexander drove up. He was holding his trusty briefcase as usual.

"Good morning John," greeted Alexander.

"Good morning, all set for this?" answered John. "Do you know the Baroda area outside Newbridge? Gerry Hoban lives about a mile from Baroda Stud."

"I know where Baroda Stud is," replied Alexander. "You can direct me when I get closer."

Alexander put the car in gear and they began their short drive from Naas to the outskirts of Newbridge. He knew to turn left towards Baroda Stud just before entering the town. "There's a right turn coming up, the house is a half mile down that road on the right," instructed John.

Alexander followed the instructions and arrived outside a modest two storey 1950's style dwelling with well maintained lawns on either side of the driveway and colourful rose beds on both sides. The car pulled up in front of the house and just as they were about to knock on the front door, it was opened by a slim man in his late thirties holding a toddler in his arms. The man held out his free hand to shake the hand of John Muldoon.

"Hello I'm Jerry Hoban, please come in."

"I'm John Muldoon and this is Alexander de Bruin who is assisting the police with this enquiry," said John Muldoon.

Jerry Hoban showed the two men into a front sitting room with a pretty bay window. There were flowery pink curtains and cushions of the same colour strewn on the sofa and armchairs.

"Please sit down gentlemen, I'm just going to put Liam to bed for an hour or so, and then we will have some peace and quiet."

John and Alexander sat down in the armchairs in front of the fireplace and waited for Gerry Hoban to return to the room. John Muldoon opened his briefcase, took out his notebook and pen and placed them on a small coffee table in front of him. Alexander looked around the room and thought how homely it all looked. There were photos on the mantlepiece and on the wall. There was a family portrait which showed Gerry Hoban, a plump dark haired woman and two children.

"So there must be a second older child," Alexander thought.

His musings were interrupted when Gerry Hoban entered the room and sat opposite them on the sofa. He explained that he was alone in the house with the toddler today as his wife was at work and his older boy was in school. His wife worked as a school secretary and wouldn't be home until after five o'clock. He himself was a self employed carpenter, so was able to facilitate the interview that morning. John Muldoon picked up his notebook and pen from the table, opened it, and began.

"As you know Jinny Galdstone was murdered in her milking parlour, and we are investigating the crime. We have learned that you have a connection to the area through your deceased cousins Ena and Kitty Hoban. It has come to our attention that there was some ill will between you and the Galdstones after you inherited your cousin's lands."

"There certainly was," answered Gerry vehemently, "and with just cause."

"I wonder would it be easier if you gave us the complete background to the story so that we can get a better understanding of the different relationships involved," suggested Alexander. "I must also tell you that I knew your cousins. My wife Monique and I moved to Briarstown ten years ago with our children, and your cousins were very kind and welcoming to us. Monique had afternoon tea with the two ladies at least once a week and was extremely fond of both of them."

"My family has been living in Briarstown for generations. My father and Ena and Kitty were first cousins. Jim Hoban inherited the land from his own father. Ena and Kitty were the only children that Jim had, and they in turn never married nor had any children themselves. My father passed away twenty years ago, so really I was their only close relative. I spent most of my summer holidays at Briarstown helping out on the farm. Ena and Kitty farmed themselves until it became too much for them, and then they let the land to the Galdstones. I had set up my own business in Newbridge as a carpenter. It had done very well for a number of years. I bought this house here and married. I would visit Ena and Kitty every chance I got.

Unfortunately the recession hit my business badly and I had very little work. Margaret my wife, and I decided that we would have to go to England to get work for a few years until things improved at home here. We also had to pay the mortgage on the house. I didn't tell Ena and Kitty about our financial troubles as I didn't want to worry them. I remember visiting them the weekend before we left for London. I really wanted to check up on them – that they were OK before Margaret and I left. I also wanted to assure them that we would phone them every weekend and that we had every intention of coming back to Ireland. Chatting with them on that weekend, I learned that they did not really trust the Galdstones. They did not seem to be getting a fair price for the land letting. Ena laughingly told me about having to drive through the laneway on occasion so that their right of way would not be taken away by the Galdstones. I asked them why they hadn't let the land to someone else, but I really didn't get an answer to that, nor did I want to interfere too much in their affairs as they had always been very independent women.

We left for London and rang them every week. Everything seemed OK for a few years, but then poor Ena got very ill and did not last long. We came home for the funeral and made up our minds to come back to Newbridge as we were all that Kitty had left. Things were hard enough for us for a while. I didn't have much work, but fortunately Margaret got herself a job in one of the schools. I visited Kitty quite often. She was not the same after Ena died, so it was not very long before she passed away as well. I always knew that I would inherit Briar's Cottage and the lands, and so I did. There was very little money which I didn't understand as the ladies didn't spend much on themselves. Margaret and I had hoped to move into Briar's Cottage and work the farm ourselves. We knew we'd have a huge amount of inheritance tax to pay, but we thought we might be able to manage, if we sold this house and got a mortgage out on the land. I knew that the Galdstones still had the land let, so I called to them to try to come up with an arrangement that they would vacate, and I could put my plan into action. I was in for a great shock. When I called to the house both Adam and Jinny were there. She was quite adamant that there was no way in hell that they would leave the land. I found out that six months before Kitty died that she had signed a ten year outright lease with them. Poor Kitty had not put in what I would call an "out" clause so that the lease would be void if anything major happened, such as grave illness or death. I told the Galdstones about my financial predicament and my plans to farm myself. I could see that Adam felt a bit sorry for me and might have relented, but Jinny's demeanour just hardened. She actually smirked at me and said that I could do what I wanted with the land in ten years time. I told her that I couldn't possibly last ten years financially without working the place myself. She really didn't care at all. Then she offered to buy the whole place, cottage and all, as her son John could live there himself.

I left Briarstown that day very despondent. I knew the family solicitor in Naas well. He got hold of all the financial dealings that my cousins had with the Galdstones. He told me that the lease was solid, and the only way of getting out of it was by the Galdstones agreeing. He also said that my poor cousins were only getting a pittance for the land, and this explained why there was very little money in the accounts. Despite not being able to take back the land, I would still have to pay enormous inheritance tax within a year. I would not even meet the favourite nephew clause. I could take them to court, but there was no certainty that I would win and it would have cost me thousands of pounds. Nobody else wanted to buy the land with a ten year lease on it. So, I ended up selling beautiful Briar's Cottage and all the lands for about half its value. John Galdstone is now living there with his family. Those people treated my cousins so badly and they did me out of my home and my livelihood. Between inheritance tax and fees I was left with enough to pay off the mortgage on this house and a little more to restart my business. My work has picked up in recent times. My wife has quite a good job and we have two beautiful children, so on the face of it we're doing OK."

Gerry Hoban took a breath and stared at Alexander and John. The two men looked back at him. John stopped taking notes and asked.

"So would you say that you feel resentment towards the Gald-stones?"

"What I feel," answered Gerry "is the nearest thing to hatred. I've lost my beautiful Briar's Cottage and a future that I thought I would have with my wife and children in Briarstown. How would you feel if all this had been taken away from you. I do my best to count my blessings, but it's very difficult. Jinny Galdstone was the monster behind this. She orchestrated the whole thing. She manipulated my elderly cousins. God only knows how they were treated when I was away. Jinny played the whole system so that I would have no choice but to sell to them or go bankrupt."

Gerry Hoban went silent again. He sighed deeply looking down at the floor. Then he raised his head and asked.

"I suppose you want to know if I killed her now? Well I wanted to. I wished her dead on numerous occasions. I even planned it in my head. But I didn't. Maybe I'm too much of a coward or I was afraid of getting caught. I suppose mostly I have too much to lose."

"Have you an alibi for that Tuesday morning between 6am and 8am?" asked John.

"Margaret and I got up at 7.30am, got the kids ready for school and had breakfast. Margaret usually leaves at 8.45 to bring the kids to creche and school and then on to her own work. I had a job starting at 9 o'clock in Naas."

"I have one more question Jerry," added Alexander. "May we see any Wellington boots either you or Margaret have please?"

"I usually wear work boots, but I think all the wellies are in the back kitchen."

He led the two men through the house to the back kitchen. Lined up in a row were four different size wellies. John checked the soles of the two bigger pairs.

"Thanks for all your help," said John. "Could I have the number of the job you were on that morning, and we'll just have to verify your alibi with your wife."

The three men went into the kitchen where Jerry took out a notebook and wrote down two phone numbers – one for his wife's place of work and one for the people for whom he was doing the carpentry work on that Tuesday morning. Alexander looked around the kitchen noticing all the utensils. There was no sign of a set of knives.

Two minutes later John and Alexander were making their way back to the car. They sat in and Alexander started the engine and they headed back towards Naas.

"He wasn't holding anything back about his feelings towards her," said John. "He certainly has a very big motive. She really was some piece of work, Jinny Goldstone. She showed great ingenuity and manipulation to carry that off."

"Wellingtons have different threads. There were no signs of steak knives. Once again both he and his wife had to be in cahoots to carry out the murder if she substantiates his alibi," returned Alexander.

"I'll phone the wife when I get back to the station. I may as well phone his workplace as well but I don't even know how that will help."

"We have so many people with strong motives, so many people who absolutely detested her. A husband who is completely downtrodden," added Alexander

"Yes indeed," said John. "I checked with their solicitor. It would seem that Adam is now quite a wealthy farmer. All the mortgages and loans will be paid off, even the one on Briar's Cottage, where the son John lives. So now we have John Galdstone with a motive, a monetary one, although he's the only one who seemed to have had no major rows with the mother. We have only completely ruled out Frank and maybe the vicar. Have you ever come across someone like Jinny Galdstone before Alexander?"

"Unfortunately, I have," answered Alexander. "There have been psychopaths and sociopaths and terrorists popping up in my past investigations. There are more of them out there than we would like to think. I was discussing these phenomena with some friends the other night. One of the ladies in the company referred to Jinny as resembling some sort of mythical monster."

"That's a bit of a coincidence," observed John " When I first saw her corpse in the dairy parlour, lying on it's back, cold blue eyes staring at the ceiling, her long blond tresses splayed out behind her head, some of it matted with her blood, Medusa immediately sprang to mind." John shivered a little as he remembered the ghastly sight. "I wonder was she born with that type of personality or did she develop it over the years," thought John to himself.

The two men sat in silence as they continued on their drive back to the Garda Station in Naas.

Ten minutes later Alexander had dropped John off in front of the station and was on his way back to The Lodge. He was thinking about his conversation with John and wondering had something happened in Jinny's childhood to have turned her into a person with no morals or remorse. He made up his mind to discuss this further with Robert as his friend was more au fait with this sort of psychological trauma. He also pondered whether the murderer was also some sort of psychopath, or was he/she just a victim of Jinny's manoeuvrings who just couldn't take anymore and lashed out. He thought once again about all the unfortunate people who had been badly affected by Jinny's actions, who might have led very different and perhaps happy lives if they had never met her.

CHAPTER 14

A PHONE CALL

On Wednesday morning Inspector Muldoon did not arrive into the office at Naas Garda Station until noon. He had attended a meeting at Garda Headquarters in Dublin from nine to eleven. He hated these meetings. There were a certain number of officers who would dominate the conversation and loved the sound of their own voices. Every month there was such a meeting so that all the main cases could be discussed. There were only two murder cases on the agenda and his was one of them. He always found it extraordinary how certain people had opinions on subjects that they knew nothing about. Inspector Muldoon had given his briefing on the way his case was progressing. This he had done concisely. Unfortunately, there followed an hour and a half of what he considered bullshit. He was always very relieved to leave Garda Headquarters and head back to his own domain. He walked into his office carrying his briefcase. He sat down at his desk, opened his briefcase, took out his notebook and just as he was about to study his notes on the case once more, Sergeant Dunne walked into his office.

"Good morning, Sir," he said. "I have some news for you, Inspector."

"Well spit it out Sergeant," answered Muldoon.

"Young Liam Kelly was on duty in the station yesterday evening when he received a phone call at eight o'clock. The caller was a female, but would not give her name. She said that she had information pertaining to the murder of Jinny Galdstone. She told him that she was driving past the Galdstone farm at 7 am on the morning of the murder, when she saw someone running from the farm yard covered in spatters of blood. This individual ran towards a parked car which was described as mid-sized and red. Fortunately, she got the registration number ZIP 962. Liam asked the caller whether it was a man or a woman. She said she wasn't sure, but thought that it was a woman. He also asked her why it had taken her so long to come forward. She told him that that was all the information that she had and hung up the phone."

John Muldoon had listened very carefully to this narrative . He sat quietly behind his desk and allowed the new information to sink in. Sergeant Dunne handed him the notes that young Liam Kelly had taken down and Muldoon studied them carefully.

"We'll have to find out who owns that car," said Muldoon. "It's in the works, Sir," answered Dunne.

"First thing this morning I got on to the Transport Office in Shannon. They are to get back to me as soon as possible. The girl I had been talking to said that it would take her about two hours to get the answers, so I'm expecting a phone call back any minute now."

"Great work Michael. This could be our breakthrough. On the other hand it could be someone playing silly buggers. Seems very strange that this woman hadn't come forward with this information earlier and then wouldn't give Liam an explanation for not doing so. But we can only go on what we have. Let me know when you get the info from Shannon."

Twenty minutes later Sergeant Dunne returned to Muldoon's office.

"I have it, Sir," he announced. "The car belongs to a Pippa Mc Hugh of Castle St. John Stud, Barnstown , not too far from Enfield, seemingly. So about twenty five miles from Briarstown."

"That's the first we've heard of her," added Muldoon. "They are obviously some sort of horse breeders, so I'll have to contact Alexander de Bruin who has friends in the know. I really can't stress enough how invaluable that man has been in our investigation, Michael. That farming world is alien to me. Alexander de Bruin has a close friend who is able to inform us about all the relationships in the area and the local scandals. Without him we wouldn't be so far ahead in this case. I hope he can glean some insights into this latest development. First things first, I want you to drive out to this stud and locate this woman. See what she has to say for herself. Off with you. Bring one of the young officers as well."

There was very little that Inspector Muldoon could do until Sergeant Michael Dunne returned with the information. He flicked through his notebook again, but knew that that might be all in vain if this Pippa Mc Hugh had actually committed the murder. He thought that he had never heard that name before, but then, as if a light bulb had been turned on, he remembered that he had indeed heard it before, or a similar name. A few years ago, before he had been promoted, there had been some kind of criminal damage case that his boss at the time hadn't really wanted to proceed with. He had believed that the girl involved had just been young and impulsive. Muldoon wondered was this the same girl. He recalled her Christian name because it was somewhat unusual, Pippa. He didn't recall what had happened as it wasn't his case. Two hours later Sergeant Dunne arrived back from Castle St. John Stud. He told the Inspector that when they arrived at the gates he was buzzed in by the manager. They were brought into his office and the manager, a John Wilson, was very cooperative. He informed the two guards that Mr. and Mrs. Mc Hugh and their daughter Pippa, who is twenty four years of age, were away in Newcastle in England at a horse sale. They left two days ago and are due back tomorrow. John Wilson had been asked about the car belonging to Pippa Mc Hugh and had shown them around the back of the house, where a red Corolla, licence plate ZIP 962 was parked. The two guards examined the car. Everything seemed in order from the outside.

"We'll have to get a warrant to examine the inside of the car for bloodstains. The witness said that whoever ran to the car had spatters of blood on their clothes. Will you see to that, Michael please."

Inspector Muldoon decided that it was time to give Alexander de Bruin a ring. He needed to discuss the latest developments with him. Either he Muldoon, or de Bruin, also had to have a chat with the Brownes as they might know something about the Mc Hughs, being part of the horse breeding circle. He made a phone call to The Lodge. Alexander picked up the phone and listened very attentively to all Muldoon had to tell him. He reassured Muldoon that he would call to the Old Rectory immediately and find out everything he could regarding this latest information. He rushed out the door and up the road to the Brownes. Damien answered the door.

"Well, what's up Alex?"

"A witness has come forward which might close the whole case," answered Alexander.

"Come in and tell me all."

The two men went into the kitchen and sat down at the table. Alexander began.

"The guards received an anonymous tip last night. It was a woman's voice but no name was given. She claims to have seen someone with blood spattered clothes running from the Galdstones' farm yard to a red Corolla parked down the road, at 7am on that infamous Tuesday morning. She fortuitously got the number plate which was connected to a woman called Pippa McHugh."

"You can't be serious!" interrupted Damien, "I know the McHughs, and their daughter Pippa. They run a very successful stud farm near Enfield. They breed beautiful race horses and also train them. They have had great success at the Curragh, Ballinrobe, Newcastle and Doncaster amongst others. This just can't be right," continued Damien.

"I find this whole witness business just a little suspicious," added Alexander. "This came out of the blue. Is there any link between the McHughs and the Galdstones?"

"Well, as a matter of fact there was an unpleasant occurrence about four or five years back. Lydia would be able to give more details about it as she was directly involved," returned Damien. "Best if I were to start at the beginning and tell you as much about the background as I can. As I've just said, the McHughs are big thoroughbred horse breeders and trainers. They have a very substantial establishment and are extremely successful and wealthy. They have one daughter, Pippa, who also, always showed a great interest in horses. Pippa and Frank Galdstone were at boarding school together and became close friends. As we have established, Frank is gay and more or less estranged from his family. Being always a very sensitive young man, he needed a close kind friend and he found this in Pippa, who by all accounts was always kind and caring towards him. They are both great animal lovers. Of course the McHugh parents are also renowned for their kindness to retired race horses and have part of their stud given over to the care of these older horses. After school, as we know Frank went over to California. Pippa studied Agricultural Science in U.C.D. with the aim of continuing her studies in equine care. During one of the summer breaks Pippa went over to another stud farm near Newcastle, to work and see how they did things in England. This isn't unusual at all among the horse breeding fraternity. They visit each other's stud farms. Of course England and Kentucky are very popular destinations for work experience for our young aspiring horse breeders. During Pippa's summer work experience she became involved with an animal rights group which was active in the next village to the stud farm. You know of course, that Greenpeace and a good number of animal rights groups were getting very popular in England from the mid seventies. Many of them were inspired by the philosopher Peter Singer and particularly his book "Animal Factories" and of course "People for the ethical treatment of animals" (PETA) was founded in 1980 as well. I've read both of these books and they are certainly food for thought. I can see why someone as sensitive and caring as Pippa McHugh might get involved with a group advocating for better care for animals. Anyway to cut a long story short she came home after the summer. She doesn't seem to have been involved in any antisocial behaviour while in England. But one morning she arrived up at the Galdstone's milking parlour and wrote MURDERERS in red paint on the wall. She was seen by Adam. The guards were called and Pippa was arrested. Of course the McHughs offered to pay for the damage and Pippa was asked to apologise. She refused, which antagonised Jinny Galdstone particularly. Jinny insisted that she be charged with vandalism and destruction of private property. This is when Lydia became involved as Pippa's solicitor. The parents virtually begged the Galdstones not to proceed. Even the guards at the time did not want to take Pippa to court. But there was no moving Jinny. She was adamant that Pippa should suffer the consequences of her actions. If Pippa were convicted, it would be on her record and she would not be able to travel to Australia or Kentucky, where it was hoped she would continue her education in Equine Science. Jinny Galdstone was informed of the serious consequences for Pippa of a conviction but she really couldn't care less or be swayed. So, the case went to court and the judge handed down a conviction and a fine. None of us could understand why Pippa had painted MURDERERS on the milking parlour wall, but during the trial the judge asked Pippa why she had taken this action. The young woman explained that several years earlier she had been visiting Frank at the farm, where she had wanted to see a pony that he had. While there she witnessed the loading into a truck of all the two week old male calves who were not yet weaned from their mothers. The mother cows and baby calves were all crying. Frank was also upset according to Pippa and he explained to her that his father Adam would drive them to the continent to be slaughtered for veal. Male calves were no use to his mother. So, Alexander, that was the explanation. It would appear that Jinny Galdstone had as much care for her calves as she had for people in general," concluded Damien.

"That must have been an awful shock for a young woman who is a serious animal lover," said Alexander. "I wonder though, if it's a motive for murder. I can't see, that not being able to travel to America or Australia would cause you to murder another human being. You say that she is a kind, caring, sensitive young woman. How on earth does this tally with stabbing Jinny Galdstone five times and more or less gouging at her heart?"

"It may have been her car, but someone else driving it, and committing the crime," said Damien.

"Or it may be a complete red herring and a false witness statement," said Alexander.

The two men sat looking at each other for a few minutes. Suddenly Damien stood up, walked over to the counter and switched on the kettle. They had a cup of tea and then decided to go outside for a walk to clear their heads. It was cool outside. There was a slight breeze as they strolled towards the stables. Harriet, Lydia's quiet old black horse had her head over the half door. Alexander stroked her mane and then the top of her nose. How very beautiful he thought. Animals are so trusting and a lot of the time we let them down. The two men walked around the land for about twenty minutes. It was extremely peaceful as they watched some of Damien's other horses grazing in the fields. The birds were twittering in a small copse and two rabbits scurried across the grass nearby. In the distance cows were lowing, not crying this time.

CHAPTER 15

—— ✦ ——

ENIGMAS

Inspector Muldoon read the message on his desk that had been left there by Sergeant Dunne. Tests on Corolla complete. No sign of blood. No sign that inside of car had been recently washed. No sign of bleach. Unlikely that anyone with clothes spattered with blood had sat in the car. No signs that anyone sitting in this car had been near a milk parlour. John Muldoon wasn't particularly surprised by the results. He had been suspicious from the outset of this mysterious phonecall. There was just something about it that didn't ring true. At three o'clock that afternoon, Alexander de Bruin collected Inspector Muldoon from outside the Garda station and they began their twenty mile journey to Castle St. John Stud to interview the McHugh family.

"Tests came back on the inside of the car – all clear," said John. "I'm not a bit surprised."

"Nor I," replied Alexander. "An anonymous caller who only now decides to come forward with information, – very fishy indeed."

A half an hour passed and they reached their destination. They drove through the entrance to the stud. There were two natural stone pillars with a horse head sculpture atop each. The old wrought iron gates interlaced with rearing horse motifs were wide open. They continued down a long winding avenue. On either side there stood lines of majestic oak trees, beech, horse chestnuts and sycamores. The manicured green fields were divided into paddocks by post and rail timber fencing which had been recently creosoted. As they drove along, they noticed a graceful, sleek bay horse cantering along the gallops between the avenue and the paddocks being ridden by a slender young woman wearing a black riding hat, white jodhpurs and a blue body protector. She waved at them. Alexander slowed down to allow her to safely reach the house before them. They watched her ride up to the front of a beautiful Georgian building. She alighted and loosened the saddle immediately. A groom appeared, a young lad of about sixteen and took the saddle and the reins and led the horse away under an archway that led into the stable yard.

The car came to a stop and Alexander and John made their way towards the young woman.

"Hi there," she greeted them. "I'm Pippa McHugh."

She was a very beautiful young woman, looking far younger than her twenty four years, with warm dark brown eyes, wavy brown hair tied back in a pony tail, and a delightful smile.

"Good afternoon, I believe you and your parents are expecting us," said John Muldoon.

He introduced Alexander and himself.

"Mam and Dad are in the office in the yard, I'll show you the way."

Pippa led the two men under the archway into the stable block. At the end of the stables there was quite a large office. Pippa entered first and the two men followed. At a large mahogany desk, sat a couple in their early fifties. The woman was an older version of Pippa with the same eyes and hair. The man had grey hair and a kind face. They both stood up to greet the two men.

"Mam, Dad, let me introduce you to Inspector Muldoon and Mr. de Bruin," said Pippa.

"How do you do," said both, and they all shook hands. "Please take a seat,"

They all sat around the large table.

"How can we help you?" asked Mrs. McHugh.

"As you know, per my explanation during our telephone conversation, we received an anonymous telephone call claiming to have seen your daughter's car and a person running from the Galdstone farm yard at 7am the morning of Jinny Galdstone's murder. We have done some forensic tests on the inside of the car and have found no sign of blood. However we are also aware of Pippa's relationship with the Galdstones and her conviction for vandalism a number of years ago. Therefore we need to check everyone's alibi for that morning," concluded John Muldoon.

"I didn't kill her," interjected Pippa "I couldn't stand the woman. She was just a dreadful person. She was really cruel to those poor calves and they're still at it, still taking the poor babies away from their mothers and trucking them over to the continent in awful conditions to be slaughtered so that horrible people can eat veal." Pippa was obviously very upset. "Jinny Galdstone was a nasty piece of work. She was so cruel to Frank and really horrible when Clara got pregnant. I can't imagine my parents doing that to me. Clara was left penniless, in a small flat with a a baby and no support at all. If anyone deserved to die, that woman did, but I didn't do it."

The tears had welled up in her eyes and her hands were shaking. She looked beseechingly at her parents who were looking lovingly back at her.

"Don't upset yourself anymore Pippa," said her mother calmly.

"We weren't here at all, any of us," said Mr. McHugh. "We weren't even in the country. We were in England selling one of our two year olds. All three of us and two of the grooms took a ferry from Rosslare to Fishguard on the Friday before Jinny was murdered. We got the ferry back on the Thursday after the murder. There are dozens of witnesses who will attest to that. I have the name of the hotel where we were staying the Monday and Tuesday night also if you would like to check that," continued Mr. Mc Hugh, who handed over a written list of everything that he had just described, which he had ready to hand over, together with Ferry tickets and receipts.

"That's very helpful, thank you," replied John Muldoon, placing the paperwork into his briefcase.

"I have a question about your car Pippa," said Alexander. "Could someone have used it in your absence?"

"No," replied Pippa. "I had the only set of keys with me in my handbag. I always keep them there in a particular pocket in the bag because I lost the other set somewhere on the land about six months ago, so I have to be very careful with this set. The car was in the exact place where I left it. No one had been near it, as I went to visit my friend in Clane the day after we came back from England. I took the keys from my bag which had been with me in England and drove the car to my friend's house."

"So, I suppose we can only conclude that the car never left it's spot during our absence," suggested Mr. McHugh.

"I think you may be right," replied Alexander. "Do any of you have the faintest idea as to who might want to implicate Pippa in this murder?"

"To tell you the truth, we haven't a clue," answered Mrs. McHugh "We have wracked our brains. Honestly, we have had nothing to do with the Galdstones since the trial. It was such an unpleasant business and we just wanted to put it all behind us and get on with our lives. I believe we've managed to do this. Pippa has no enemies as far as we know. She has a good number of close friends."

"Are you still in contact with Frank?" Her mother looked over at her daughter.

"No, Mam, I haven't spoken to him in a few years, sure he's in California."

"Ok," replied her mother, "of course we were not invited to the funeral. I can't remember the last time we were in Briarstown. Our solicitor Lydia Browne is from there."

"I know," said Alexander, "the Brownes are our neighbours."

"We haven't had need of her expertise in a while," smiled Mrs. McHugh.

"I think we've covered everything there," said Inspector Muldoon, as he stood up, picked up his briefcase and proffered his hand to each of the McHughs. Alexander did likewise and the two men left the office, thanking the family for all their help and cooperation. The two men walked past the stables, under the archway and towards the car. Alexander admired once more the beautiful house and it's surroundings. They drove back down the tree lined avenue, noticing the magnificent thoroughbreds in the paddocks until they reached the exit, turned right and made their way back towards Naas.

"That was a right old puzzle," said John "We've been rightly set up. I've never met a less likely murderess in all my days as a police officer. Whoever made that phone call was either trying to throw us off the scent, with smoke and mirrors, or there's someone out there with a weird sense of humour. It's not the first time that the gardai have received such calls and it is usually a prankster. I'm not so sure in this case."

"There are a number of puzzling events here. We need to think about whether they are coincidences, or someone is cleverly or not so cleverly, when it comes to Pippa, trying to divert our attention away from them," added Alexander.

"I will get Sergeant Dunne to check the alibis etc., but I have no reason to doubt those people at all. Whoever made that phone call obviously did not know that the McHughs were not even in the country, and that there was no way of driving the car without the sole set of keys which were in Pippa's possession in England," said John.

"Yes indeed," returned Alexander, "but the caller had a great deal of information about Pippa. They knew the registration number and were aware of the altercations with the Galdstones. Of course it would seem that Pippa has owned that car for several years and only uses it as a run around because she has the use of the four wheel drives from the stud farm. ZIP is very easy to remember as well."

"So, we don't know if the caller is actually the murderer or his/her accomplice or a prankster. Either way the choice of Pippa McHugh as a target was clever. Just bad luck on their part that the McHughs have such solid alibis. On the other hand the discarding of the knife in your ditch leaves another question – was the murderer trying to frame you or were they just careless? But not so careless as to forget to remove the fingerprints. Have we a murderer who, on two occasions attempted to throw the blame onto two different people. When it failed with you, they moved on to Pippa, or are the two puzzles unrelated?" John mused." I'm beginning to think that this might be close to home. We need to go back again to the Galdstones. We haven't interviewed John Galdstone yet. I'll phone him to see if he has any objections to your being present. I don't know if he has the same animosity towards you as do Adam and Clara. He had very little to say when first we met."

"If the caller had not been so exact with the type of car and the registration number we would have had to extend our travel further afield. We would have wasted even more time. They really wanted to give us a target, but it has backfired for them."

The two men drove back through the rich Kildare countryside. Alexander was looking forward to bringing his two Bernese out on the land for a long walk. John Muldoon was deep in thought and putting pieces of the puzzle together in his head. He found it difficult to compartmentalise his life. His wife complained at length that he always brought his work home. On the other hand, Alexander was able to put different parts of his life into different compartments. Otherwise it would have been very difficult for him to survive some of the events that he had witnessed down through the years. The car stopped in front of the station. The two men said their goodbyes with the intention of being in contact again as soon as John had checked on John Galdstone's attitude towards Alexander.

CHAPTER 16

∗

BRIAR'S COTTAGE

Monique left The Lodge at ten o'clock in the morning. It was parent's day at the girl's boarding school. Normally both parents would attend, but today it was decided that Alexander may be required to attend the interview that John Muldoon had arranged at Briar's cottage, and so he remained at The Lodge, awaiting a phone call. Alexander was thinking about his two girls who were very happy at their school. Alice was very good at maths and science and took after her parents with her logical thinking. Maeve was more into languages and literature. She was also very interested in art and design. This in turn reminded him of his own mother who loved visiting art galleries, and who had brought him one summer to visit the Louvre and the Palais de Versailles. His reveries were interrupted when the phone rang. He went over to the desk and picked up the receiver.

"Alexander de Bruin speaking."

"Good morning, John here. I've had a chat with John Galdstone. He doesn't seem to care one way or the other whether you come to the interview or not, so I'd be grateful if you'd tag along. If you are available I'll collect you in an hour and we'll head over."

"That's no problem, see you in an hour," answered Alexander.

The two men walked up to the front door of Briar's cottage. The front garden looked more or less the same. The same shrubbery and flowers, but not kept with quite the same amount of care. When they entered the old house, all the beautiful antique pieces of furniture and porcelain figurines were missing. Perhaps their cousin Gerry Hoban had taken them. The sitting room also looked very different from his first visit to the two old ladies, Ena and Kitty. Gone were the old sofas, cushions, and colourful rugs. Instead there was a more modern looking suite of furniture, with children's toys strewn on the floor. Despite the obvious presence of children in the house, there wasn't a very happy atmosphere. The sitting room could no longer be described as warm and welcoming.

The three men sat down on the new suite of furniture. John Galdstone looked very much like his father Adam. He did not have a happy countenance. His light blue eyes avoided contact with the other eyes in the room. John had blond hair that was slightly curly, and had a slight frame. He seemed more wiry and robust, than thin and weak.

"I suppose you're here to talk about my mother," he grunted.

"Yes indeed we are," answered Muldoon. "Once again let us offer our sincere condolences on your terrible loss. Thank you for allowing Commandant de Bruin to join us for this interview. As you know he has been very helpful in our investigation to date."

"No problem," retorted John, "you may as well get on with it."

Alexander was sitting quietly on the sofa. He had decided to intervene very little in this interview, but instead watch and listen, not wanting to cause annoyance to John Galdstone.

"Can you tell me where you were the morning of your mother's death, between 6am and 8am?" asked Muldoon.

"I was here," replied John Galdstone. "My wife was here too. I wasn't feeling very well so I didn't get up until 8 o'clock. Then my father rang me and I went up to their farm. I mean I went up to the house."

"Would you usually help your mother with the milking in the mornings?" asked Muldoon.

"Sometimes I would, sometimes I wouldn't," retorted John Galdstone.

"Would you be able to elaborate more on what you usually did on the farm?" said Muldoon. Despite the short responses Inspector Muldoon showed no evidence of impatience.

"Well, I'm usually up much earlier, but I was feeling sick as I said. My mother would ring me at about a quarter to six if she wanted help. Sometimes she preferred to be on her own in the mornings. She never liked Dad to help. She used to say that he didn't know what he was doing. Since Clara came back, she might help out sometimes, but my mother usually just got her to clean up afterwards."

Alexander watched and listened attentively. He concluded that John was very much like his father, docile, not very bright and under Jinny Galdstone's thumb.

"If your father didn't get very involved with the cows, what was his function on the farm?" asked Muldoon.

"My father never liked milking, he prefers being in his truck. He's really a drover like his father and grandfather before him. He has his own truck and moves cattle for other people and then travels to the continent with the male calves that are no use to anyone. Taking the male calves to the continent was my mother's idea. She said we could get rid of them young and get a good price for them."

"Could you tell me about your and your family's relationship with your brother Frank?" asked Muldoon.

"Frank was always a bit of a nancy boy. My mother was very disappointed with him. We didn't want the whole world to know that he was queer. He used to even cry about the calves. My mother used to shout at him that he'd end up in jail for being queer. "What you are is against the law," she used to say. So Frank just went off to America. He didn't stay with us for the funeral. He stayed in the village with a friend of his. My father said that your mother wouldn't like it – him staying in the house that is."

"Tell me about Clara," said Muldoon.

"Clara is the clever one. She was always real good at school. She was up in UCD doing architecture. But she got knocked up and my mother was having none of it. My mother said that she broke the rules. Jack's father wanted nothing to do with them. So Clara was left with nothing. Do you know, it was the thing that my parents argued about. My father wanted to help her, but they didn't in the end. She had to leave the university and fend for herself. I don't know why my mother changed her mind after all these years, but she took Clara back in and even decided to renovate one of the outhouses for herself and Jack. They are living in the main house while the work is being done. Clara would have gotten a great job you know. She made the rest of us look stupid."

"What about yourself, John, did you get on well with your mother?" asked John Muldoon.

John stood up, walked over to the mantlepiece where he picked up a packet of Carrolls cigarettes and matches, took out a cigarette, struck a match, placed the cigarette in his mouth, lit it and inhaled deeply. He blew out white smoke which permeated the room. John grabbed the ashtray from the table, sat down again, placed the ashtray on his knee and looked straight ahead. His brow was furrowed and his eyes looked empty. He stirred slowly in his chair before answering Muldoon's question.

"I suppose I got on fine with my mother. I was always going to go into the dairying. I wasn't any good at school and I always did jobs for her whenever I was home and during the holidays. It had to be me. There was no one else. And I always followed the rules. My mother even half approved of my wife Heather. We bought this place here so that I could start my own herd and we'd share the milking parlour – you know, use it at different times."

"Is your wife here at the moment?" asked Muldoon.

"No. She's taken the children to visit her mother in Carlow. She said she wanted to give me time to adjust, and I have a lot more work to do now that my mother is gone."

"I must ask this question John," continued Muldoon, "Have you benefitted financially from your mother's death?"

Both Alexander and John Muldoon knew the terms of the will already but wanted to hear John's version in his own words.

"Well, I suppose I did. Briar's Cottage and the land with it is now completely mine. It was a sort of joint arrangement between myself and my mother. We had a mortgage insurance on it, so I don't have any debt on it now. But it's going to be very hard to run this place without her. I'm going to have to bring people in to help with the milking. My father has no interest in the cows and Clara only helps when she wants. I suppose you're suggesting that I had a reason to kill my mother. Well, I didn't do it. I was here with Heather and the kids until I got a phone call from my father to tell me the horrible news. I told you already that I was in bed late because I was feeling sick."

John Galdstone turned very pale sitting in the chair. He looked very gaunt and defeated.

It was hard to fathom whether he was upset because his mother was dead or overwhelmed by the thought of running the whole enterprise by himself. Alexander also thought it was quite bizarre that his wife had chosen this time to take the children to visit her mother and just abandon him in his hour of need. He was a lonely figure sitting in the armchair, in a quiet house that should be bustling with children. Toys on the floor that were not being played with. Quite a sad sight. He looked a lot older than his years. "Could you ask your wife to ring me at the station so that I can verify your alibi, please. I think that will do for now. We may be back again if we have more questions, and of course, we will keep your family informed of any developments."

The two men left Briar's Cottage and headed back towards The Lodge.

"What do you think?" asked Muldoon.

Alexander drove the car slowly down the road.

"He's certainly a suspect. He has inherited a beautiful house and lands. His wife and he are definitely in some sort of crisis. If all was hunky- dory between them, she would be by his side with the children supporting him through all this. He's a very sad lonely figure. Submerged and floundering is how I would describe him."

"Now would be a good time to pay a visit to Adam and Clara before John can have a discussion with them. I'd like to go back to The Lodge and phone them. I intend asking them if they are OK with you attending the interview. I really would prefer if you were there."

Twenty minutes later following the phone call, both de Bruin and Muldoon were making their way towards the front door of the Galdstone house. Whilst not being overly pleased with the prospect of Alexander coming to the house, Adam had agreed to allow it. Muldoon was glad that it had been Adam who had answered the phone. Clara might have been a different kettle of fish.

They were greeted at the door by Adam and led into the kitchen where Clara was standing in front of a green Aga cooker, sipping a cup of coffee. She didn't look at all pleased to see them.

"Well, have you caught the killer yet?" she demanded in a cutting tone of voice.

"We are continuing with our inquiries," answered Muldoon. "We actually have quite a number of suspects."

Muldoon and Alexander, although not having been offered a seat, sat down at the kitchen table. Clara remained standing obstinately, but Adam meekly joined them at the table.

"We have a few more questions for you both as you can imagine," stated Muldoon, "and thank you again for allowing us both to be present as I'm sure you would like us to solve this dreadful murder as quickly as possible."

Clara didn't look one bit impressed and Adam had a similar forlorn expression that they had seen earlier at Briar's Cottage.

"We really need to discuss who profits from Jinny's death. We know that your son John inherits Briar's Cottage and it's lands. Did your wife have an insurance policy and what about the farm and house here?"

Once again John Muldoon already knew the answers, but wanted to see the reaction from both Adam and Clara.

"Dad gets everything," retorted Clara. "The insurance of £200,000 and the house and lands. If he had died first, she'd have got it all."

"That makes me a suspect, I know," whispered Adam, his head bowed and his leg twitching under the table, "but I tell you, I didn't see her that morning until I went looking for her and found what I found in the parlour."

"Dad couldn't have done that to her. He's a good man and she was a wonderful person."

"Could I ask you about the rows you had with your wife? I'm sure like every married couple there were some rows."

Muldoon stared straight at Adam.

"We didn't have that many rows. Sometimes I'd annoy her but never anything serious."

"What about the vicar?" interjected Muldoon

Adam went very white in the face. His upper lip twitched and his hands began to shake. He didn't appear able to speak.

"That's only idle gossip," snarled Clara.

"It would appear not, several people have informed us about your mother's interest in the vicar. We interviewed the vicar himself who had noticed a coldness towards him in this house after your mother's death. Arguments were heard between the two of you."

"Who said that?" growled Clara.

"We know that your mother had made many enemies over the years. I think it is time to dispel the proposition that your mother was universally loved. Unfortunately, we have learned through our investigations that there were many people, not only in this townland but in other parts of Ireland, who had anything but warm feelings towards her. We now know a lot about your mother's relationships with people. We now need to call a spade a spade, and dispense with the charade that you can't think of anyone who might want to dispose of her. From interviewing people, we have learned that she has hurt many individuals and caused havoc in some people's lives. We all need to get serious here if we are to find the culprit. We have a number of suspects and we have only been able to eliminate very few. So, from now on, we must proceed with candour and we need all our questions answered honestly."

Both Adam and Clara appeared quite shocked. They stared at each other and then at the two men seated at the table. Both Muldoon and Alexander stayed silent, waiting patiently for some sort of reaction or response.

"Well if you know, you know," said Adam despondently. "Yes, she had a way of rubbing people up the wrong way. She did whatever she wanted, whenever she wanted and damn the consequences. She had rules for us all, except for herself. I know she was chasing the vicar and I blamed him, not her. She didn't care about other people. She threw Clara out of the house when she got pregnant. I admit we had some rows about that. We also had rows about her making a fool of herself with the vicar. I always gave up though. I couldn't even stand up for Frank. I couldn't even ask him to stay in the house after she was dead. What kind of coward am I?"

Adam put his head in his hands and started to whimper. His whole body shook and Muldoon was reminded of the first time he had seen him sitting on the steps of the milking parlour the morning of his wife's death, head in hands shaking.

"Perhaps you could get your father a cup of tea, Clara?" said Alexander.

This was the first time that he had spoken since he had sat down at the table. She clicked on the kettle, took out a mug, put a single tea bag in the mug and waited for the kettle to boil. About two minutes passed in silence as Clara prepared the tea and handed the mug to her father. He sipped it slowly and little by little began to compose himself.

"It's hard pretending that she was someone she wasn't. But I know it's hard to believe that despite everything she did and the way she treated everyone, that I still loved her and needed her. She made all this happen for us. I couldn't have killed her."

Clara was standing behind her father's chair with one hand on his shoulder. She did not look quite as defiant as earlier, but she certainly looked stoic.

"Now that everything is out in the open Clara, how did you feel about your mother?" asked Muldoon, resuming his questioning.

"Of course I was very unhappy when I had to leave all those years ago, but I moved back in and we never got along better. She insisted on building my little house for Jack and me.... Mother and daughter relationships are very strong. Even if you have bad arguments, the bond is unbreakable, I think – in our case anyway."

"Were you left anything in her will?"

"She didn't expect to die," interrupted Adam. "She was only a young woman. I'm going to look after Clara, Jack and Frank. John was different because of the mortgage and the bank insisting on insurance. I'm going to look after Clara."

Father and daughter looked at each other, and Clara patted Adam's shoulder. Adam sipped his tea again.

"Remind me again, where you were that morning Clara," said Muldoon.

"I was in bed until nearly eight. I don't help with the milking in the morning. I have to get Jack his breakfast and ready for school. Why would I kill my mother now when everything was going so well? I know that I broke the rules. I know that I disgraced the family and my mother was good enough to take me back into the house. I let the family down. My mother did everything for this family and I was expected to maintain the standards."

CHAPTER 17

—— ◆ ——

THE SPRING BALL

I t was Mrs. Hannigan's day for cleaning at The Lodge. She was in the kitchen organizing the cutlery and putting the knives, forks and spoons into their correct sections in the drawer. The de Bruins just tended to throw them into the drawer willy-nilly, and Mrs. Hannigan always had a chuckle when she opened the drawer. Monique came into the kitchen with the post in her hand.

"I see we've left the cutlery in a mess again," she laughed. She sat at the table and sorted through the various envelopes – mostly invoices and bills. There was one that had an army stamp on it addressed to Commandant A. de Bruin. She knew immediately what it was, as she had been expecting it. It was an invite to the Spring Ball at the Officer's Mess in the Curragh Camp. Alexander and she went every year religiously, and it was one of the highlights of their social calendar. All the serving officers attended with their wives and girlfriends, but an invitation was also extended to retired officers. It was always a formal dinner with entertainment. The ladies wore long evening dresses and the officers wore their dress uniforms. Retired officers were not permitted to wear uniform, but instead a tuxedo and bow tie were required garb.

"It's our invite to the Spring Ball, Mrs. Hannigan. I must go into the office and tell Alexander. He's working on the accounts for a big company in Dublin. He has been very busy for the last few days between his accountancy work and the murder case."

When Monique left the room Mrs. Hannigan thought fondly about her years living in the Curragh. She remembered the nights of the Spring Balls and other social occasions when she had minded the de Bruin children. Her own children were older, but they used to play with them. The de Bruins always brought presents, and she always thought how wonderful the couple looked in their finery as they headed off. She continued to reminisce as she pottered around and came to the conclusion that they were all very lucky to be part of this wonderful army family and despite retirement, the strong bond was still there.

Alexander was hard at work when Monique entered the room.

"The invite has arrived as usual," she said.

He knew immediately what she was talking about. Alexander enjoyed these evenings, even more so now that he had retired. It gave him the chance to meet up with old comrades and particularly to spend another evening with their very good friends, the Kings.

The two couples travelled together to the Spring Ball. Robert King drove. It would cause less confusion as they had to go through security at the camp. Colonel Robert King was dressed in his military dress uniform. Lydia sat in the passenger seat wearing an elegant green chiffon dress. Seated behind Robert was Alexander attired in a tuxedo, beside him Monique, in a sleek black long Dior dress with sequins at the collar. They drove along the Curragh plains and entered the village turning left after the church. They stopped at the barrier where there was a soldier on duty. He had a clipboard in his hand. Firstly he checked the reg number of the car and made a tick on his clipboard. He walked over to the driver's side of the car.

"Good evening Sir," he said. "May I see your I.D.s." Both Robert and Alexander showed him their army I.D. cards. The soldier checked them, ticked another box on his clipboard. He walked back to his station, lifted the barrier and saluted as the car drove past him.

"Is security tighter than usual?" asked Monique.

"There are a number of important prisoners in the military prison at the moment," answered Robert. "They are taking a lot of precautions with them. We don't want another escape attempt."

The car drove past the red brick buildings and came to a halt outside an imposing building, also red bricked, in front of which there was lots of activity. Officers of all ages and their wives and girlfriends chatting animatedly to each other. They all filed in through the entrance and into the dining room where they took their designated seats. The gathering fell silent when the Commanding Officer came in and took his place at the top table. Sitting beside him was the Chaplain who said grace. The formalities over, they sat down again to enjoy a sumptuous meal. The food as usual was top-notch. The army cooks were as good as you'd find in the best hotels. When the meal was over, the gathering was treated to the singing of a young soprano with renditions of Italian and Irish songs. She had a really beautiful voice and everyone was enthralled. She was accompanied by a harpist who continued playing in the background after the singer had completed her repertoire. There had been the usual after dinner speech from the Commanding Officer, but thankfully he had kept it short. After a decent interlude the most senior officers took their leave and the atmosphere became more relaxed. The two couples retired to one of the drawing rooms where after dinner drinks were being served. They sat in a corner in front of one of the fireplaces which had a warm turf fire. They chatted about everything and anything and finally Lydia asked.

"How is the murder case coming along?"

Monique laughed and replied. "I wondered how long it would take one of us to bring it up."

The three looked at Alexander and waited for his input.

"To tell you the truth, it's not moving very swiftly. We have a plethora of suspects. They seem to be growing daily. We have only been able to eliminate a few from our enquiries. The whole family except for the son Frank are still in the frame."

He explained about what had happened with the so called sighting of a suspect and the red Corolla and the time that had been spent investigating the sighting.

"If whoever had made the phone call hadn't been so precise with the registration number, the guards would still be wasting their time looking for the suspect."

"Did anyone at all like this woman?" asked Lydia.

"Her husband admits that his marriage wasn't exactly happy and that she was a very difficult woman to live with, but that he still loved her and needed her. Clara is the only one who still claims that she had great affection for her mother and that there was a strong bond between them. Everyone else we've spoken to, to be quite frank, couldn't stand the woman."

"Have any of you ever met someone like that, someone who doesn't care about anyone else except themselves, who doesn't seem to have any redeeming qualities?" continued Lydia.

"My aunt was a bit like that," interjected Monique.

"Who are you talking about?" asked Lydia with surprise.

"Oh, you met her when we were living in camp. We had her to stay the time of Maeve's christening. She arrived with her Spanish companion who was actually her maid, and wasn't a bit impressed with our accommodation in quarters. She was on a kind of European tour after her husband died."

"She met a wealthy Swiss man when she was in university in Paris in the Sorbonne. He and his family were involved in jewellery and watches. They got married and mostly lived in Switzerland. Their main house was in Geneva. They also had holiday homes in Crans-Montana and in Nice in the south of France. They had two daughters whom they dispatched to boarding school in England and later to a finishing school in Switzerland. They both married minor Italian aristocrats, and I lost contact with them."

"Did you ever spend much time with her in Switzerland?" asked Lydia.

"I went on holidays to visit her in Crans-Montana. It's a beautiful village in the Swiss Alps. In the winter the rich go skiing there. It's really a paradise in the heart of the Swiss Alps, famous for it's sunshine and fresh air – a playground for the wealthy in both summer and winter. I remember flying from Paris to Geneva, taking the train then to Sierre and a wonderful Funicular to Montana which is 930 metres higher up. Her home is a half timbered mountain style chalet. Now, to call it a chalet was a bit of an understatement. It was more of a mansion. To tell you the truth I had a fantastic time there."

"But she wasn't impressed with Ireland."

"Not a bit," replied Monique. "She's such a demanding selfish woman. I don't know how her Spanish companion put up with her. When they left us, they went on one of those luxury trips that are mainly geared towards wealthy Americans coming back to Ireland visiting their roots. They started out in Dublin and then toured the ring of Kerry, Galway and Mayo. Needless to say, they stayed in the best hotels. They went from Ireland to Italy for another grand tour.

Thankfully we haven't seen her since but I did receive a very long letter on her return to Switzerland in which she excoriated the whole trip here, the service, the food, the accommodation etc. etc. So, I know somebody with a similar personality to Jinny Gladstone but my aunt Amelie Muscio is still alive and kicking and probably complaining in her beautiful chalet in Crans- Montana. I always thought she was a bit of a sociopath as well. She really didn't seem to have any empathy towards others. I can see someone knocking her off as well."

"Speaking of knocking someone off," interjected Robert "Do you remember that case in France during your secondment there Alex?"

"Oh yes," said Monique "That was an interesting case. We spent six months in Paris, Lydia, when Alex sort of did a swap with a French intelligence officer. They do that sort of thing on and off, so that the intelligence officers can learn how things are done in other countries. Tell her about it, Alex, it's one of your more interesting cases and in lots of ways the victim's personality resembles that of Jinny Galdstone."

"As Robert said I was studying the methods of the "centre d'exploitation du Rensignement Militaire" when I was asked to help out in a murder investigation. My senior officer knew that I had some experience in this area. Because the victim was a Colonel in the "Forces armees francaises", a French army officer was to liaise with the Gendarmerie, and I was asked to tag along. It was a very interesting case. Colonel Alain Gilbert was found murdered in his holiday home in Nantes by his wife. His wife Madame Gilbert had left the house at nine o'clock that morning to go shopping with friends, and later they had lunch in a restaurant in the centre of Nantes. She returned home at four o'clock to find her husband dead on the living room floor. He had severe head injuries and there was blood everywhere. He was only wearing his dressing gown. Madame rang the gendarmes immediately and a thorough investigation ensued. The murder weapon, a bronze statuette which had been on the mantle piece was found near the body. There wasn't any sign of a break in. Nothing had been taken from the house according to Madame Gilbert. She said to the gendarmes that she couldn't think of anyone who might want to murder such a wonderful man. According to the Medecin Legiste, the Colonel had died between ten and twelve that morning. He had died from blunt force trauma to the head. He had been struck on the left temple with a bronze statuette, had then hit his head on the corner of a marble table, and finally his head had hit the marble floor. Death would have come very quickly. So Madame Gilbert had an alibi. She had been shopping with two friends at the time of the murder. When Madame was asked who else might have keys to the house, she stated that their two adult children, along with the cleaner and a kind of concierge com handyman, all had keys to the building. She insisted that her two children were both abroad, one working in Australia and the other in Canada. The cleaner was not due to clean the house until the following week when she and her husband would have returned to Paris. She couldn't give any information on the whereabouts of the concierge. As it happened, the concierge had an airtight alibi for the time in question. It didn't appear to be a burglary gone wrong as there was no sign of forced entry. So, now we had to delve into the life of this, on the face of it, well respected Colonel in the French army. A bit like Jinny Galdstone, there was a lot more to him than met the eye. First of all we looked into his army life. He turned out to have been a very unpopular army officer, neither liked by his men, nor respected by his fellow officers, being described as arrogant, selfish, cruel, without morals and only interested in self-advancement. He had crawled over everyone in his way to get to where he was, and caused the dismissal of quite a number of his subordinates. So, we painstakingly went through all the army suspects. The man was really despised by most of them, described by many of them as manipulative, hostile, aggressive with no conscience. The gendarme with whom we were working examined his personal life. As his wife had stated, their two adult children were abroad and had alibis. But then he located five mistresses which the Colonel had had over the previous ten years. When they were interviewed, none of them hid their hatred for him. Monsieur Le Colonel had used, abused and abandoned all these poor women. It transpired that his wife knew about all his shortcomings but they had an understanding. She seemed to care not a whit about her husband, and that it was more a marriage of convenience, the couple getting together on occasion but leading, to all intents and purposes, separate lives. Madame Gilbert, herself had her own lover, with whom she had a relationship for the previous six years. So, she wasn't exactly heartbroken but definitely had an alibi.

Then we thought that perhaps she had sent a hitman to eliminate him but really it would have been easier to divorce him and she was independently wealthy. The Colonel was also a landlord and not a good one. There had been complaints made to the "Conceil muniscipal" by many of his tenants. They were living in very poor conditions. Children were getting ill because of mould and damp in the apartments. But of course the man couldn't be bothered to fix anything and really didn't give a damn about his tenants. I think we can see a lot of similarities here between the case in France and the one in Briarstown. The suspect pool was growing in size. We couldn't find anyone who liked the man. Nothing good was said about him, apart from, some people who were just being polite. We really didn't know how we were going to solve the murder. It creates huge problems when one has a victim who is universally disliked and despised with virtually no redeeming qualities.

The gendarmes and ourselves spent weeks interviewing suspects. There were absolutely no witnesses. The Colonel was alone in the house, there didn't seem to be a break in, unless the burglar got in without leaving any signs. The people with keys weren't around. The fingerprints obtained were, as expected. There were smudges on the statuette as if the killer had worn gloves."

"So what on earth happened? Did you catch the culprit?" asked Lydia.

"Conscience cracked it," replied Alexander. "The young cleaning lady who was only twenty years of age and a veritable beauty with long brown hair and deep brown eyes came into the gendarmerie one morning and announced that she had killed Monsieur Le Colonel. She wasn't meant to be there that week. Madame Gilbert had booked Louise Santos, an immigrant from Portugal, to clean the house after the couple had returned to Paris. Poor Louise had got the dates mixed up. Madame Gilbert had never wanted the young woman to be in the house with her husband as she was well aware that the Colonel would make moves on the young, beautiful, innocent woman. When Louise Santos arrived at the gendarmerie that morning, she was in a dreadful state. She hadn't slept in weeks. She described what had happened that morning. Louise had arrived at the house at ten o'clock and had used her own key to gain entry. She hung her coat on the rack inside the front door, made her way through the living room and into the kitchen where she put on her full apron and rubber gloves to begin cleaning. She heard a noise from one of the rooms off the living room. She was afraid as the house was meant to be empty.

"Qui est la?" she asked.

The Colonel replied "C'est seulement moi, Colonel Gilbert.

Louise made her way into the living room and was standing beside the fireplace when Colonel Gilbert appeared from the room wearing only a bathrobe. She said that she knew immediately what was going to happen by the look in his eyes. He made a lunge for her and grabbed her around the waist and started kissing her. She tried to push him away but he was a very big, strong man. She managed to grab the statuette from the mantlepiece with her right hand and strike him on the left temple. He fell backwards and hit his head on the side of a table and then she heard a crack as his head hit the marble tiles. She said that she was absolutely terrified and stood watching him for a few moments. She knew he was dead as his lifeless eyes were staring at the ceiling. The blood began to ooze from his head, nose, mouth and ears. She doesn't know why she decided to run. It was instinct. The weapon had been thrown on the floor near the Colonel. She put on her coat and went out the door. She didn't meet anyone. She was still wearing the apron, which had splatters of blood under her coat, and the rubber gloves. She took the gloves off, put them in the pocket of her coat and walked back to her flat as quickly as she could. She waited and waited for the gendarmes to arrive at her door. When she checked her calendar she realised her mistake and that Madame Gilbert had probably told the gendarmes that she wasn't due in the house. But Louise became exhausted and ill and decided she couldn't live with what had happened so she gave herself up."

"What happened to her?" asked Lydia.

"Well her version of the story was believed. Madame Gilbert pleaded her case. The procureur decided that it was self defence and she ended up doing some community service instead of going to prison. Everyone, including Madame Gilbert recognised Louise as a victim of a predatory man. Not so sure that it would ever have been solved, only for her conscience got the better of her."

"So in this case it was the maid in the living room with the statuette." interjected Louise.

Alex, Robert and Monique smiled and nodded.

"Well in our Briarstown case," said Monique, "can't see it being Mrs. Hannigan in the parlour with the steak knife."

CHAPTER 18

A RECAP

Two years ago Inspector John Muldoon had decided to install a teacher's blackboard on the wall of his office. It had a wooden ledge beneath it which held a duster and sticks of chalk, mostly white with a few coloured ones. When he was at school, he always understood things much better when they were written on the blackboard with chalk. Now he himself writes his thoughts in chalk on the board. That morning he had spent an hour drawing columns and making headings on the board. He entered the names of all the suspects in their relevant columns. He stood back a few steps from the board and looked at his work.

SUSPECTS

Ruled out	Unlikely	More likely	Family	Couples acting together
Frank Galdstone	The Vicar	Vicar's wife	Adam	John and Heather Galdstone
Pippa McHugh	Lilly Healey	James Healey	John	James and Lilly Healey
A. de Bruin	Heather Galdstone	Dora Lavelle	Clara	Mr. and Mrs. Jerry Hoban

Mrs. Gerry Hoban   Jimmy Lavelle   Mr. and Mrs. Lavelle

Gerry Hoban

Mrs. Hannigan (housekeeper to many)

ENIGMAS

Knife found in de Bruin's ditch.

Phone call claiming to have seen Pippa McHugh's car and someone running away.

He stared and stared at the blackboard. Nothing was jumping out at him. He walked into the outer office and called.

"Sergeant Dunne, could you come into my office for a moment. I'd like you to take a look at something."

Sergeant Michael Dunne walked into the office as requested. He immediately saw the list on the blackboard. Both men stood still and looked intently at all the suspects. Michael Dunne had become used to Inspector Muldoon's methodology. Whenever he had gathered up all the information, written it in his notebook, read over it several times, he then put his thoughts in chalk on the blackboard.

"Anything jumping out at you, Michael?"

"Apart from the fact that we have way too many suspects – no. I see you have de Bruin in the "ruled out" column."

"Yes, he's obviously ruled out, but it's strange that he was ever a suspect. It was Adam and Clara who pointed us in his direction and the murder weapon in his ditch. It's still a conundrum. Were the Galdstones just so annoyed at him, because he had found them out for what they really were and wanted it to be him, and was the knife just discarded coincidentally in his ditch by the real murderer?

The so called witness ringing in about Pippa McHugh is also very strange. Why Pippa? Why so definite about the car reg? Was it the murderer trying to divert attention? Whoever rang in, knew a lot of information about Pippa McHugh and her troubles with the Galdstones. Bloody hell! Michael, it's not getting any clearer."

"I suppose Sir, the vicar is the most unlikely. He really hadn't a clue about Jinny Galdstone's intentions towards him."

"I agree Michael, but can't be positive about his wife. I also think that it's a bit far fetched to think of the Healey's despite the father's suicide, driving at all hours of the morning from Roscommon to Kildare to murder Jinny Galdstone and to use a steak knife for the purpose. Having interviewed them, I really got the impression that they were now content enough and moving on with their lives."

"We can't say the same for the poor Lavelles. Their lives were destroyed when they lost their boy. They have to pass by the place where he died and the Galdstone farm practically every day. There's no forgiveness there and I don't blame them. That poor couple is just existing in their own living hell. The Hobans lost a lot as well. Again, both of them had to have conspired together to have pulled this off. Don't know how the Galdstones could be forgiven for taking their homeplace and future in Briar's cottage away from them."

"And of course the family, apart from Frank, Sir. They really are a very odd bunch. There's no happiness there at all. They are still absolutely in the frame. Just wondering, why have you Mrs. Hannigan's name there at the bottom?"

"She's obviously not a suspect, Michael, but she's a fountain of information. She has links to the Galdstones with her cleaning job. She's the one, through the de Bruin's, who informed us about the relationships in the Galdstone family and all the tensions. Don't know, she might have more information that she doesn't even know she has.

I really feel that we are a bit stumped at the moment. We absolutely have too many suspects and no witnesses. Alexander de Bruin is convinced that some information will be forthcoming from somewhere. He believes that a witness will hear a titbit or someone will remember an incident that they thought was irrelevant. Murderers tend to get caught. A small piece of evidence will be uncovered or the murderer will slip up. We just have to wait and bide our time."

"That's all very well for him to say that, Sir, but he doesn't have the brass in Garda Headquarters ringing up, demanding results."

The two men once again contemplated the columns of names on the blackboard and hoped that Alexander de Bruin would be proved right sooner rather than later.

CHAPTER 19

A LULL IN THE INVESTIGATION

As the days since the murder turned into weeks, Briarstown and it's surrounds were returning to some sort of normality.

Each morning cars were stopped on their way to work or school in front of the Galdstone farm, as cows meandered across the road towards the milking parlour. The rope remained in place blocking any movement of vehicles until John Galdstone was finished, with no regard for anyone else. No greeting was proffered to the neighbours who might be late for wherever they were heading. The road was even filthier than before Jinny's death. Muck quickly turned into slush after the cars passed over it.

The inhabitants of the townland were no longer afraid that there was a raving madman about the area waiting to murder his next victim. Everyone had come to the conclusion that this crime had been personal. In a small country townland everyone eventually knows everything that's going on. The case was discussed at dinner parties, after Mass on a Sunday, at bingo, at ladies lunches, at the shops, after Sunday school. The suspects were all known, even the Healey's from Roscommon, as it began to circulate among the farmers the news about the diseased calves. Whilst it had been generally known that the Galdstones were tricksters and liked to get one over on people, it was swept under the carpet and glossed over somewhat. However, when the local farmers began discussing it at length and more stories emerged, attitudes hardened towards the Galdstones. The other farmers were no longer as willing to let things pass and do business with them. Land that was coming up for rent or lease was no longer available to them.

More information filtered through to the community about the way the Hoban's had been treated and people remembered the accident involving poor Mike Lavelle.

Before Jinny's death the Church of Ireland community had watched, some with amusement, the spectacle of Mrs. Galdstone chasing after the poor young vicar. Most had decided to ignore it or pretend that it was not happening. After the murder, of course it was chatted about at length and now the sympathy lay with Jonathan Edwards and his wife Mary. They now realised that it was not funny that Jinny was willing to destroy a young family. At the church services, there was great support for the young vicar and his family, particularly when the community became aware of the fact that they were suspects in the murder following the visit of Muldoon and de Bruin to the village.

Frank Galdstone had said goodbye to Briarstown, some thought for the last time, and returned to California. Inspector Muldoon had given him permission to leave the country as he had an alibi for the time of his mother's death. No better alibi of course than not being in the country.

Mrs. Hannigan was busier than ever with all her cleaning jobs. She still cleaned for the Galdstones, now doing both houses as John's wife hadn't been seen with the children in quite some time. Being much in demand she was finding it harder to fit in all her "families", the doctor's in Clonee, the Browne's, two other households near Newbridge and of course her favourite family, the de Bruins, twice a week. Her husband continuously told her that she was taking on too much, but Mrs. Hannigan couldn't sit still, she loved company and chatting with people. Her husband was able to relax more. He enjoyed meeting up with his army buddies and going to the local pub for a few pints and a game of cards. Mrs. Hannigan also loved socialising after work. The flower club met once a week at the parish hall in the village and of course, there was her favourite activity, bingo twice a week. She wasn't sure whether she enjoyed the bus trip there and back with the other ladies more than the bingo itself – such fun, chats and laughter on the bus.

Damien and Lydia Browne were also busy with their jobs, running their farm and looking after their horses. Damien had gone to the sales in Goffs recently and sold one of his best two year olds for a very good price. Alexander had accompanied him. They both loved watching the whole process – the horses being led into the ring, the mares with their foals at foot. They were both able to pick out the very promising animals. However, some of the price tags were astounding – way out of their financial league.

Alexander and Monique, together with their children had attended a few show jumping events. Maeve was still trying to qualify her best pony for the Dublin Horse Show, but to no avail. They had been to Kill, Mullingar and Virginia in the last two weeks and each time the pony had knocked the last bar of the treble. She wasn't able to stretch enough for the last element of the jump. Maeve had been disappointed, but she was never down for long and was now looking forward to the next competition.

Inspector Muldoon, not having received any additional information in the Jinny Galdstone murder, had made no further progress in solving the death. Every so often he received a phone call from Garda Headquarters with questions about the crime. He felt disappointed that the case had not moved on in the last number of weeks. Unless some other witness came forward or something else happened, he couldn't see where it was heading. He hoped that this wasn't going to be one of those unsolved murders that would haunt him all his life. He had other crimes to solve, break-ins, local lads fighting in the streets, driving offences, accidents, drug dealing, but it was difficult to give these one's full attention when Jinny Galdstone's murderer was still at large. He also found it somewhat disturbing that he had great sympathy for most of the suspects involved in the case. He still had his columns of suspects written on the blackboard. He no longer found it helpful, as not one of the suspects had moved to a different column, but he still didn't want to take the duster and remove it. There was still hope that one day he would come into the office and a light bulb would go off in his head. In the meantime he had to prepare his own statement for a burglary case at Naas District Court.

The vicar Jonathan Edwards and his wife were happier than ever. There was no more Jinny Galdstone appearing at any time of the day. Mary no longer had to worry about her husband being led astray by the harlot. She had taken over all of Jinny's duties. There really wasn't much to it, she realised quite quickly. Locating and arranging the flowers in the church was a dawdle. A number of ladies who had never volunteered for church work before, when Jinny was front and centre, appeared out of the woodwork and were now a great help to Mary. She noticed that the vast majority of the congregation had become much more supportive. She no longer felt that she was the butt of ridicule in the parish and would never again have to go on a camping trip with the scouts. She watched her husband prepare his sermons in the evenings after the children were in bed. Sitting in her armchair by the log fire she knitted a yellow baby cardigan and every so often she placed the palm of her hand on her tummy. Jonathan appeared so content and fulfilled. Mary had always thought that he was an absolutely beautiful man, with his perfect features and thick brown hair.

"How wonderful life is when she's no longer in this world, thought Mary as her knitting needles made a clinking sound."

The Lavelle's state of mind had improved a little since Jinny's death. They were not quite as depressed. It was as if they had found some sort of closure, as Americans might put it. Telling their story to Inspector Muldoon and Alexander de Bruin had been cathartic for them. When the inhabitants of Briarstown and Clonee became aware that the Lavelles were suspects in the murder, they rallied around them. All the people who knew them in the past, who may have forgotten about, or just put to the back of their minds, their tragedy, remembered again the so called accident that had befallen Mike. There were more visitors to the house. Mike's friends from school, who had got on with their own lives came back to see the Lavelles. Mrs. Lavelle made scones and made tea for the visitors. Everyone wanted to talk about Mike. Mr. Lavelle still passed by the Galdstone farm on his way to and from work. Sometimes he too was stopped by the rope across the road. This didn't bother him as much anymore. He thought to himself "The witch is dead" as he watched the pathetic sight of either Adam or John Galdstone waiting for the cows to pass from one side of the road to the other. "They know what suffering is now". He often wondered should he feel some sort of sympathy for them all, but he didn't. He thought that his overwhelming emotions were vindication and satisfaction. He and his wife were also relieved that they would never again have to watch Jinny Galdstone swanning around in her blue MGBGT, with the hood pulled back and her long blond hair blowing in the wind.

Life in Baroda at the Hoban's house was much as before. Gerry's work was going well and he was busier than ever. His wife was happy in her school job and children's laughter permeated the house. They had decided to no longer visit Briarstown. It was too painful. There were too many memories there. They had lost something wonderful. The person who had caused their pain was dead and as Gerry had said, " That one got her comeuppance in the end." Gerry wondered how long it would take for the empty feeling inside them to subside. Would they ever not feel regret regarding their cousins Ena and Kitty. Could they forgive themselves for nor having checked in with them more often and saved them from the mental abuse inflicted on them by the Galdstones. Would the feeling of resentment ever leave them? They would do their best to recover. The person pouring salt into the open wound was gone.

The Healeys in Roscommon had just attended the anniversary mass for James' father. There had been a good turnout from the neighbours. Lilly had prepared sandwiches, scones and cakes. At the farmhouse, they chatted with their friends about James senior and everything else under the sun, bar one topic. Nobody mentioned Jinny Galdstone although everyone knew that the Healey's had been questioned regarding their whereabouts at the time of the murder. The neighbours had all rallied around the Healeys when T.B. was found in their herd. They watched James' father as he deteriorated and lost the will to live. His suicide, though not a complete shock, caused great sorrow in the area. All the Healey's neighbours and friends hoped that the young couple and their daughter Rose were happy and well. On the surface they appeared to be recovering and getting on with their lives. Lilly and James were a very united couple who would do anything for each other and their baby girl Rose. The people who loved them hoped that revenge wasn't in their vocabulary.

CHAPTER 20

———— ◆ ————

INVITATIONS

Monique went out to the postbox to collect the post. She headed back into The Lodge and through the hall into the living room where Alexander was computing some figures.

"Anything interesting in the post?" he asked. Monique looked at each envelope and then placed them one by one on the desk.

"Oh there's one from my aunt."

"Which aunt," demanded Alexander, his tone slightly panicked.

Monique knew immediately that the letter was from her aunt Amelie Muscio in Crans- Montana. The envelope was of the highest quality paper and it was sealed with red wax and the family crest, which her aunt made with her gold ring.

"How pretentious in this day and age," she thought to herself.

"It's from Aunt Amelie," she replied. "It's in French." She read through the contents very quickly.

"Tell me she's not coming to visit," said Alexander hopefully.

"No, au contraire, it's "une invitation a passer des vacances chez elle a Cran- Montana." There's a choice," said Monique. "We can either go near the end of the summer holidays, when the weather is sunny and warm, or in winter for the skiing. Her preference is winter as she will be entertaining her daughters, and their minor aristocratic husbands, in the summer. It really would be a great holiday for the children. They've never been to Switzerland or skiing for that matter. I know she's a very difficult woman, but we mightn't have to spend much time with her during the day. I know there will be long dinners in the evenings and we'll have to listen to her pontificating on every subject."

Alexander looked doubtful, and the last thing he wanted to do was to spend time with such a self centred, opinionated, manipulating, unfeeling person. But he also recognised that Monique was right, and that it was a huge opportunity for the children to travel abroad.

"Ok," said Alexander. "We'll rule out the summer and make plans for Christmas holidays. Alison and Robert have been offering for a long time to housesit and look after the dogs and the horses, so that won't be a problem."

"Yes, and Mrs. Hannigan will do all the housework for them. Why have you ruled out the summer?" asked Monique.

"Well, as you know we have reached an impasse in the murder case. I was speaking to John Muldoon yesterday and he feels the same. I told him not to lose hope as murderers tend to make mistakes – they say something or do some little thing that gives them away. There's also the possibility that another witness will come forward. Some-one knows something, maybe they saw something suspicious, heard a conversation, noticed something not in it's place. I know it's hard for John to be patient as he's under pressure from "on high." But I'm convinced that something will happen that will lead us to solving the murder. However it may nor happen before the end of the summer. I really don't want to be abroad if something breaks. We can only hope that it will be solved by Christmas and we can all go to Crans-Montana."

"I'll write back to Aunt Amelie immediately," said Monique,

"The sacrifices one makes for the happiness of one's family," laughed Alexander.

But behind the laughter he thought about the similarities in the personalities of Jinny Galdstone and Aunt Amelie, and hoped that he wouldn't have to solve another murder in Switzerland.

An hour later Mrs. Hannigan arrived at The Lodge to perform her housekeeping duties. Monique offered her a cup of tea and some biscuits on arrival. She was very excited to tell her about her planned holiday to Switzerland. Monique told her all about the invitation that she had received in the post that morning, and their plans to visit Crans-Montana at Christmas. She also checked with Mrs. Hannigan that she was available to help out in the house while the Kings were housesitting.

"That's wonderful news," said Mrs. Hannigan. "The children will have a fantastic time. There will be no problem at all with helping out over the Christmas holidays. I have exciting news of my own."

She smiled broadly at Monique, and her eyes seemed to dance with happiness.

"Do tell," said Monique.

"Well, Jean phoned last night. She has met this lovely young man called David and they're getting engaged. They are both coming home in two weeks time so that David can ask Liam for permission to marry Jean. She said that they have the ring already, but not to tell her father, as you know the way these army fellas are sticklers for rules and regulations. So I have to try to keep their secret for the next two weeks."

"That's wonderful news Joan, have they set a date yet?"

"They are thinking about next summer. They are not sure what size wedding they would like yet. If they decide on small, it will be in the Curragh Church, if bigger they will choose Newbridge Church. They think that the Keadeen Hotel will be the best place for the reception. They can cater for any size wedding there, and do things really well."

The excitement was palpable. Mrs. Hannigan was beaming with happiness. Although Mrs. Hannigan was always good humoured, Monique had never seen her so delighted with life.

"I hope you and the Commandant will be able to come."

"We wouldn't miss it for the world."

"I'll have so much to do since Jean will be in England. My goodness, there's the cake, the invitations, the flowers, the band...."

"Don't worry about it Joan, it will be great fun and I've never seen such a wonderful organiser as yourself – and you have loads of friends to call on, including Alison and myself."

"Where will Jean get her wedding dress?" asked Monique as she sipped her tea.

"I don't know, we didn't talk about that. Of course they have wonderful boutiques in London. I wonder will she want me to go over and help her pick it out. I've never been to London, you know. I've never been out of Ireland. Will I get the boat or fly?" she asked excitedly.

"You have so much to look forward to when Jean and David come home. I'm sure they have it all worked out already. There's no need to panic. You'll know all about it in two weeks time and don't forget you'll have lots of help."

The two women sat quietly for a few moments and finished their tea. Mrs. Hannigan went upstairs to start her work and Monique returned to the office.

An hour later Alexander arrived back from his walk on the land with the dogs. He gave the pair their feed and fresh water in the kitchen having left his boots outside the back door. He slipped on his loafers and made his way into the office.

"I have more news," said Monique as she entered the room. "We have another invitation. Alexander feigned a look of horror. "Mrs. Hannigan's daughter Jean is getting married in the summer. She is over the moon about it. I don't think I've ever seen her looking so joyful. Of course she is in a bit of a panic about all the organisation involved, and she can't tell Sergeant Hannigan yet as her daughter wants to do things in the traditional way. Her fiance David is going to officially ask for her hand in marriage when they come home in two weeks time."

"It's going to be very difficult for Mrs. Hannigan to keep her secret," smiled Alexander.

They heard Mrs. Hannigan's footsteps on the stairs. Alexander, who had been sitting beside Monique at the desk stood up to greet her as she entered the room.

"Well, Mrs. Hannigan, I hear congratulations are in order," he said, as he walked over to shake her hand. "That's wonderful news. I hope the lucky couple will be very happy. Please convey my congratulations to Sergeant Hannigan, although Monique tells me that you have to keep it all a secret until Jean and her man come home."

"I know it's going to be very difficult, but I'm determined to keep my mouth shut for once."

They all laughed and Monique decided that it was time for coffee.

The three sat around the kitchen table and sipped coffee and Monique produced some scones that she had baked the night before.

"Are you still as busy as ever?" asked Alexander.

"I'm overstretched at the moment," returned Mrs. Hannigan. "Clara Galdstone asked me to do a few hours at Briar's cottage as well as Galdstones' house. To tell you the truth, I don't like doing either house. John is very grumpy. His wife is still away with the children, I think at her mother's. I'm not sure she is ever coming back. Clara is very demanding – change the sheets, polish this, clean out the presses.

I really don't need to be told what to do. I've been working for her mother for ages and I know where everything is and what's to be done. I want to leave them but I feel guilty about it. I suppose I'll give it another few months and see how things are then."

"Do they appear to be coping?" asked Monique. "It seems that Adam has gone from being bossed around by his wife, to being bossed around by his daughter."

"Do they still intend renovating the outhouse for Clara and Jack?" wondered Alexander.

"There's no talk about it anymore. Clara and Jack are still in the main house. I did overhear a conversation about Clara going back to college. Adam actually said to her that her mother wouldn't have wanted that. There was a bit of a row and Clara shouted at him "She's dead, she can't tell you what to do anymore. Be a man and make your own decisions." I didn't hear anymore after that as I had to finish my work at the other side of the house."

"You don't have to feel guilty Joan," interjected Monique. "You work very hard. You have people like ourselves and the Brownes who really appreciate you, and what you do. You don't need to work for them. You must do what's best for yourself."

There was a moments silence as Mrs. Hannigan thought about her situation.

"How is the Sergeant?" asked Alexander to break the silence.

"He's in very good form. He goes to the pub twice a week to have a few pints and play cards. He does a lot of gardening now, and goes for walks most mornings. He complains sometimes that he doesn't see enough of me – that I'm either out working or out socialising. Oh, I meant to tell you that Mrs. Lavelle from down the road has joined the flower club. She seems to have come out of her shell a little bit. Also, the last time I saw the vicar's wife Mary at the club, she spent quite a while with her hand on her tummy, so the ladies suspect that she's pregnant again."

Alexander smiled to himself as he wondered how on earth Mrs. Hannigan was going to keep her daughter's engagement a secret from her husband.

"Are you still able to fit in your bingo?" asked Monique.

"Oh yes," replied Mrs. Hannigan. "I wouldn't miss bingo. It's very handy as I just have a five minute walk from the house to where the bus picks up the women from the village. The bus driver is always on time. He arrives at exactly 7.30 and leaves at 7.35."

The three finished their coffee. Mrs. Hannigan went back to her household chores and Monique and Alexander decided to go out to the stables to check on the horse feed. Monique linked Alexander's arm as they walked towards the stables, the two Bernese behind them. There was a slight breeze, but the sun was shining and they felt it's warmth on their faces. The ponies were in the paddock and looked up from the grass in their direction for a moment, but then continued feeding on the rich green meadow.

"Well," said Monique "Two invitations, one to a summer wedding and another to a skiing holiday at Christmas."

"Indeed," replied Alexander. "But we have to solve this bloody, perplexing murder in the meantime. There are so many suspects and most of them are really nice, decent people, whom you don't want to be guilty. Would you mind checking the feed stock and putting in an order? I'll go over to Naas tomorrow to collect it. I have to meet up with Inspector Muldoon again. There may be something we've missed. I'm going to go to the Garda Station. I want to study this chalk board of his. I think I'll take a walk over to the Brownes – you know clear my head – maybe Damien might have a few new ideas or might have picked up some titbits on the grapevine."

"You go ahead, darling, I'll take the dogs back to the house with me."

Monique watched her husband as he made his way across the fields towards The Old Rectory. She had great faith in her husband's ability to solve puzzling mysteries. He had never failed in the past. He treated these murders like jigsaw puzzles. Each piece of evidence has it's place in the puzzle and little by little the whole picture becomes clear. Unfortunately, there are always extra pieces that don't belong and cause confusion, and these have to be discarded. Of course, the last few pieces may be missing and if they are never found, the murderer gets away with it. Hopefully Inspector Muldoon and Alexander will complete the puzzle sooner rather than later.

Monique checked the store, then made her way back to the house with the dogs. Mrs. Hannigan was just finishing up and putting away the hoover in it's cupboard in the utility room.

"That's great Joan," said Monique. "Thanks for everything. Once again don't be worrying about the wedding plans, it will all work out. Please don't hesitate to ask for help if you need it and try your very best to keep schtum."

Mrs. Hannigan laughed, put on her coat, said goodbye and walked out the front door towards her little car.

Monique walked back to the office, picked up the handset and dialled the number of the feed store in Naas. She spoke to a very chirpy sounding girl on the other end of the line, and placed her order. Monique replaced the handset, picked up a file with a red cover and began to read.

Two hours later Alexander returned from The Old Rectory where he had been told by Damien Browne that there were no new developments and, apart from a few stories regarding the Galdstones' methods of doing business with other farmers, there was no news. Although nothing new had come from the visit, it was always good to chat with his old friend.

After dinner the couple sat down to watch a film. Monique had a collection of DVDs in French, which she acquired on holidays in France to visit her parents and relatives. Tonight they chose "Les Enfants du Paradis", a romantic drama film set in 1830s Paris, directed by Marcel Carne. It tells the story of a courtesan and four men who were all in love with her. Believed to be one of the best films of all time, Marlon Brando called it "Maybe the best movie ever made." The film is divided into two parts, "Boulevard du Crime" and "L'Homme Blanc". The first begins around 1827, the second several years later. It is set mainly in the Boulevard du Temple" in Paris. Alexander and Monique had watched it before but it was one of those films that one could watch over and over.

They were about half way through the film when the telephone rang.

"I'll get it," said Monique as she jumped up, paused the DVD and ran to answer the phone. "Hello, Monique de Bruin speaking."

"Monique, it's Joan Hannigan. Sorry to bother you, but I forgot to tell you that I'll be about an hour late to your house on Thursday as I have a doctor's appointment."

"I just hope everything is OK Joan."

"Oh yes, just a check up. There was something else that I wanted to mention to you too which I thought was very strange. They weren't there, they just weren't there Monique."

"Who wasn't there," demanded Monique. "I don't understand. What are you talking about?

"Oh! look at the time, I have to rush to get the bingo bus. I'll miss it if I don't run. I'll tell you all about it when I meet you on Thursday, bye."

The line went dead and Monique replaced the handset and returned to the living room.

"Who was that?" asked Alexander.

"It was Mrs. Hannigan. She was just letting me know that she was going to be about an hour late on Thursday."

Monique sat down beside Alexander, looking very pensive.

"What's up?"

"She said something very strange about someone not being where they should be, but then had to rush off to catch the bingo bus. I'm sure it's nothing, and sure, she'll tell me all about it on Thursday."

CHAPTER 21

—— ∙ ——

A SECOND DEATH

Alexander and Monique were still sleeping when the phone rang at 7.45am. There was a telephone extension in the bedroom on Alexander's side of the bed. He turned on his side, picked up the handset and groggily said, "Hello, Alexander de Bruin speaking."

Monique sat up on her side of the bed and watched her husband as he listened to the person's voice on the other end of the line. She saw the colour drain from his face and his expression became very serious.

"Oh I'm so sorry, Liam... yes... where are you now?...who is with you?... we'll come down to your house this afternoon."

Alexander returned the handset and sat up straight in the bed. He looked over at his wife who seemed petrified sitting beside him.

"It's dreadful news Monique. That was Sergeant Liam Hannigan. Joan was killed last night in a hit and run on her way to catch the bingo bus. So just after her phone call here."

Monique was speechless, sat very still in the bed and just stared into space. After a few moments she put her head in her hands and started to weep. Alexander put his arms around her and she sank into his chest, her tears running down her cheeks. They lay there quietly for about ten minutes, neither able to speak.

"What happened?"

"Liam had left the house at 7 o'clock to go to the pub for a game of cards and to watch some soccer match. He said that Joan always left the house at 7.20 to make sure she was on time for the bus. Seemingly, it's just about a five minutes walk. She was found on the road by a neighbour who rang the ambulance, told his wife to find Liam, and ran back to stay with Joan. She was taken to Naas Hospital where she was pronounced dead. Liam is there now. Two of his good army friends are with him. The guards are there as well. He said that he thought he'd be back home at about 2 o'clock. As you heard, I said that we'd call down this afternoon."

"How life can change in a second. Yesterday she was so happy about the engagement. They had so much to look forward to. She was so full of life and so full of joy. Life isn't fair, Alexander."

"I know my love, it isn't." He held her even more tightly in his arms.

"I have to tell Alison," whispered Monique as she started to cry again.

"No, my dear, I'll phone Robert. I should get him before he leaves for work. He should be with Alison when she hears the news. Stay here, I'll make the call from the office."

Alexander kissed his wife on the forehead, got out of the bed, put on his dressing gown and slippers and made his way downstairs to the office. After Alexander left the room, Monique jumped out of the bed and headed for the shower. "Stop feeling sorry for yourself, get it together, other people are more important and help is needed," she thought to herself. It dawned on her that the grief that she was feeling was nothing compared to that of Joan Hannigan's husband and children. They must do what they could to help the family.

Alexander returned to the bedroom after about fifteen minutes. As he entered, he heard the shower going and realised that Monique was fine, that her brain had clicked into organisational mode. She had had her cry and was now ready for action. Monique appeared from the shower room, towel on head and clad in her white dressing gown.

"Did you get Robert?" she asked.

"Yes, he was just on his way out the door to the Curragh Camp. He's going to take the day off to be with Alison. I'm going to ring them again after we've seen Sergeant Hannigan this afternoon."

Monique began to get dressed. Alexander gave her a hug and then headed for the shower.

As the morning passed, there were many phone calls made to former army colleagues, all of whom would have known Sergeant Hannigan and his wife. The Brownes were informed, who, in turn, informed others.

By the end of the morning, everyone who should know, knew about Joan Hannigan's death. Damien Browne had informed Adam Galdstone. At three o'clock that afternoon Alexander and Monique de Bruin arrived at the home of the Hannigan's in Clonee village. Monique was carrying a cake and flowers. Liam greeted them at the door and led them into the sitting room, the same room where Monique and Joan had drunk cups of tea and gossiped about everything under the sun. The house was cold, Liam had not yet lit the fire in the sitting room. The man was like a zombie, hardly able to speak at first. Monique went into the kitchen to make tea and prepare something to eat for Liam as he looked exhausted having been up all night, with obviously nothing to eat. Alexander lit the fire in the sitting room and sat down beside Liam and waited for him to be able to speak. Monique returned to the room with a sandwich and tea for the Sergeant.

"You need to eat something Liam," she said kindly. "You'll need your strength. It's going to be a very hard week."

Liam sipped his tea and took a few bites out of the sandwich. There was silence in the room as Alexander and Monique gave the Sergeant time to compose himself. They waited until he was able to form his words and tell his story. Suddenly Liam Hannigan looked up from his cup of tea. His eyes had turned from a blank stare, to anger.

"They didn't even stop," he said abruptly. "My poor Joan, just left there. I should have been with her, not down at the pub."

"Please don't do this to yourself," said Monique. "Joan wouldn't want this. She did the same things twice a week every week. All her friends knew that she left the house at 7.20 to catch the bingo bus and you went to meet your pals for a game of cards and a few pints. There's nothing wrong with this. There was absolutely no reason to imagine that things would be any different last evening."

Alexander had moved behind the sergeant's chair and placed his hand comfortingly on his shoulder.

"I spoke to her before she left the house last night," continued Monique. "She wanted to tell me that she would be late to our house on Thursday because of a doctor's appointment, so, I suppose I must have been the last person to speak to her, as she said she had to rush to the bus."

Monique saw that Liam's cup was empty, so she got up to pour him another cup of tea. Alexander sat back down in his chair.

"I don't know why they didn't stop," Liam muttered, staring straight ahead of him. "If our neighbour hadn't found her, she could have been lying there for ages. It was Joe Hynes. He lives two doors down from us. He was bringing his dog out for a walk. Our lane here is very quiet and dark, being a cul-de-sac. I don't know why anyone would be speeding along here. She was still alive in the ambulance, you know, but then she died, just as they were bringing her into the hospital. The doctors told me that she probably didn't know what had happened to her – that she would have been unconscious immediately after the car hit her – I suppose that's some consolation."

"Have you been able to speak to Jean and John?" asked Alexander.

"Yes, I spoke to them early this morning. They are getting a flight home as soon as they can. Jean's boyfriend is coming with her as well."

Monique thought about Mrs. Hannigan's joy as she told her about Jean's engagement, and all the excitement at the thought of meeting him and organising the wedding.

"We won't be able to have the funeral for a while. The guards said that there had to be an autopsy because of the way she died. The guards came early this morning, while I was at the hospital to collect up any evidence. When I got home, there was a tent around the place where Joan was found."

Liam Hannigan looked down at the floor and began to cry. The tears streamed down his cheeks. Monique handed him down some tissues from her handbag. Her heart was breaking, watching this strong, proud man disintegrating before her eyes. After a few minutes, he did his best to pull himself together. He stood up from the chair, straightened himself and headed for the back door.

"I need a breath of fresh air."

Alexander accompanied him into the back garden. Monique picked up the dishes and cutlery, walked towards the kitchen, placed the dirty dishes in the sink and began to rinse them. She watched the two men stroll around the small neat garden. She knew that the poor man was virtually helpless. She knew that she would have to mobilise all of Joan Hannigan's friends to help out with the catering in the house. When the sad news filtered through, there would be a flood of people calling to the Hannigan's home to sympathise. Monique thought about all the practical things that had to be done when someone dies, despite the painful grief. She decided to make a few rounds of sandwiches, wrapped them in tinfoil and left them on the kitchen table, together with the cake that she had brought and some scones and biscuits that she had found in tins in the kitchen. She laid out cups, saucers, plates, a milk jug and sugar bowl. She left the tea bags, tin of instant coffee and tea pot beside the kettle. Everything was ready for the next visitor. "This would do," she thought "until she could organise a rota."

Ten minutes later, there was a knock at the door. The two men were still strolling around the garden. Monique answered the door and she recognised the callers. It was Sergeant Byrne and his wife Maria. They used to live in quarters in camp near the Hannigans. She led the couple into the sitting room, explaining to Maria about her plans for a rota. Monique was tired now, not physically but emotionally drained. She called out to Liam Hannigan that he had visitors. The two men came in from the garden and Liam went into the sitting room to greet his friends. They hugged each other. Alexander entered the room and shook hands with the couple. He too knew Sergeant Byrne and was very glad that he had arrived to sympathise with Liam.

Monique and Alexander stayed for ten more minutes, then took their leave of the company. They walked up the laneway to where they had parked the car. En route they passed the spot where Joan Hannigan had lain on the ground. There was a rectangle of yellow tape. There was no debris around the area – the guards must have removed it all that morning. But there were spatters of blood on the kerb and on the road. Monique took a deep breath as her heart pounded in her chest.

"Oh my God," she sighed.

Alexander put his arm around her shoulder and led her gently towards the car. They both got into the car and sat there quietly for a few moments before Alexander turned the key, put the car in gear and headed home. On arriving at The Lodge, Alexander immediately rang the Kings to let them know the lay of the land. Robert and Alison had plans to visit Liam Hannigan that afternoon and then to call to The Lodge, where the two ladies, together, could organise a rota to cater for the visitors.

Alexander was very grateful that their good friends, the Kings, were calling that evening. Alison and Monique needed each other's support.

"Lets take a stroll over to the Brownes," said Alexander. "They'll be very keen to know what's going on as well. I'm quite sure that they will want to help in any way they can. They too were very fond of Joan."

As they strolled through the fields towards The Old Rectory, Alexander was very pensive. On reaching the Brownes, he had determined to ring Inspector Muldoon on his return home. He wanted to know about every single detail concerning the hit and run. What exactly had befallen poor Mrs. Hannigan?

CHAPTER 22

—— ◆ ——

999 CALL

Inspector John Muldoon had received a phone call at his home at 8.30pm on the night of the accident. The Garda who had received the 999 call at the station knew that this was out of his league and had decided to phone his superior.

Inspector Muldoon was slightly taken aback when he was told the address of said accident. He was informed that it was a hit and run to boot. He then rang the home of Sergeant Michael Dunne who was also off duty that night to request that he accompany him to the site of the accident.

When the two men arrived at Clonee village, Mrs. Hannigan had already been taken to hospital by ambulance. The man who had found her, Joe Hynes, was waiting for them. The ambulance crew had asked him to stay put and wait for the guards. He was leaning against a window sill, staring down at the blood and debris that had been left behind, his little Jack Russell dog at his feet.

"Would you like to move indoors somewhere?" asked John Muldoon after he had introduced himself.

"Yes, we can go down to my house, the wife is there. She's the one who went down to the pub to tell Liam Hannigan about his wife.

He's followed the ambulance into Naas in his car. She looked a mess. I didn't think she was going to make it."

Inspector Muldoon recognised the name immediately. Mrs. Hannigan was the housekeeper to the de Bruins, Galdstones, Brownes and others in the area. He recalled all the information that she had proffered regarding the murder case.

"I don't like coincidences," he thought to himself.

On entering the Hynes home, he asked for permission to use the phone, as he wanted to organise a liaison officer to go immediately to the hospital, to look after Mr. Hannigan and to speak to the doctors.

Mr. Hynes wasn't exactly a witness. He had just found Mrs. Hannigan injured on the laneway. He hadn't seen the accident nor heard anything out of the ordinary.

Inspector Muldoon then made a second call to organise a forensics team to attend the scene as soon as possible. He left two young officers guarding the area until they arrived.

The forensics team were there within the hour. A tent was erected and a bigger area was taped off. They did what they could that night but would have to wait until daylight to collect up all the pieces of glass and other pieces of debris from the accident.

Inspector Muldoon and Sgt. Dunne left the village and drove to Naas Hospital. They located the liaison officer who had bad news for them. Mrs. Hannigan had died of her injuries. Liam would be there for a while as he wanted to see his wife's body.

Muldoon decided to leave well enough alone and to put off questioning the husband until at least the following day as the poor man was in an awful state.

"Is Mr. Hannigan's car in the hospital carpark?" asked Muldoon.

"Yes," replied the liaison officer. "My colleague has already taken a look at it. Clean as a whistle – no sign of any damage. It clearly wasn't involved in any hit and run."

"Well done," added Muldoon. "We'll leave it to you and speak to-morrow."

The two men walked along the hospital corridor. On their way to the front entrance, they noticed a small room to their right with a glass partition. They saw a young man, in his early thirties, dressed in a white coat, standing in front of another much older man, explaining something very serious to him. The older man was listening very intently, a look of shock and horror on his face.

"Someone getting very bad news," thought Muldoon to himself.

Muldoon and Dunne continued on their way into the carpark. They sat into their car.

"We have to organise a door to door tomorrow," said Muldoon. "The sooner the better. We'll have to get help from other stations like the last time."

"I'll organise that and the questionnaire," replied Dunne.

The following morning at Naas Garda Station, Sergeant Michael Dunne had assembled his band of young officers, handed them their questionnaires, explained, in great detail, their duties for the next couple of days and sent them on their way. He then walked into the office of Inspector Muldoon to report what he had done.

"All that has been organised, Sir," said Dunne.

"Well done Sergeant," replied Muldoon. "I hope we find some wit-nesses. I rang the owner of the pub in Clonee. Liam Hannigan arrived there before seven and didn't leave until Mrs. Hynes ran into the pub to tell him about the accident. So he's completely in the clear."

"There were a lot of people in their homes watching the football match," continued Dunne. "Sure we'll see what the lads come back with, from their door-to-door. Seemingly the pub in Clonee was crowded enough as well."

"I was on to the hospital. There's going to be an autopsy today, although there can be no doubt as to the cause of death. Will you get on to forensics, John, to get them to hurry up with their findings."

Sergeant Dunne left the room just as the phone on Muldoon's desk rang. He picked up the handset. It was Monique de Bruin.

"I just wanted to let you know Inspector Muldoon, that I was probably the last person to speak to Mrs. Hannigan," she said. "She rang me just before 7.20 to let me know that she would be late for her job here on Thursday. We only spoke for a moment as she was rushing for the bingo bus at 7.30."

"Thank you Mrs. de Bruin."

The inspector realised that there was only about an eight minute window in which the accident could have occurred. He had already checked with the bus driver, who stated that he arrived at the pick-up point in the village at 7.30 and had left at 7.35. There was no sign of Mrs. Hannigan, but the other ladies were all on board, so, presuming that she wasn't going to bingo last night, he left.

John Muldoon picked up his coat and briefcase, left the room and called out to Sergeant Dunne. "I want to visit the scene again. I need to get a feel for what happened. We probably won't hear anything from forensics for a couple of hours. Come with me Sergeant."

Dunne stood up from his desk and followed the Inspector to his car.

Twenty minutes later they were standing in the laneway where Mrs. Hannigan used to live. They made their way down to the end of the cul-de-sac.

"Look Sir," said Dunne, pointing at the ground. "There are what look like tyre marks here."

Muldoon bent down and examined the marks.

"That really looks like a car was parked, revved up, and took off at speed leaving these rubber tyre marks on the ground."

They walked from there up the laneway slowly, until they came to the area surrounded by the yellow tape. They both stared at the ground but couldn't find what they were looking for.

"There are no skid marks, John. The driver didn't brake."

The two men stood still and in silence for a moment, taking in the whole scene.

"It looks like they accelerated all the way from the end of the cul-de-sac there, ran her down, and kept going. This is beginning to look less and less like an accident," answered Dunne.

"I think it's time we asked Mr. Hannigan a few questions, but we'll handle him with kid gloves- we know he's not involved and is in a dreadful state after the loss of his wife. We also don't want to inform him about our suspicions just yet. It would be an awful shock for the man to be told that his wife might have been murdered. We are not sure of the facts yet anyway."

The two men made their way to the Hannigan home. They noticed the young officers with their clipboards going from house to house talking to the neighbours.

There were a number of visitors in the Hannigan home. Muldoon noticed that Mary Edwards, the vicar's wife, was serving tea in the sitting room. There were two other women, who were not known to Muldoon making sandwiches in the kitchen.

"I'm sorry to disturb you Mr. Hannigan but I'm the detective in charge of your wife's accident – John Muldoon, and this is my Sergeant, Michael Dunne. We are very sorry for your loss. Do you think that you'd be up to answering a few questions?"

"Yes, of course," answered Liam Hannigan. "We'll go into the garden. As you see I have a lot of callers. The ladies from Joan's flower club have been very kind and are helping with the catering. I don't know what I'd do without all the help from Joan's friends. I think they must have some sort of a rota going, no doubt organised by Commandant de Bruin's wife," he smiled.

The three men walked into the garden and Liam Hannigan sat down on a wooden bench. There were three other wrought iron chairs available to the two officers. so they too sat down.

Muldoon did not want to give any indication that he thought that the death was suspicious so he decided to ask very general, vague questions.

"We don't know how or why this accident occurred as yet. It is very early days in the investigation. So, I suppose what we would like to get from you is a sense of what Joan was like."

"Well my Joan was a wonderful wife and mother. Our two children are on their way home from England. She was really looking forward to meeting Jean's boyfriend – he's coming too."

The tears welled up in his eyes and he straightened in the bench and was obviously trying to control his emotions.

"She was a bundle of energy, always working. I told her she shouldn't take on so many jobs. We didn't need the money. I have a good army pension. But there was no talking to her. I think she liked the gossip. She really liked going to the de Bruin's. Herself and Mrs. de Bruin got on like a house on fire. We have a lovely home. She kept it so well and she was a great cook."

"What about her social life?" asked Muldoon.

"Well, there was bingo and the flower club. Same things every week. She was going to get the bus to bingo you know when it happened.

She'd leave the house at 7.20 to be on time. You could set your watch by her."

Muldoon wanted to ask the question. "Did she have any enemies?" But decided against it. It would set off alarm bells and he didn't want to upset the man anymore than he had to. He wanted to be sure of his facts and nothing was clear as yet.

"Thank you for your time, Mr. Hannigan. Once again please accept our sincere condolences."

"I suppose it was those young joy riders did it? The young lads don't know how to drive and lose control of the cars. Although our cul-de-sac is a strange place for joy riding. It's a pity they didn't stick to the Curragh plains – plenty of room there."

"We really don't know what happened as yet," replied Muldoon. "We'll contact you as soon as we have any information at all."

The two men made their way back to the car.

"Do you think that it could be young lads who just made a dreadful mistake – hit the accelerator instead of the brake and then panicked?" asked Dunne.

"Anything's possible," replied Muldoon. "I suppose we can't jump to conclusions. We have to investigate every single angle. Let's hope the forensics are back by the time we return to the office. They might tell a tale."

They drove back to Naas Garda Station. En route, they spoke very little. Sergeant Dunne was making notes, sitting in the passenger seat. John Muldoon was wondering was there a link between the cases.

Before reaching the station Muldoon had made up his mind to discuss this with Alexander de Bruin. He would study the forensics and the post mortem results and take it from there.

On returning to his desk, Sergeant Dunne saw the folder with the label "Forensics Hannigan". He picked it up and went straight into the office of his superior.

"It's arrived," he said, and handed it straight away to Inspector Muldoon.

John Muldoon opened the file and read it carefully, then handed it back to his sergeant so that he could peruse it before their discussion.

"So, they found glass from a headlight that broke in the impact and some flakes of blue paint on the kerb. They concur that there were no skid marks where Mrs. Hannigan was hit, so therefore no braking. They also mention the rubber tyre marks at the bottom of the cul-de-sac. We now know the colour of the car, but they were not able to determine the make or model from the glass. OK, while we are waiting for the post-mortem, will you check if there are any blue stolen cars reported. Get a few squad cars to drive around the usual estates. We have a good idea what young lads could be involved in joy riding. Of course they could have come down from Dublin. Ring Garda Headquarters and get some extra help from there. We need to rule out the stolen car scenario first."

Sergeant Dunne left the office and went back to his desk to make the relevant phone calls. Several more hours passed before the post-mortem results landed on Muldoon's desk.

The document was not an easy read. Mrs. Hannigan's injuries were horrendous. It was estimated that her body had been impacted by the car, travelling at 45mph/50mph. Her legs had been swept from under her and both broken in several places. There were multiple head injuries as her head hit the hood and probably made impact with the windscreen. There were no glass shards imbedded in her skull, so it was unlikely that the windscreen shattered but most likely cracked.

She then bounced off the car and landed, crashing her head against the pavement,. There were small stones imbedded in her skull. Her whole body was broken. There were rib fractures, one punctured lung, brain bleed and a ruptured spleen. She would have been knocked unconscious on impact. As the ambulance crew testified, she was barely breathing when they got to her. This was a traumatic, unsurvivable impact. It was also noted that there were flakes of blue paint imbedded in the back of her knee. Muldoon read through the report twice.

"That poor woman," he thought to himself. "The only saving grace is that she probably didn't know what hit her. She had been impacted from behind. She would not have seen it coming."

Muldoon wondered was she just in the wrong place at the wrong time, or was someone waiting at the bottom of the cul-de-sac for her to emerge from her house at the usual time to catch her bus, so that they could run her down and silence her.

CHAPTER 23

— • —

A SECOND FUNERAL

Two days after their mother's death, the Hannigan children arrived back to Clonee from England to a very sad homecoming. Their father was very happy to see them. There had been a delay in the releasing of the body due to the post mortem. Jean and John Hannigan were very grateful to all of their mother's friends for having stepped up to the plate, and having helped their father through the first few very difficult days following the accident. Now they had to organise a funeral. Both the Parish Priest from Newbridge and the Chaplain from the Curragh camp had offered their services. Lengthy discussions ensued regarding where Mrs. Hannigan's funeral mass should take place. Both the Curragh Military Church and Newbridge Parish Church had been very important to her. The Hannigans had attended Mass in the Curragh every Sunday while they lived in quarters. The children had been christened there, as had many of the children living in camp including the de Bruin and King children.

Jean and John had attended secondary school in Newbridge, so there had been many an occasion when the family took part in ceremonies in the parish church. Sergeant Hannigan had also bought a family plot in the graveyard in Newbridge.

Finally, they decided on the parish church in Newbridge. A very big crowd was expected to attend. When an army wife died, there was always a huge army attendance. The walk from the church to the graveyard was also doable.

The Hannigans had decided that there would not be a removal the night before, which was unusual, but they wanted to keep their wife and mother with them in the house for one more day. The removal and the Mass would be on the same day, followed by the burial.

The hearse left their home in Clonee at eleven o'clock on Saturday morning followed by the cars carrying Mrs. Hannigan's family and relatives. It was decided that they would drive through the Curragh before they continued their journey to Newbridge Church. Alexander and Monique de Bruin arrived at the church at eleven forty five. They took their seats about half way up the church. The Kings arrived a few minutes later – Robert in full army uniform, as were all the serving personnel. The church was full by the time the coffin arrived. The congregation stood up when the choir began the entrance hymn "Be not afraid". The coffin was wheeled up the aisle by the undertaker, followed by the family. Liam, John and Jean walked slowly up the aisle. There was a young man holding Jean's hand.

"How sad," thought Monique. "Their first time up the aisle should have been their wedding day."

The choir from the girl's secondary school where Jean had been a pupil sang beautifully, accompanied by their music teacher on the organ. During the offertory procession when gifts were brought to the altar they sang "Ave Maria".

At communion as the choir sang "Bread of Angles" Alexander contemplated the beauty of this particular church. He admired the High Altar which had been imported from Italy and behind it, the magnificent stained glass windows.

The mass was celebrated by the Parish Priest and the Army Chaplain but it was Fr. Jones, the chaplain, who gave the homily, a very fitting homily that acknowledged the unique life of Mrs. Hannigan and the significance of such for all who had known her.

Then finally..... "For our brothers and sisters who have gone to God before us, we thank the Lord for their lives and ministry and pray that they might truly know God's eternal presence and peace. May they rest in peace and rise in glory. Eternal rest, unto them, O' Lord , and let perpetual life shine upon them."

Then the coffin was blessed and wheeled down the aisle to the strains of "Amazing Grace". The congregation filed out behind the family. As the de Bruins and Kings made their way out of the church they noticed Inspector Muldoon and Sergeant Dunne sitting in the back pew. They nodded at each other. They also noticed Clara, John and Adam Galdstone standing beside the wall outside the church.

Following the very moving burial, they retired to the Keadeen Hotel for refreshments. It was a very sad affair. People stood around making polite conversation, nibbling finger food and drinking tea or coffee. The Hannigans were in too much of a daze to say that much to anyone. They gave monosyllabic answers to questions posed by concerned friends. It was a very difficult few hours for them but it was part of the ritual. Finally it was all over and everyone went home.

Inspector Muldoon and Sergeant Dunne had gone to the funeral to detect and observe. They knew that it was very likely that whoever had killed Mrs. Hannigan, either by accident or intentionally, would be present at the funeral. Apart from all the army people who were present in their uniforms and the obviously retired army group and their wives, they noticed that all the suspects in the Jinny Galdstone murder, bar the Healeys from Roscommon, were also present. There was no sign of any young lads from the estates who might have been involved in joy riding though.

Alexander and Monique de Bruin arrived back at The Lodge at five thirty. They were emotionally exhausted. Monique hung up her coat in the hallway, walked into the sitting room and threw herself down on the couch.

"I think I'll have a glass of wine," she said. "Will you pour me one please Alexander?"

Alexander went over to the drinks cabinet and poured a glass of red wine for his wife and a brandy for himself. He walked over to the couch with the two glasses, handed one to Monique and sat down beside her on the couch.

"What a dreadfully sad day," whispered Monique. "The mass was lovely and the singing was superb and the chaplain was wonderful, but I'm really fed up. She should still be here. She should be organising Jean's wedding and watching Liam's reaction to the engagement."

"I know my love," replied Alexander, putting his arm around Monique's shoulder as she snuggled into him for comfort. "She never did anyone any harm. She was a force for good. Joan was such good company. It's going to be so hard for Liam to cope without her, especially when the two kids go back to England."

"Monique, tell me again exactly what Mrs. Hannigan said to you on the phone that evening."

"She said that they weren't there," replied Monique.

"Did you mention to Muldoon when you rang him that you were probably the last person to speak to her before her death?"

"Yes, I think I did, but I don't recall telling him what she said to me."

"I'll ring him first thing in the morning. I need to have a catch up with him anyway about the other case. He certainly has his hands full at the moment."

"I presume that Jean meant that someone wasn't there when she said "they" maybe it was something! Do you think she saw someone or something that made her suspicious about the murder?" asked Monique with a tone of slight panic in her voice.

"I don't know, darling. We're tired and emotionally wrecked so we may be putting two and two together and getting ten. What she said to you on the phone may have nothing at all to do with her death."

Alexander and Monique decided to watch one of their French language films. They sat in front of the television screen but neither really concentrated on the film. They were both thinking about poor Joan Hannigan and her family, wondering who was missing or what was missing. What on earth had Mrs. Hannigan been talking about when she said, "they weren't there."

He was under extreme pressure now with two cases to solve. A phone call had been put through to his office first thing that morning from head office, a superior officer demanding that he get a move on, and solve the murder case and the accident as quickly as possible.

Muldoon thought to himself that some of these fellows from head office couldn't organise a "piss-up in a brewery" never mind solve a murder case. They just loved the power. His thoughts were interrupted by Sergeant Dunne entering the office.

"Bad news, Sir, nobody saw anything. The lads managed to question everyone in the village. There are only two houses that are unoccupied at the moment. Most of them were watching the football match either at home or in the pub. It was a school night, so the kids were at home, inside. Anyone who was getting the bingo bus was already down at the stop. So, for that eight minutes, no one was out on the laneway, and no one noticed any sort of car in the vicinity. The squad cars have also been patrolling the streets watching out for the banged-up blue car – but no luck yet. There have been no reports of stolen cars in the area, but there were three in the Dublin precinct – of course none of them was blue. So for the moment, Sir, we're at an impasse. But it's early days."

"Thanks for all your work Michael, you've done a very thorough job. By the way, Alexander de Bruin is calling in to the office in half an hour. We are going to discuss both cases. He and his wife were very close to Mrs. Hannigan."

Sergeant Dunne left the office and returned to his desk.

Half an hour later Alexander de Bruin climbed the stairs of Naas Garda Station and made his way to the office of Inspector Muldoon.

"Good morning John, how are you?"

"Not bad, considering." replied the Inspector.

Alexander sat down at the desk and noticed that the names on the chalk board hadn't moved. He also observed that John Muldoon was looking exhausted, his brow was more furrowed than usual and there were puffy bags under his eyes.

"I may have a piece of interesting information for you regarding Mrs. Hannigan. I know that Monique rang you to inform you that she was the last person to speak to Mrs. Hannigan before she left her house to catch the bus, but during the brief conversation between the two women, Mrs. Hannigan had said something very strange. She said that she was worried by something, that "they weren't there." She didn't explain as she was running a bit late. We don't know whether this is relevant. I suppose it depends on whether Mrs. Hannigan's death was actually a hit-and-run or something more sinister."

"Any idea whether the "they" are persons or things?" wondered Muldoon.

"No idea at all, Monique and I discussed this and couldn't come to any conclusion. Have you made any progress with the hit-and-run theory?"

Inspector Muldoon explained about the progress that they had made regarding the questioning of all the neighbours in Clonee and Briarstown. He admitted that they had found no witnesses, that everyone in the area seemed to be indoors during the window of eight minutes. He related everything that Michael Dunne had reported to him with respect to the stolen cars and failure to find any banged up blue cars during patrols.

"I suppose you have the post-mortem report and forensics back?"

"Yes, we have, and it's looking somewhat suspicious. First of all the car is blue, it has broken headlights, probably a cracked windscreen and damage to the bonnet. It looks like it was parked at the end of the cul-de-sac. It took off at speed, revving up and leaving rubber tyre marks on the ground. It hit poor Mrs. Hannigan at 45-50mph. There were no brake marks anywhere near where Mrs. Hannigan was found. The unfortunate woman didn't stand a chance. Her injuries were horrendous. Muldoon handed the post-mortem file to de Bruin who studied it very carefully. When he was finished he left it on the desk.

"It's a wonder she wasn't killed instantly. If this wasn't an accident, whoever did this is a very evil person."

"We have two theories at the moment, either it was young lads who were inept drivers and kept their foot on the accelerator instead of braking, then panicked and kept going, or this was intentional. Someone waited for Mrs. Hannigan to emerge from her house and deliberately ran her down. But if this is the case they had to get the timing right."

"There are a lot of people who would have known about Mrs. Hannigan's bingo. She told just about everyone about her bingo nights and when she left the house to catch the bus. We all knew her rituals. Her husband even said that you could set your watch by her." continued Alexander.

"The conversation that she had with your wife lends credence to the second theory."

"Well then, if it is the latter, it only stands to reason that the two deaths must be linked and that Mrs. Hannigan became aware of someone or something being missing that made her suspicious and she wanted to speak to Monique about it."

CHAPTER 24

— ◆ —

A STRANGE OCCORANCE

Following his meeting with Inspector Muldoon, Alexander drove home to The Lodge. He thought carefully about what he was going to say to Monique. He reached the conclusion that he would not tell her that he had seen the post-mortem report because if he did, she would ask for details and he knew how upset it would make her if she learned of all the traumatic injuries that Mrs. Hannigan had suffered.

Monique was at the desk working on a file with a blue cover when Alexander entered the office.

"Well, what news?" she asked.

He told her about the two theories that the gardai were working on. He reassured her that her friend hadn't suffered, and had been knocked unconscious by the impact and that she wouldn't have known what was about to happen to her. Monique looked relieved on hearing this.

"So does Inspector Muldoon believe that what she said to me is relevant?" she enquired

"He thinks, as we do, that it's very suspicious, particularly if they can rule out the first scenario – joy riders. He also believes that if it's the second scenario, and she was killed to silence her – then the two cases are linked. It's all just too much of a coincidence, two violent deaths, in the same small country area, of two women who knew each other and Mrs. Hannigan knew all the suspects except the Healeys from Roscommon."

"She wasn't anywhere near the Galdstone's farm on the morning of the murder. As she said to me, she was still tucked up in bed at that ungodly hour. So it was something she noticed in the intervening weeks," continued Monique.

There had been a lot of rain that week, so the fields were sodden. It was not conducive to walking the dogs through the fields as they would get completely covered in mud, therefore Alexander decided to take them for their daily exercise along the road. He did not expect to meet much traffic at this time of the day, as anyone going to work had left, and they would not return for another couple of hours. He also decided that he would not go past the Galdstone farm as the road would be completely covered in dung, the mess on the road exasperated by the heavy rains.

He returned to The Lodge after about twenty minutes. Monique had been expecting him to stay out longer as the dogs usually needed at least an hours walk when they couldn't run around the fields.

"What happened? you look very pale," she asked as her husband entered the kitchen.

Alexander was ashen faced and there was muck on the bottom of his trousers and on his shoes. Monique knew that there was something amiss, as her husband, as well as looking shocked, would never have brought mud through the house and into the kitchen.

"What I would call a strange occurrence," answered Alexander "I was walking along the road with the dogs on their leads when I saw the Galdstone's jeep coming towards me. Clara was driving and John was in the passenger seat. As they neared, the jeep swerved towards me and I had to jump out of the way and into the ditch dragging the dogs in after me. They obviously saw what had happened to me but just kept driving."

"That's really weird," said Monique "Do you think they did it on purpose?"

"I don't really know. If it hadn't been on purpose I believe they would have stopped to see if I were OK but they didn't, they just kept going."

"What strange behaviour! Why on earth would they do such a thing? You could have been injured or the dogs could have been struck by the jeep. Why would they have such animosity towards you?"

"At this stage, I don't really know, the mind boggles. Muldoon made it very clear to them that I was not a suspect in Jinny's murder and they know that I am helping with the case. Is it possible that they are still annoyed about the land? You'd think that should not even be in the equation anymore with all they have to deal with."

"I suppose there's nothing we can do about it, your word against theirs. There's the off chance that it wasn't done on purpose and it was just a lapse of concentration. But then the decent thing to have done was to stop and check that you were OK and apologise for shoving you into the ditch with the dogs."

"We'll just have to put it behind us," said Alexander. "Hope that it doesn't happen again. I'll have to be very light on my toes if I see any of them driving in my direction in future," he smiled.

Alexander and Monique decided not to tell any of their friends about the strange occurrence. They didn't believe that the Galdstones would try to frighten any other pedestrians and cause them to jump into the ditch. He was convinced that they were still suspicious about him, had not forgotten that he had words with Jinny (although as far as he was concerned – a very pleasant conversation) and resented the fact that they had been caught out by him in underhand behaviour.

An hour later Alexander was at his desk, writing a report and sipping coffee when there was a knock on the door. It was Damien Browne.

"Well, I see you're still in one piece. I was up at the top of the small paddock when I saw what happened. By the time I got down, you were gone so I presumed you were OK. Couldn't see which one of them was driving, did you?"

"Yes, it was Clara," replied Alexander.

"That young lady is for the birds and just to keep going – what dreadful behaviour!" continued Damien. "Just called in to check that you were OK."

"Are you coming in?" asked Alexander.

"No, sorry, have to rush off – have to check on one of the horses. She's a bit lame. Hope it's not laminitis. It's so hard to cure that."

Alexander watched as Damien walked quickly down the path and towards The Old Rectory.

"Monique," called Alexander as he rushed into the office. "You'll be glad to know that I haven't gone mad. Damien saw the whole thing and just called in to check on me."

"I hadn't thought that for one minute, my dear. You're not one to imagine things or exaggerate events," Monique smiled as she returned to her work.

Alexander wondered were the Galdstone children taking up where the mother left off – did this sort of sociopathic behaviour run in the family?

CHAPTER 25

— ❖ —

LIFE GOES ON?

Inspector Muldoon had rung The Lodge early the following morning to make arrangements for both he and de Bruin to visit Liam Hannigan. They had decided that Muldoon would collect de Bruin at 10.50 and travel to the Hannigan home for eleven o'clock.

Alexander waited at the gate for John, as he didn't want to be late for the appointment. Muldoon arrived precisely at 10.50. De Bruin jumped into the passenger seat.

"Good morning," greeted John Muldoon.

"Morning," returned Alexander de Bruin.

"We've hit a dead end with the hit-and-run, boy racer theory – that's not to say that we're not continuing with that idea – the lads are still on the look-out for the elusive blue car. Just thought it was time to have a chat with Mrs. Hannigan's husband. She may have said something to him. He may know something that he doesn't even know he knows."

They arrived at the Hannigan house ten minutes later. Liam Hannigan was standing in his doorway ready to greet them and led them into the sitting room.

"How are you, Liam?" asked Alexander in a kind tone of voice.

"Just putting one foot in front of the other, Sir," he replied.

"Alex, please call me Alex."

"Force of habit, Alex."

"Jean, John and David went back the day before yesterday," continued Liam Hannigan. "The house is very quiet now. It wasn't too bad when we were busy – but now!"

He sat down on an armchair and stared out the window. Then he looked up at Alexander.

"Jean and David are engaged, you know. Joan knew before they arrived but was keeping the secret from me so that David could ask me – you know, proper like. She'll never get to organise the wedding now. My poor Joan."

The two men looked down at this poor, broken man sitting in his armchair. Alexander thought that he looked as if he had aged ten years since his wife's death. He had been such a strong, capable man and now he was a shadow of his former self.

"Sit there Liam and I'll make a cup of tea for all of us before we start. We have a few questions for you and we want to explain what has been happening with the case."

Alexander left the room and made his way into the kitchen. He opened the presses above the cooker to look for the teabags. He noticed the teapot on the counter beside the fridge. There were mugs and spoons beside it. He looked around the kitchen and remembered Joan Hannigan fussing about in there. He could see in his mind's eye Monique and herself chatting at the kitchen table. "What a sad ending for a lovely lady," he thought to himself. The kettle switched off. He threw the tea bags into the teapot and filled it with water. He noticed a tray standing against the wall above the counter, and put everything he needed on it. As he was lifting the tray to carry it into the sitting room, he observed a set of steak knives in a wooden holder on the left side of the counter, just underneath a glass cupboard which held drinking glasses. They were exactly the same set of knives that they had in their own kitchen at The Lodge which had been examined by the guards when he was originally a suspect – the same knife that was the murder weapon found in his ditch. He knew nothing about knives or cutlery and presumed that they were fashionable and popular at the moment. There was a full set in their wooden holder in front of him in any case.

He walked into the sitting room, carrying the tray. He laid it down on the small coffee table and poured the tea. Liam took a sip from his cup.

"Have you found anything out?" he asked. "Did you find them?"

"There have been a few developments," answered Muldoon. "There are several possibilities. We have been looking for the blue car – as you know there were flakes of blue paint found at the scene. It wasn't a stolen car. We are searching high and low for it. Unfortunately we have found no witnesses. Everyone in the area appears to have been indoors at the time of the incident."

"We have to ask this question, Liam, as there's another possibility," added Alexander. "Did Joan have any enemies to your knowledge?"

Liam looked extremely shocked and surprised. "What do you mean? Do you think someone did this on purpose? Do you think that someone murdered Joan?"

He was visibly upset and shaken by the insinuation.

"Joan was harmless. Everyone loved her. She was kind and thoughtful. She just worked hard, looked after me and the house, and went to bingo and the flower club to have fun with the other women. Why would anyone want to hurt her? It's ridiculous! Is there something I don't know?"

"As you know, Monique was probably the last person to speak to her before the incident. Joan said something strange to Monique. She said that she was puzzled that, to quote "They weren't there". But she was rushing to catch the bus so didn't explain. We were just wondering if she had said anything to you of this nature."

"No, she said nothing like that. She was in great form when I left for the pub. She didn't say anything like that in the days before either. What does it mean?"

"We don't know," answered Alexander. "We don't know whether the "they" she mentioned are people or things. We don't know when she noticed the anomaly. Will you think carefully, Liam, did she say anything to you about the Jinny Galdstone murder?"

"So, you think she knew something about that murder and that's what got her killed?" Liam stuttered.

"As we said," interjected Muldoon." We are considering all angles. We just find some of the circumstances a bit suspicious."

"Do you think she might have told anyone else?" asked Alexander.

"I think if she needed to discuss anything serious she would have asked your wife first or Colonel King's wife. She thought the world of them."

"Since we believe that there may be a link between the two deaths and if so, the suspects in one may be the suspects in your wife's death. So I need to know about Joan's relationships with the Galdstones, the vicar and his wife, the Lavelles, the Hobans and a longshot – the Healeys from Roscommon."

"Well, first of all she had never heard about, nor met the Healeys. We only got to know about them through the gossip after Jinny's death. It went all around the village the way the Galdstones ruined them and about the suicide. She knew Mrs. Lavelle from the bingo and the flower club – Dora Lavelle only joined them recently. She seemed to come out of her shell a bit after the murder. Mary Edwards, the vicar's wife is a member of the flower club. Joan really liked her, she thought that she was a lovely young woman. Joan knew the old ladies, Ena and

Kitty Hoban. I don't think she knew the young cousin. The others were all people she worked for. She did the Galdstone's main house and then after the murder, she started at Briar's Cottage. She didn't like going to either of those but felt she couldn't leave because of the situation. She loved going to your house Alex and the Brownes. She had the doctors in the village as well and two others in Newbridge."

"So, she never mentioned anything strange about the suspects?" John asked once more.

"No, I'm sorry," answered Liam. "Maybe it just came to her when she was on the phone to Monique. Of course Joan would think a lot about things. Maybe she knew that there was something strange and was turning it around in her head – she did that a lot – and when she couldn't solve it, decided to talk to Monique about it."

"We are so sorry about all of this and all that you are going through, Liam. Thanks so much for seeing us. These new developments, we know are very surprising and upsetting for you. We will let you know if we find out anything new."

The two men took leave of Liam Hannigan. As they walked to the car, he was standing at his front door, looking dazed and bewildered. Muldoon and de Bruin realised that they were really none the wiser or any closer to finding the killer, or killers. As Liam had said, no one knew when Mrs. Hannigan became aware of the puzzling event.

Unless the first scenario was correct and some young lad was arrested for the accident, then they would have to begin questioning the original suspects in the Jinny Galdstone murder once again, and this time checking alibis for the eight minutes in question.

Muldoon dropped Alexander off at the front gate and went on his way. He wanted to get back to the station to check with Sergeant Dunne if any developments occurred in his absence. He wasn't really hopeful as he was becoming more and more convinced that the two deaths were linked and poor Mrs. Hannigan had been murdered because of something or someone she saw, or didn't see.

Alexander went into the house and immediately went to locate Monique so that he could relate to her everything that had been said at the Hannigans. Monique always had a slightly different perspective on things. He valued her opinion greatly and always found it helpful to talk through events and conversations with her. Sometimes she was able to pick up on a nuance or meaning that he had missed or misinterpreted. Monique listened very carefully to what her husband had to say, but this time she had no new insights to give him.

Alexander had noticed that one of the ponies looked a bit lame in the paddock just before he had been collected by Muldoon that morning. He thought now would be a good time to walk out into the fresh air and check it out.

It was Cailin, Maeve's really good jumper. He was hoping that it wasn't laminitis – it's such a horrible affliction. He had seen it often before. Ponies are more prone to it than horses. It is caused by eating too much rich grass. The hoof becomes inflamed and it's really painful. There really isn't any cure but it can be managed. Alexander knew that this would spell the end of her jumping career, because once they got laminitis it came back again and again. But more importantly, he didn't want to see the pony in pain and Maeve would be really upset. He went into the paddock, carrying a lead rope, slipped the clasp into the headcollar and led her into the stable. He picked up the front leg to check the hoof using the hoof pick. He cleaned away the muck and there was an abscess. He was never happier to see a yellowy brown abscess full of puss. He breathed a sigh of relief – not laminitis just an infection that could be cured. He returned to the house, as he needed to prepare a poultice for the hoof. It required hot water and Epsom salts.

When he reached the kitchen. Monique was there having a short break from work.

"What's the verdict,?" she asked.

"Just an abscess," he replied. "She must have picked up something in the paddock that caused the infection. I'm going to prepare a poultice and keep her in the stable for a few days."

Monique watched her husband as he measured out the hot water, added the Epsom salts, stirred it with a spoon, then added some bran until it had the consistency of porridge.

"Life goes on," she said as she sipped her coffee.

"Maybe for the likes of us, but life has irrevocably altered for poor Liam Hannigan. Need to rush back before this cools."

Alexander took the small basin with the mixture and hurried back to the stable. Cailin was a very quiet, well behaved pony. She never objected to her hooves being cleaned. Alexander picked up the hoof again, scraped out any remaining dirt with the hoof pick, brushed it, then washed it before applying the hot poultice. Cailin jumped a little as she felt the poultice meet the abscess but Alexander was able to calm her. He then wrapped a bandage around the hoof to keep it in place. He kept it from unravelling with a tiny clip. Job done, he brought in more straw in the wheelbarrow to make her bed thicker and softer, so easier on the pony to have the offending hoof on the ground. He put some hay in the net and checked the water. There was something niggling at him, something that he had heard maybe during the conversation with Liam Hannigan, but couldn't put a finger on it. He wandered around the land trying to remember everything that had been said. He noticed that the daffodils and tulips were on their way out. The snowdrops had finished flowering a month earlier. It was time now for the roses, peonies and lily of the valley to bloom. Tiny pink flowers were beginning to blossom on the clematis that hugged the archway, that led into the back garden. Life really does go on. Death in nature makes way for new life in it's place. Not quite as straightforward for the human circle of life.

CHAPTER 26

—— ✳ ——

MORE ALIBIS

Muldoon and Dunne were sitting in the office, browsing through their notes. Inspector Muldoon now had two cases written in chalk on his blackboard. He had divided the blackboard into two, the column relating to Jinny Galdstone's murder on the left and the ones relating to Joan Hannigan's death on the right, using coloured chalk to make the links between the two. There were many arrows leading from one side of the board to the other. He had only given over a small section to "boy racers and accident". All the garages had been checked for repairs to blue vehicles in the surrounding areas and in Dublin, to no avail.

"I've made arrangements for us to visit the Galdstones again," Muldoon said, looking up from his notes.

"The two of us will go to the main house on the farm at 2 o'clock. I had asked to speak to each of them separately but Adam insisted that they were too busy and wanted us to speak to the three of them together. I led them to believe that we were just going to give them an update on the murder, so we'll have to manoeuvre our questioning in the direction of alibis for Joan Hannigan's death. They also said that they didn't want de Bruin to come with us. I've made them aware several times that there is no question that the man was involved in

Jinny's murder and that he is officially helping us with the case but no go this time."

"Maybe they think that we're not as clever as him," laughed Dunne. "Maybe indeed."

At precisely 2 o'clock Muldoon and Dunne arrived at the Galdstone farm and were shown into the sitting room by Clara. Adam and John were sitting on a couch by the fireplace. The two gardai sat on the chairs indicated to them by Clara. Clara sat on the arm of the couch beside her father. They were not offered any refreshments, to their disappointment, as drinking tea together usually leads to a more friendly atmosphere.

"Have you news then?" asked Clara glaring at the two men.

Muldoon looked at this young woman who had lost her mother in harrowing circumstances and thought that her facial features had hardened since he last saw her. She looked more like her mother, her nose seemed longer, her light blue eyes harder and more devoid of warmth. Her long blond hair was loose and somewhat unkempt. Muldoon had, what he would later describe as a kind of flashback to the morning in the parlour. The strands of blond hair appeared to move and slither. The monster with snakes for hair came to his mind. He shook himself out of his chimera and concentrated on the task in hand.

"Unfortunately we have not made much progress to date," Muldoon admitted. "As you know we have ruled out a number of suspects, but we are still hopeful that a witness will come forward. I was hoping to talk to your wife as well John."

"She's not around. She's still at her mother's with the kids," answered John gruffly.

He was dressed in his work clothes and hadn't bothered to remove his boots. He too had shaggy, blond, unkempt hair and light blue cold eyes like his mother and sister. There was sadness and strain etched into his face. His eyes were bloated with dark rings as if he hadn't slept in weeks.

Adam also looked exhausted and broken. He had lost weight and his clothes were hanging off him, at least one size too big for his shrinking body. All the extra work was taking it's toll. He looked lost.

"So, you're here to tell us that you know nothing!" said Clara.

"Not exactly," replied Muldoon. "We were hoping that you might have remembered something that might be helpful – that in the intervening weeks, some small detail may have come to mind."

"Well, nothing comes to mind," answered John in a most sarcastic tone. "You're expecting some sort of light to go off in our heads that will help you because you can't do your job."

"It happens more regularly than you might think," added Muldoon. "We also hope that you might be able to help us in another matter. We are making enquiries about everyone's whereabouts when Mrs. Hannigan was knocked down. We are aware that this must be very upsetting to you all as Mrs. Hannigan was your housekeeper. This is just routine and we are calling to all households in the area to ask these questions. It just has to be done."

All three Galdstones looked slightly irritated. Clara sat still and just stared at the two guards. Adam shuffled in his chair and John looked at his sister.

Clara answered. "It was a school night, so I was here in the house. Jack had his homework to do, so he was in his room and I was probably making his lunch for the next day and getting his uniform ready."

"What about you John?" asked Muldoon.

"I was in my own house, on my own, watching the television – there was a match on."

"I was in my bedroom," said Adam. "There's a small black and white T.V. there. I like a bit of peace and quiet in the evenings after the dinner and a hard day's work."

Muldoon had noticed that Adam had given Clara a glancing look when the question had been posed. It might be quite innocent but it might not.

"Well, we'll take our leave," said Muldoon. "Once again thank you all so much for your time and help. We'll let you know as soon as we have any more information on the case."

The two guards gathered their notes together, stood up, and showed themselves out of the house as the three Galdstones remained seated.

"The ravages of grief," thought Muldoon as they made their way back to the car.

"What did you make of that Michael?" asked Muldoon as he drove the car back towards Naas.

"I think they're hiding something," answered Dunne.

"They weren't very forthcoming with their answers. They all looked worried and stressed. It's obvious that the young lad's wife has probably left him, so that might account for his demeanour. Did you see the look that Adam gave Clara when you asked the question about the alibi? He moved very uncomfortably in his chair and gave her a quick, frightened looking glance out the side of his eye."

"Yes, I saw that too. It was very fleeting. Clara, is the really tough one to fathom," continued Dunne. "She's very angry. Maybe 'tis grief does that to you. She claims to have been very close to her mother."

"Did you notice that none of them showed any concern about what happened to Mrs. Hannigan? They didn't ask any questions either about the accident or about how the poor Hannigans are coping. Most people would have shown some empathy towards a bereaved family especially as they are going through the same grieving process themselves."

Mary Edwards was sitting in her usual spot in front of the fireplace in the sitting room, knitting yet another baby cardigan. Her bump was beginning to show a little and her morning sickness had subsided in the last couple of weeks. The children were playing in the corner of the room with their Barbie dolls. Mary looked over at her two beautiful girls, placed a hand on her growing tummy and sighed with contentment. Her life was so much happier since Jinny Galdstone had met her maker.

Her husband Jonathan entered the room carrying a bunch of papers. He had been preparing yet another sermon for his flock. The tiles on the church roof also required mending so he had been busy doing the maths to see when his church could afford to pay for the work.

"Mary, darling, I've just received a phone call from Inspector Muldoon. He and Alexander de Bruin are on the way here. They want to ask us a few more questions."

Mary sat upright in her chair and then slowly stood up.

"I wonder what they could possibly want now," she said. "I thought that we had answered all their questions about that woman."

"It may not be about her," replied Jonathon. "Perhaps it's about the death of poor Mrs. Hannigan."

"Perhaps indeed," sighed Mary "I'll prepare some refreshments for them."

She made her way into the kitchen to ready a tray of tea and cakes. Twenty minutes later there was a knock at the vicarage door. Jonathon answered and showed the two men into the sitting room. Muldoon and de Bruin sat on the two armchairs. They were offered their tea and cakes.

"We need to ask you a few questions about the death of Mrs. Joan Hannigan," began Muldoon. "Are the children OK to be in the room?"

The two little girls had cakes on a small table and orange drinks in plastic cups. They were pretending to have afternoon tea with their Barbie dolls. The dolls were seated at their own tiny table with a dolls tea set in front of them. The children were chatting to each other and to the dolls.

"Oh, they will be fine," answered Mary. "They are in their own Barbie world and won't hear a thing."

"You do know that we've already filled in a questionnaire about that night. A young officer called here shortly after the accident," said Jonathan.

"Yes indeed and thank you for doing so," replied Muldoon. "We are following a different line of inquiry – we have to cover every eventuality. We are not certain that it was an accident. Some of the circumstances are suspicious."

Both Jonathan and Mary looked shocked.

"You mean, she may have been murdered?" asked Jonathan. "That's dreadful news. Two murders in our small area."

"We really just have to cover every base," said Alexander.

"Did you both know Mrs. Hannigan?"

"I had never met her," replied Jonathan "She wasn't a member of our congregation."

"I knew her from the flower club," added Mary. "She was a lovely lady. She welcomed me with open arms when I joined. The thing I like most about the ladies in the flower club is that there's no talk of religion. No one cares that Jonathan and I have a mixed marriage, or at least they didn't mention it. Of course the Church of Ireland women are outnumbered by the Catholics. Mrs. Hannigan was a very caring, thoughtful woman. She was always very positive, great fun, and loved all the harmless gossip. She was always talking about her two children – she was so proud of their achievements."

"May we ask you again about the night in question,?" said Muldoon "Where were you both between 7.15 and 7.30 on the night Mrs. Hannigan was fatally injured?"

"We were here together," answered Mary. "It was a school night. We usually bathe the children at around seven o'clock, then put them to bed, reading them a story before putting out the light. We were here together for the rest of the evening and didn't hear about the dreadful accident until the following day."

"Did Mrs. Hannigan ever do cleaning here for you or in the church?" asked Alexander.

"No," retorted Mary. "I do my own housework. We really can't afford a cleaner on a vicar's salary. There's an elderly lady called Mrs. O'Connor who does the church once a week but there are also volunteers who help out. My only interaction with Mrs. Hannigan was in the flower club."

"Did you ever go on the bingo bus?" continued Muldoon.

"No," replied Mary. "I don't really like bingo and don't have time to go out at night, with the children and helping my husband with his parish work takes up a lot of my time. I only really started going to the flower club because of having to help out with the flower arranging in the church."

"I think we have all we need," said Muldoon standing up. "Thank you very much for all your cooperation and of course for all the delicious tea and cakes."

Alexander also thanked the vicar and his wife for their hospitality and followed Muldoon out to the car.

"Next port of call – the Lavelles," said Muldoon, as they headed for the cul-de-sac where Dora and Jimmy Lavelle lived, past the Galdstone's farm, the Old Rectory and The Lodge.

They arrived at their destination less than ten minutes later. They parked the car outside the gate and walked towards the entrance. Alexander noticed that there were flowers planted in the garden. There were potted plants at both sides of the front door. They were greeted at the door by Jimmy Lavelle, who ushered them into the sitting room. Dora Lavelle entered from the kitchen and smiled at the two men.

"How are you both?" she asked. "Please sit down. Would you like some tea and biscuits?"

"Just a cup of tea please," answered Muldoon. "We've just come from the vicarage where we had cake."

Neither Alexander nor John really wanted another cup of tea but Muldoon always insisted that they take the tea if proffered, as it helps to put people at their ease if everyone is sipping tea together.

Alexander looked around the sitting room. There was a different ambience in the place, not as cold and depressed. There was a single log burning in the fireplace which gave a sense of warmth to the room. He thought that the cushions were new, as well as a colourful rug in front of the hearth. The demeanour of the couple had also changed. They appeared more content in themselves as if a load had been lifted from their shoulders. Mr. and Mrs. Lavelle had both smiled at them. They no longer looked haggard and drawn. The suffering and worry were no longer writ large on their faces. In fact they both looked ten years younger.

"What can we do for you?" asked Jimmy Lavelle, as they all sat around the hearth, cup of tea in hand.

"We are just making inquiries about Mrs. Hannigan's death and everyone's whereabouts on the night of the hit-and-run between 7.15 and 7.30," said Muldoon.

"We were both here together, early evening. I came home from work at the usual time. Dora had dinner ready for me. We ate together. I dropped Dora to the bingo bus and watched a bit of telly. I went back to collect her and there was a lot of commotion around the place. Dora got straight into the car, and home, so we didn't know anything about it until a friend of Dora's from bingo rang her the following morning to tell her about the dreadful news."

"Did you know Mrs. Hannigan well?" asked Alexander, directing the question at Mrs. Lavelle.

"To tell you the truth after Jinny Galdstone's murder, I felt great relief and so did Jimmy. We didn't have to look at her anymore. It was as if God had punished her and her family for what they did to our Mike. People began to call to us a bit more. Jimmy said that it would be good for me to get out and about. I had turned into a bit of a recluse after Mike's death. That was how I met Joan Hannigan. I started with the flower club and she was so kind to me, as if she knew how I had suffered. She asked me to go to the bingo with her on the bus. We all had great fun chatting about all sorts on the bus. She was a great woman and a great friend to me. I was surprised when she didn't get the bus, herself, that night – but now we know why."

"So," interjected Muldoon, "you were both in your car between 7.15 and 7.30 that evening. Did you see a blue car in your travels? Mrs. Hannigan was hit by a blue car down her laneway during that time on her way to catch the bus."

"We didn't see any car at all on the road, did we Dora?"

"No, Jimmy, it was very quiet. The other women who get the bus there are from the village, and walk. We don't pass the laneway where she lived. Jimmy just dropped me and turned around and went home."

De Bruin and Muldoon knew that Jimmy Lavelle did not drive a blue car and his car was parked in front of the house, in perfect condition. Muldoon made a mental note to check that Jimmy's car had been seen by someone on the bus that night. If so, this would rule out the Lavelles as they couldn't be driving two cars at once.

The two men left the Lavelle's house, got into the car and sat quietly for a moment.

"If it's the same killer, and their story holds water – they're exonerated," said Muldoon.

"Yes," answered Alexander, "and I think the vicar and his wife are also looking less likely. There's such a chasm between how everyone felt about Jinny Galdstone and Joan Hannigan. They reviled and detested Jinny Galdstone and didn't even hide it. They are relieved that she is dead and one could say even happy about it. On the other hand Joan was loved and admired, certainly by Mrs. Edwards and Mrs. Lavelle. Although the Galdstones don't seem to care much,"

"We'll call to the Hobans in Baroda tomorrow although according to Liam Hannigan, Joan didn't know him – only his elderly cousins. We won't go back to Roscommon. I'll just double check with the local guards that the Healeys have no access to a blue car and let them check their alibi as well – they didn't know her in any case."

At ten o'clock the following morning, de Bruin and Muldoon arrived at the Hoban residence in Baroda. Both Mr. and Mrs. Hoban were waiting for them.

"We won't keep you both long," said Inspector Muldoon. "Just a few follow up questions."

They all sat down in the front room. They both had taken an hour off work so that they could meet the two men in their own home.

"We believe that there may be a link between the deaths of Mrs. Galdstone and Mrs. Hannigan," said Muldoon. "We just would like to know if you knew Mrs. Hannigan, and also could you tell us your whereabouts between 7.15 and 7.30 on the evening of her death."

"Neither of us knew her," replied Gerry Hoban. "We heard about the accident of course but my wife doesn't go to bingo either, so I can't even think of any sort of a link that could be made."

"What about the evening in question?" continued Muldoon.

"We were here. I usually get back home at around six o'clock. We have dinner and put the kids to bed. It was no different that night," his wife concurred.

"I don't think there's anything else," said Muldoon.

Both men stood up and left the house.

They drove back to Naas Garda Station and made their way up the stairs to Muldoon's office. As they entered, Alexander noticed once more the blackboard with it's columns of suspects. Muldoon went straight over to the board, picked up a yellow coloured piece of chalk and put a squiggle line underneath the Hoban's names.

There were yellow squiggly lines underneath the Healeys, the Edwards, the Lavelles and the Hobans. Alexander understood at once that these were the people who were more or less ruled out of the equation if there was one murderer. Standing out from the rest were the three Galdstones.

"Unless someone else pops out of the woodwork," said Muldoon, "or we find out that the two deaths are not linked, then we're down to three main suspects."

"

CHAPTER 27

—— ◆ ——

AN EPIPHANY

Damien Browne had asked Alexander to help him with some fencing that had to be repaired in his paddock. They always gave each other a hand with these types of jobs. Three of the posts were rotting and had to be replaced and creosoted. Alexander held the posts steady as Damien used the large post hammer. When this part of the job was complete, they brushed the posts with creosote and replaced the rails.

"Any developments in either case?" asked Damien, as they strolled across the paddock to the house for refreshments.

"We think that they may be linked. If they are, we can rule out a number of suspects."

"Muldoon and his men have searched everywhere for signs of the car, all the garages, round the estates – that angle doesn't seem plausible anymore."

"So, if it is the same person who committed both murders, who's left?"

"Unless another suspect appears out of the blue from left field, we're left with the Galdstones. Probably back to the husband. The husband is always first port of call."

When the two men reached the back kitchen, they removed their wellington boots, put on their shoes and walked into the kitchen.

They walked over to the counter where Damien switched on the kettle. Alexander was standing very still staring at something on the counter in the corner near the fridge.

"What are you thinking about?" asked Damien. "You've gone very quiet. What's up?"

"That set of steak knives, where did you get them?" asked Alexander, pointing at a set of six steak knives in a wooden holder.

"I haven't a clue," replied Damien. "I'd have to ask Lydia. Why? Is it important?"

"I don't know yet. Could you ring her and ask her about them?"

"Do you want me to do it now?" asked Damien with a very confused look on his face.

"If you wouldn't mind," retorted Alexander.

Damien made his way into the sitting room to make the phone call to his wife who was in chambers for the day. He hoped that he wouldn't interrupt Lydia's work. He returned to the kitchen a few moments later where Alexander was deep in thought.

"Well, Mrs. Hannigan gave them to us as a Christmas present the Christmas before last."

"I have to go. I'll explain later," said Alexander rushing out the front door.

He ran across the fields, back to his own house. Monique was in her office, typing up a report. She heard her husband rush into the room.

"Are you ok?" she asked in surprise as she saw her husband, standing there, red faced and out of breath.

"Where did you get our set of steak knives? – you know the ones that the guards took away for forensic examination, the ones that are identical to the murder weapon, found in our ditch?"

"Mrs. Hannigan gave them to us as a Christmas present."

"When?"

"Let me think, oh, it was the year before last. She gave us the lamp in the sitting room last Christmas. Why, Alexander, what's wrong?"

"Something has been niggling at me since I was in Liam Hannigan's kitchen. I know what it is now. I saw the exact same set of knives in his kitchen. I was over helping Damien with the fencing. When we went back to the kitchen, low and behold, but what was sitting on the counter, but a set of identical steak knives as our own and the Hannigans. All three sets exactly the same. I'm going down to see if Liam Hannigan is at home. I need to speak to him."

Alexander grabbed his car keys from the small table in the hall and rushed out the door. He took a deep breath before opening the car door. He needed to compose himself before he spoke to Liam Hannigan. Five minutes later, he had arrived at Clonee village and was sitting outside the home of Liam Hannigan. He thought about how he would phrase his questions. The last thing he wanted to do was to upset the poor man. He alighted from the car and strolled up to the front door. Liam Hannigan had seen the car arrive and opened the door just before Alexander was about to ring the bell.

"Hello, Sir, Please come in."

"Hello, Liam, how are you?" replied Alexander as he followed him into the kitchen.

They both sat down at the kitchen table and looked at each other.

"I'm not too bad. There are still a lot of people calling to see me. I've started going back to the pub for a few pints and game of cards. It gets me out of the house. Night time is very lonely here without Joan."

He fidgeted with his fingers and his shoulders slumped.

Jean and John ring me twice a week at six o'clock to check up on me. I always tell them that I'm improving all the time. I'm very bad at cleaning the place and at cooking. I never used to do any of it. Joan did all that."

Alexander felt enormous pity for this unfortunate man, who has been left on his own to cope with the mundane things in life to which he had never given a thought before his wife's death.

"One foot in front of the other, one day at a time, is the only way to deal with this grief," Alexander advised.

Liam Hannigan nodded his head, straightened his shoulders again.

"How are Monique and the children? Your wife has been very good to me, calling down with dinners and the like – so has Mrs. King."

"They are all well, thank you Liam."

Alexander decided that he might as well just ask his questions.

"Liam, the last time I was here, I noticed a set of steak knives on your kitchen counter. They gave me pause for thought and it was just today that I realised that they are identical to the ones that I have, and to those that the Brownes have. Monique tells me that they were a gift from Joan for Christmas. Can you tell me, did she give the same knives to anyone else?"

Liam Hannigan looked over at the set of knives, still perched on the counter and thought for a few moments.

"Yes, I remember that – the Christmas before last. You see her cousin Mary Mc Cann works in Newbridge Cutlery. She told her about a sale that was coming up – you know end-of-line stuff – getting rid of old stock. The long and the short of it is that Joan thought that these sets would be great for Christmas presents for her "families" as she called all the people she cleaned for. So, I think she bought about eight sets and to be fair she said that they were very good quality and a great bargain. I remember her being delighted with herself and wrapping them all at the table here."

"So, would you know to whom she gave the sets?" asked Alexander expectantly.

"Anyone she was working for that time – yourselves, the Brownes, the Galdstones, the doctor, the two families in Newbridge and we kept one for ourselves. Not sure if there was someone else – I thought she got eight and that's only seven. Never mind, it might have been only seven. What's so important about the knives?"

"I'm not sure yet Liam. It's just that Jinny Galdstone was murdered with a knife identical to the one in our sets."

"Do you think Joan knew something about the knife and that's why she's dead?" muttered Liam, his voice now trembling.

"Please try not to think too much about it. I'll let you know as soon as I find anything out – I promise you."

Alexander left Liam to his thoughts and drove home. Immediately on reaching the house, he headed straight for his office and dialled the number for Naas Garda Station.

"Please put me through to Inspector Muldoon – Alexander de Bruin speaking."

The receiver was picked up by John Muldoon on the third ring.

"Inspector Muldoon, how can I help?"

"Alexander de Bruin here. I think I have some interesting news."

John Muldoon listened carefully as Alexander explained about the seven or eight sets of steak knives that had been given as Christmas presents by Joan Hannigan to her "families", and the one kept for her own use. Also that there may or may not be one that isn't accounted for.

"So, you believe that the murder weapon came from one of these sets," stated Muldoon. "Do you not think that there may be dozens more around?"

"You may be right John, but I don't like coincidences. Then I began to think about what Mrs. Hannigan said to Monique on the phone.

"They weren't there". What if she hadn't been talking about people? What if she had been talking about a set of knives?"

CHAPTER 28

AN ARREST

Liam Flynn, the young garda, had delivered the post to Inspector Muldoon's office at 9 o'clock precisely, as he did every morning. He placed the letters, of which there were eleven, in the basket on his desk.

On entering his office, John Muldoon placed his briefcase beside his chair, sat down, picked up the letters and began leafing through them. There was one large brown envelope at the bottom of the pile.

When he looked at the address, he immediately became suspicious. His name and address were neither typed, nor hand written.

Someone had used the letters from a newspaper or magazine and stuck them on the envelope. He knew at once that there would be many sets of fingerprints on the outside of the envelope, but perhaps there might be only one set on whatever was within.

There was also the possibility that there might be something more sinister inside.

He rang the forensics department in Dublin and made arrangements for the envelope to be delivered to them for examination. The envelope was boxed and sealed. Liam Flynn placed it in the back of his squad car and drove to Dublin.

John Muldoon remained in his office endeavouring to work on other cases, but was finding it difficult to concentrate, as he awaited news of what exactly was in the envelope.

Six hours later Liam Flynn returned to Naas Garda Station, envelope and sheet of paper sealed in an evidence bag in his hand.

"How did you get on Liam? What's the verdict?" asked Muldoon.

"There are loads of fingerprints on the outside of the envelope as you might expect and nothing on the sheet of paper inside."

John Muldoon inspected the sheet of white paper. The same type of lettering was glued onto said sheet.

It read.

SAW JOHN GALDSTONE DRIVING HIS MOTHER'S SPORTS CAR ON NIGHT JOAN HANNIGAN WAS KILLED.

That was the message. There was no signature, nor sign of who might have sent it.

Muldoon's reaction was to ring Alexander de Bruin. De Bruin was in his office at The Lodge when he received the phone call. Muldoon explained the situation to him.

"That sport's car that Jinny Galdstone used to drive in the summer months is blue," said Alexander "We really should have thought of that."

"To be fair to ourselves," replied Muldoon. "It's a bit of a leap to think that the first victim's car that is stored away would be used to mow down the second victim."

"So what's the next move?" asked Alexander.

"I hope to apply for a search warrant for the Galdstone farm and outhouses as well as one for Briar's Cottage and it's outhouses."

"You know that this could be another red herring to lead us astray again."

"I'm very aware of that, but we must investigate every lead. It may be tomorrow by the time I get the warrant."

"You need to check if the set of steak knives is missing from the Galdstones as well," added Alexander.

"Yes, we are going to do a thorough search. By the way, Michael Dunne has checked out the two families in Newbridge and the doctor in Clonee who received the set of knives as Christmas presents. They all still have the sets intact and none of them ever had anything to do with Jinny Galdstone. We now have six sets of steak knives accounted for – now only the Galdstone's outstanding."

"Maybe there's one more as Liam Hannigan wasn't sure if there was an eight."

The following day the search warrants arrived and a large number of gardai descended upon both houses simultaneously to search the properties. Sergeant Dunne served the warrant on Adam Galdstone, much to his surprise. Inspector Muldoon served the warrant on John Galdstone who appeared quite shocked. There was a team of gardai searching both houses and another team searching the outhouses and barns. Twenty minutes into the search a young garda came rushing towards Inspector Muldoon who was seated in his car looking at some notes.

"Sir, Sir, we've found the car."

Muldoon got out of the car and stood in front of the excited young guard.

"Well, spit it out."

"We found it in a locked barn right at the bottom of the farm. It's the one alright. The headlight is broken. The hood is dented and the windscreen is cracked. There seems to be traces of blood as well. It's blue."

"Seal off the barn. I'm sending for forensics," said John Muldoon as he went in search of Michael Dunne, whom he found leading proceedings at the main Galdstone house.

"The car has been found Sergeant. It's definitely the one used in the hit-and-run. Will you come with me. We have to make an arrest."

The two men sat into the squad car and headed for Briar's Cottage. When they arrived, John Galdstone was sitting on a window sill outside the house smoking a cigarette. The two men got out of the car and approached him.

"We need to speak to you John," said Muldoon. "We can use one of the rooms that has been searched."

The three men walked into the front sitting room, having been told that it was clear. John Galdstone looked very apprehensive as Muldoon beckoned to him to take a seat.

"Can you tell me again where you were the night Joan Hannigan was killed?" asked Muldoon.

"I was here, on my own as I've already told you, why are you asking me again?"

"Information has reached us that you were seen driving your mother's sports car in the vicinity of the hit-and -run at the precise time in question," continued Muldoon.

"That's daft," replied John Galdstone, panic in his voice. "I was here all evening. I never drove that car, ever. Nobody drove it except my mother. It's locked away in the barn where it always is."

John Galdstone lit another cigarette, his hand trembling slightly. His face had turned a very pale colour and his eyes looked like those of a frightened fox being chased by hounds.

"The car has been found and has obviously been involved in some sort of collision," added Muldoon. "We would like you to accompany us to the garda station for questioning."

"Am I under arrest?" asked John Galdstone, alarm in his voice.

"Not at present, but I believe that it would be in your best interest to cooperate with us."

John Galdstone just nodded his head in defeat. The three men drove back to the station.

John Galdstone was led into a sparsely furnished interview room. In the middle of the room was a table with four chairs. There was brown linoleum on the floor and the walls were beige.

Muldoon and Dunne sat opposite Galdstone but didn't speak for a few minutes which must have seemed to John Galdstone to be an eternity. They sifted through their notes in front of him. Finally Muldoon spoke.

"As I told you at the farm, we are in receipt of information which places you at the scene of the hit-and-run. We have located the blue sports car which belonged to your mother and forensics are presently examining it for evidence. Have you anything to add to your previous statement?"

"And as I told you," answered John Galdstone angrily, "I've never driven that car. No one ever drove that car except my mother."

"Well someone drove it the night of Mrs. Hannigan's death. It has obviously been in a collision and the paint matches the flecks of paint found at the scene and on the victim."

Muldoon stared very intently at Galdstone. He saw him move uncomfortably in his chair.

"Can I smoke?" he asked, taking a packet of Carrolls and a lighter from his shirt pocket.

"Yes, go ahead."

Galdstone lit the cigarette, took a long drag of it, inhaled deeply then blew puffs of smoke that permeated the room.

"I don't know why this is happening to me. Why on earth would I run over Mrs. Hannigan. I barely knew her, only to see her doing the cleaning. She does my mother's house and lately started to do mine when Heather's away. Why would anyone say that they saw me driving the car. I told you I was in the house. Who said I was driving anyway? Whoever did is lying."

He sat up very straight in his chair, his lips tightened and he glared across the table at the two men.

Muldoon recognised that look – the look of a suspect that was about to clam up and ask for a solicitor.

"We have to leave the room for a while. We'll send in another officer to get you some tea or coffee."

Muldoon and Dunne stood up, gathered their notes and left the room.

"He's going to stop cooperating soon," said Muldoon. "We really need to stall until the forensics come back."

Muldoon told Liam Flynn to ask John Galdstone what he would like to drink.

"Take your time about everything Liam, slow motion please."

"If he asks for a solicitor, we're going to have to charge him. We can't have him running around the place to murder again. He is a danger to society if he did commit these crimes. Let's hope forensics come back with something soon."

There was a phone call two hours later from the forensics department – no results until tomorrow morning at the earliest. It was getting quite late in the day, so Muldoon decided to inform John Galdstone that they intended to hold him in a cell overnight and would recommence questioning him in the morning. John Goldstone put up no resistance as he was led down to his cell which contained a single bed with a blanket, a sink and a bucket in the corner for emergencies.

At ten o'clock the following morning, Muldoon received a written report from forensics, together with an evidence bag containing a pair of men's work gloves. There were blood stains on the woollen cuffs. The gloves were made of pig-skin and canvas, apart from the cuffs. Muldoon read the report carefully. The blue paint definitely matched the flakes at the scene. The inside of the car was wiped clean. There were no fingerprints on the steering wheel, the dashboard or gear stick. Strands of long blond hair were found in the car but this was no surprise as it had been Jinny Galdstone's car. The only real evidence were the gloves with blood stains located under the driver's seat.

"How strange," thought Muldoon "to have wiped all the surfaces clean and then stick the bloodied gloves under the seat!"

Liam Flynn informed the inspector that John Galdstone had eaten his breakfast, freshened up and was keen to talk to Muldoon.

The detective gathered the report and the evidence bag and headed towards the interview room. En route, he asked Michael Dunne to join him.

John Galdstone was sitting in the same chair as the previous night. He looked tired and slightly dishevelled, but he did not have the same look of defiance on his face.

"Good morning, John," said Muldoon. "Did you manage to get any sleep at all?"

"On and off," replied Galdstone.

Muldoon placed the evidence bag containing the work gloves on the table.

"Do you recognise these?"

John Galdstone looked fixedly at the bag.

"Yea, they're my gloves. Where did you get them?"

"They were found in your mother's car, under the driver's seat. There's also blood on them."

"That's crazy! I keep them in the barn with the hay. I need them for lifting the bales, otherwise the twine cuts into your hands. I also use them for fixing the tractor. That's my own blood. I get cut sometimes."

John Galdstone's brow was furrowed and he had a look of utter bewilderment.

"What's going on here? Is someone trying to set me up? I wasn't driving the car. Why would I want to kill Mrs. Hannigan? Those gloves were in the hay barn where I always leave them. I've had enough of this. I want a solicitor."

"John Galdstone, I am arresting you on the suspicion of the murder of Mrs. Joan Hannigan....."

John Galdstone listened to the inspector, in a state of disbelief. He was then led out of the interview room and back to his cell. The inspector and sergeant returned to Muldoon's office.

"You're not sure, are you sir?" said Dunne

"How are you so careful to remove your fingerprints and then leave your gloves for us to find?" returned Muldoon pensively. "If he's lying, he's a very convincing liar. He looked completely puzzled when we told him where his gloves were found. His motive for killing Mrs. Hannigan had to be to shut her up. He also had to have murdered his mother. We'll have to speak to his wife again. Although he has no alibi for the time of the hit-and-run, his wife gave him an alibi for the time of his mother's death. We need to get the blood analysis back as soon as possible."

That same afternoon, Michael Dunne contacted Heather Galdstone at her mother's house in Carlow. He asked her if she would prefer to answer some more questions at the station or at her mother's house. She chose the station.

Heather arrived at Muldoon's office at 2pm as agreed. She wore an old fashioned tweed coat, flat shoes and carried a black patent handbag, that had seen better days. Adam Galdstone had telephoned her early that morning to tell her of her husband's arrest. Heather looked extremely worried – her face pale and without any make-up.

"Please take a seat Mrs. Galdstone," said Muldoon.

Heather sat in the chair, with her hands clasped tightly on her lap. She had placed her handbag on the floor beside her. She looked beseechingly at Muldoon but said nothing.

"As you know, we have arrested your husband on suspicion of the murder of Mrs. Hannigan, because of new evidence that has come to light."

"Why would he kill Mr. Hannigan? I don't understand."

"Am I correct in saying that you are now living with your children in Carlow at your mother's home?"

"Yes, I left Briar's Cottage shortly after Jinny's funeral, it was all too much. To tell you the truth, I thought things might improve after her death, but they didn't. It's very difficult to be part of that family. It's their way or no way."

"Would you know, Mrs. Galdstone, who might have driven Jinny Galdstone's sports car over the years?"

"Oh, no one was allowed drive it – you could admire it, but it was Jinny and Jinny alone. Why do you ask?"

"A witness claims to have seen your husband driving it on the night of Mrs. Hannigan's death and as I'm sure you've been informed it was your mother in law's blue sports car that ran her down."

"That's impossible! That doesn't make any sense at all," she insisted.

"Can I ask you about the alibi you gave your husband for the morning of your mother-in-law's murder? He claims that he didn't leave the house at all early that morning because he was feeling ill, that he was in bed at the time of his mother's murder and you concurred with this version of events."

"That's right inspector."

"So, you're saying that you were in bed with your husband until eight o'clock when you got up to get your children's breakfast."

"Well, we weren't in the same room. We've had separate rooms for a long time, but he was there when I got up and he was definitely sick."

"So, you didn't see your husband until eight o'clock that morning?"

"Yes."

"Can you remember what he was wearing?"

"Yes. Yes. He was wearing his pyjamas – I remember because after the phone call he had to get dressed and run up to the farm."

"Thank you very much for coming in to answer our questions. You may leave now. If we need to contact you again, we'll telephone you at your mother's. Sergeant Dunne will see you out."

Heather Galdstone picked up her patent bag, stood up, straightened her coat, nodded at the inspector and followed Dunne out of the office, down the stairs and out into the fresh air where she breathed a sigh of relief before hurrying to her car.

Back in the office, Inspector Muldoon was pondering the latest developments – John Galdstone did not have an alibi for the time of his mother's murder. He could have gone to the parlour, murdered her, disposed of his bloodied clothes, thrown the murder weapon into de Bruin's ditch, returned to his own house, changed into his pyjamas and pretended to be ill when his wife and children woke up, just in time to receive a phone call.

Time to have a another chat with John Galdstone.

When John Galdstone heard the latest developments, and that the guards did not consider that his wife was able to give him an alibi for the time of his mother's death, he became very despondent. He sat silently and hopelessly in the chair facing Muldoon and Dunne. Finally, he said.

"I didn't kill my mother, I didn't kill Mrs. Hannigan. I'm not saying another word. Get my solicitor."

John Galdstone was returned back to his cell. Dunne closed the door behind him and then pulled back the door viewer, and saw the prisoner sitting on the bed with his head in his hands crying. He closed the door viewer and returned to Muldoon's office.

"Do you believe he did both murders?" asked Dunne.

"Not convinced he did either as yet, but of course they are linked. He had means and opportunity to kill his mother. Everyone who knew her seems to have motive. Have the results from the blood on the gloves come back yet?"

"Yes. It's definitely his blood type, but he didn't deny that they were his gloves, just that he left them in the haybarn and never drove the car."

Muldoon received a phone call that afternoon from Garda Headquarters asking for an update. He relayed all the information to his superior who insisted, despite Muldoon's protests, that John Galdstone be charged with both murders and sent post haste to Mountjoy Prison.

Muldoon, despite his reservations, followed his orders and that evening John Galdstone was on remand in Mountjoy Jail, charged with two murders and awaiting trial.

CHAPTER 29

THE DOG

Alexandra de Bruin and Monique were sitting at the kitchen table discussing the latest developments in the case. Muldoon had rung Alexander to inform him about John Galdstone's arrest and to discuss the doubts he had regarding the evidence. He too thought that the arrest and charges were premature.

"Heather Galdstone is back in Briar's Cottage with the children. This whole business must be dreadful for her," said Alexander.

"Oh, I'll pay her a visit and see if there's anything I can do to help her out," replied Monique. "Actually, I'll go right now, I'm not busy at the moment."

Monique put on a light coat and decided to walk to the cottage, as it was a lovely warm day.

She was greeted at the door by a very tired looking Heather Galdstone. As usual, she wore very unflattering, matronly clothes – a tweed skirt and brown jumper, with a white blouse.

"Oh, Mrs. de Bruin, how nice to see you, please come in."

Monique followed her into the sitting room where they both sat down. The children's toys were strewn around the room.

"Are the children here?" asked Monique.

"My mother has taken them to the playground in Naas. They won't be back for a couple of hours."

"I was so sorry to hear about John," continued Monique. "Is there anything at all we can do for you?"

The tears welled up in Heather's eyes and then flowed down her cheeks. She searched for a handkerchief in the pocket of her skirt and blew her nose.

"I don't believe he did this, Monique. He couldn't have. I know we've had our rows and troubles and I had to leave here for a while, but it's just not in him. He was bullied by his mother, but he just did everything she told him to do. I don't believe he hated her like that."

The tears continued to fall down her cheeks as she swept them away with her handkerchief. She sat there, a broken, pathetic figure. The collie dog, which had been asleep beside the fireplace stood up, went over to Heather, pushed at her hands which were placed now on her lap and nuzzled her.

She stroked his head which lay on her lap and then hugged him tightly.

"Rover is just a lovely dog, he knows when I'm really down. I have him in the house now – Jinny would never allow animals in the house, so John was the same."

Suddenly a man's voice came from the doorway.

"Are you okay, Sis?"

"I'm fine Rory, just a bit weepy. This is my neighbour Mrs. de Bruin. She just called to see how I was."

"How do you do," said Rory. "Lovely to meet you."

He was a tall, slim, good looking young man, of about twenty two years of age, with a shock of red hair, dark brown eyes and a wide grin.

"You too," answered Monique. "Are you staying for long in Briar's Cottage?"

"I don't really know. I'll see how Sis is doing. If you'll excuse me I have to go down to the far field to check the fence. I'll be back in about half an hour. Will you still be here, Mrs. de Bruin?"

"Yes, I believe I will. Heather and I will have a cup of tea and a good long chat. I'll be here when you return."

Monique knew that he had been hinting that she should stay with his sister, who was obviously very fragile.

Rory strolled out into the garden, leaving the two ladies and Rover in the sitting room.

"He's in third year in the Veterinary College in Ballsbridge. While he's staying here, he can drive up to his lectures and practicals. He has nothing on this morning."

The two ladies spent ten minutes indulging in chitchat and making tea. As they sat once more in the sitting room, Monique knew there was something worrying Heather.

"I know that there is something very serious troubling you, Heather," said Monique, placing her hand over Heather's to comfort her. "If you want to talk about it, I'm here to listen and help in any way I can."

Heather was just about to speak when she heard Rover scratching at the door to get out. She stood up, walked over to the dog, rubbed his head, opened the door, walked down the corridor and let him out into the garden, through the front door. She returned to her seat in the sitting room and began.

"First of all, I've all this worry about John, I don't know what's going to happen to him. Then, there's Adam and Clara, they have not been one bit helpful to me since John was arrested. You see, Jinny organized buying this place and then she guaranteed the loan, so she really thought it was hers, and so do the other two. Clara and Adam called yesterday and told me to go back to my mother's – that I had no right to be here, when John wasn't here. They told me, if John goes to prison, that I'm out on my ear – that this is Galdstone land. I couldn't believe my ears. I thought they were calling to offer their help and support."

"That's just dreadful," said Monique soothingly. "But this is John's place, I thought, and yours."

"The loan was taken out in John's name and we pay the mortgage. What Adam and Clara didn't know, is that when things were going well for John and me, he took me to his solicitors in Naas and signed a document stating, that we were joint owners of any property we had, including Briar's Cottage and the lands."□

"Well then, this is your home and they have no claim on it. What happened in the end yesterday?"

"I told them to leave my home, that I wanted nothing more to do with them and that they were no longer welcome here."

"How did they take that?"

"Adam just put his head down and walked out, but Clara said that she'd see about it. I got the impression that she just wanted to walk in here with her son - it's all just so weird and nerve-wracking. That's why Rory is here– to give me some support."

"You poor thing," said Monique. "You're having an awful time – your husband in jail and your in-laws trying to turf you out. At least you know, legally, that they haven't a leg to stand on and be rest assured that Alexander and I will support you in any way we can."

Suddenly, Rory came running into the room, a look of panic on his face.

"There's something wrong with Rover – he's lying down in the garden, not moving with sick around his mouth. He's still breathing but it's very shallow. I want to take him up to the Veterinary College. I'll get him seen to there."

The two women jumped up out of their seats and quickly followed Rory out into the garden. Rover lay very still. Heather ran over to him, knelt down and rubbed his head.

"I'm going to ring Alexander to get the jeep. He'll bring you up to Ballsbridge. You're right Rory – it's the best chance of saving him."

Monique ran into the house and phoned her husband with instructions to leave immediately – she explained the predicament as best she could. She returned to the trio in the garden and suddenly noticed a piece of liver that lay near the ailing dog.

"Don't touch the liver or the sick," she instructed. "I'm going to get a container to put them into from the kitchen – you can bring it with you to the College for analysis."

Monique ran into the kitchen and frantically searched for a plastic container which she located under the sink.

Having collected the untouched piece of liver and the dog's vomit she waited, container in hand, for her husband to arrive. The jeep pulled into the driveway shortly afterwards. Rory and Alexander lifted Rover into the back of the jeep. They jumped into the front seats and drove off in the direction of Dublin. Monique put her arm around Heather's shoulder and gently led her back into the house where they sat and waited two hours for a phone call with news of Rover's condition. It was a very long two hours. They tried to make conversation, but for a lot of the time, they just sat in silence watching the clock and listening for the ringing of the telephone.

Finally the phone rang. Monique jumped up to answer it. She listened carefully as Alexander spoke on the line. She replaced the handset and smiled at Heather.

"He's going to be OK. Looks like he was poisoned. He was lucky that he got sick. They gave him an emetic which cleared his stomach of the poison. He's on a drip and recovering."

Heather sat down and started crying again – this time tears of joy.

"They are going to analyse the liver etc. Rory and Alexander are going to collect him in a few hours and bring him home if the vets are happy with him. They are just going to get a bite to eat."

Soon afterwards Heather's mother arrived back to Briar's cottage with the children. Monique hugged Heather, who held on to her new friend very tightly, said her goodbyes and walked slowly back to The Lodge.

It was 9 o'clock that night before Alexander returned home. He was exhausted after the ordeal. Monique was waiting for him in the living room and offered him a brandy which he gladly accepted.

"That young lad, Rory, is very impressive. He's going to make a great vet. When we got to the college he was in his element and acted very promptly. Of course there was an older man there as well to supervise proceedings and a veterinary nurse. It was a treat to watch them work. The main saving grace of course was that the dog had been sick shortly after swallowing the liver. When we arrived back to collect the dog they had the analysis of the liver pieces complete. Someone had injected sodium fluoroacetate into the liver. Farmers would have this for killing foxes."

"What a dreadful thing to do," said Monique. "Who could have done such a thing?"

"We had a good chat about it on the way home. There were two pieces of liver, one ingested by the dog and one seemingly untouched. It would seem virtually impossible for a bird to have picked two pieces up and drop them in the garden. Not likely either, that the dog would have picked up two pieces elsewhere and carried them home without putting some sort of dent in the second piece. So we came to the conclusion that they were thrown into the garden with the sole purpose of poisoning the dog. The liver was fresh enough looking and wouldn't have been in the garden for long."

"I wonder was it thrown in while I was in the house with Heather, and Rory was down fixing the fence?"

"Possibly – but what a dangerous careless thing to do – there are children in that house."

"Rory and I discussed who might want to hurt his sister, and of course he told me about the Galdstones insisting that they leave Briar's cottage. Remind me to check with Damien and Lydia that she is legally entitled to be there. It seems a very cruel way to treat her and her children. Of course it just might be some random nutcase going around trying to poison other people's dogs."

"Then again it may be someone who had it in for the Galdstones in general which leaves us once again with a very long list," added Monique.

The couple sat on the couch, sipping their drinks, exhausted after the very eventful day. Tomorrow morning Alexander would ring Muldoon to inform him about the dog and ask Damien to double check on Heather's position at Briar's Cottage.

At 9 o'clock the following morning, Alexander rang the Old Rectory. The phone was answered by Damien. Alexander explained about what had transpired between the Galdstones and Heather and about the forms that John Galdstone had signed to make her joint owner of all property that they possessed. Alexander was quite relieved to learn that what John Goldstone had done was absolutely airtight and legal, and was common enough. Therefore Adam and Clara Galdstone had no claim whatsoever on Briar's Cottage and it's lands.

Next, he rang Muldoon at his office, who was very suspicious that this may have something to do with the murders – what exactly, he couldn't fathom, but once again another coincidence – neither man liked coincidences.

"I'll send two of my men out to check if there are any more incidences of dog poisonings. Sometimes we don't hear about these incidents, particularly in the countryside, as some farmers lay down bait for vermin, and domestic animals die by accident. I don't really think there's much chance of finding out who did this unless we get very lucky. That poison you mentioned, sodium fluoroacetate, is very easy to get hold of."

Following the phone calls, Alexander made his way into Monique's office to recount to her the two phone conversations. She was delighted to hear that Heather was safe and that Muldoon was going to do some sort of investigation into Rover's poisoning, however futile.

"I'm going to call up to Briar's cottage now to check on Heather and reassure her about her position there. I don't know how long I'll be."

"Take your time, darling. That poor girl needs all the reassurance she can get."

Monique left The Lodge immediately and walked up to Briar's cottage.

Heather was delighted to see her. She still looked very worried and tired.

"Please come in. I'm on my own today. Rory had to go to college, and my mother has taken the children back to Carlow for a few days after what happened to poor Rover."

They entered the sitting room and Rover was lying on a very comfortable looking fluffy bed in front of the fireplace. He looked up for a moment and then put his head back down on his front paws and closed his eyes.

"He's a lot better," said Heather. "He hasn't eaten anything yet but has drunk lots of water, which is the important thing."

"I'm delighted that he's recovering. You really had an awful fright yesterday on top of everything else that you are going through. I hope you don't mind but Alexander double checked your legal position here with Damien Browne and it's clear that Briar's Cottage belongs to you and John and no-one else. Adam and Clara have no claim on it at all. By signing that legal document John secured your future if something were to happen to him."

"Thank you so much. I thought that that was my position but with everything, I was beginning to have doubts. I haven't been sleeping either and when I do sleep, I have nightmares. I became completely frazzled. It's great to have people like you and Mr. de Bruin to look out for me. I don't know what I would do without Rory, and my mother either."

Heather went over and rubbed Rover's head. He nuzzled into her hand, his big brown helpless eyes looking up at her.

"How cruel some people are to want to hurt an innocent animal like that," thought Monique to herself.

"I've decided that I'm going to visit John in Mountjoy," said Heather suddenly. "I don't believe that he did these murders. I think someone has set him up. We were happy at first you know, before Jinny ruined everything with her interference. I believe John signed those papers to protect me from her. I need to tell him face to face what his father and sister tried to do to me and our children."

Monique was a little surprised but very glad to see this new determination in Heather's demeanour. She looked stronger and more composed.

"I think that's a very good idea," answered Monique. "I presume Rory will go with you. It will be a strange experience for you, – visiting a person in prison."

"Yes he will. We spoke about it this morning before he left for college. I'm going to ring Inspector Muldoon to see how I am to go about it. I think he's a good man, and I believe with all my heart that he and your husband will get to the truth in the end."

"Yes, I hope they will," answered Monique.

Ten minutes later Monique was making her way along the country road home. The hedges were lush and green. Wild flowers were growing along the ditches. She breathed the fresh air deep into her lungs. She wondered what was the truth of all this. Was John really the murderer, and so Heather would be disappointed and alone with her children. If it weren't John, who was it? And why were his gloves found in Jinny's car? Who on earth was the anonymous witness who had sent the message, not typed or hand written, but mysteriously, with letters taken from a newspaper or magazine glued to a sheet of paper. Why would he, if he were the murderer, have thrown suspicion onto Alexander and then onto Pippa McHugh, only to have left incriminating evidence against himself in the car. "Just as well that Alexander is very good at puzzles," she whispered to herself.

CHAPTER 30

LOUGHFARRAIG HOUSE

"Alexander, I hope you haven't forgotten that we are heading west tomorrow with the Kings."

"No, darling, I haven't. It's all organised. I've spoken to Damien about looking after the dogs and the horses and keeping an eye on the place. He'll keep the dogs in the house and only take them out on their leads."

Following the poisoning incident at John Galdstone's, everyone in the area was very wary. The young guards had done a very good job questioning and warning people about the danger. The locals could be seen checking for bait on their land a few times a day.

"By the way, Lydia is going to check on Heather in our absence. There is a great deal of sympathy for her at the moment," said Alexander. "I also rang Muldoon to let him know where we will be for two days."

At 8 o'clock the following morning, Monique and Alexander were en route to Mayo. They had been going to this hotel twice a year since they had come across it by accident on their travels along the Atlantic coast. It was a Haven of Tranquility out on the West Coast. In fact, you couldn't go any further west – next stop New York, as Alexander said the first time he stood on the shore, and looked out to sea. After their friendship grew with the Kings, they invited them to join them for a weekend, and they too fell in love with the place.

The journey from Briarstown to Loughfarraig house took four hours, leaving the flat plains of Kildare, through the Midlands, over the majestic Shannon in Athlone. Alexander pointed out the turn off for the Healey's house as they drove through Roscommon.

As they headed deeper west, the land was getting boggier, covered in heather and wildflowers, the fields separated by famine walls. There was an odd green field that had been reclaimed. They drove through Castlebar and on to Westport, where they took a road that led to nowhere except their beloved Loughfarraig House hotel. They hadn't seen a house for 5 miles and then, there it was, the entrance, with its two white pillars. The avenue was long and winding with rhododendron bushes, fuchsia and copper beech on either side. As they drew nearer to the hotel, on the right was the vegetable garden, surrounded by a stone wall to protect it from the elements. On the left, the beautiful freshwater lake came into view, with its tiny jetty where the rowing boats sat waiting for some guests to push them out onto the lake, for a spot of fishing. The lake was teaming with brown trout always, and sometimes a few rainbow trout would make an appearance. And then, there it was, their escape to serenity.

This old house had a long history. It was destroyed and rebuilt several times, being burned to the ground during the war of independence, as was many a manor house. Then, following peace in Ireland, it was rebuilt and has been a hotel since the 1940s.

Monique and Alexander alighted from the car and for a moment stood looking at the long grey house covered in ivy. To the right of the building there is a conservatory which leads onto a small lawn, which is used to play croquet. Just behind the lawn one could just get a glimpse of the tennis courts, and outdoor swimming pool, where the children spent hours. They didn't go immediately into the hotel but turned left and one minute later, they stood in awe, looking at the magnificent Atlantic ocean. On the beach they saw the huge rock that's always there. When the tide comes in it's completely submerged and when the tide is out one can climb to the top of it. The sea was quite calm today, but one could still hear the lapping of the water against the shore. Further out to sea, the waves were breaking and sending foam into the air as they smashed against the rocks, jutting out of the water. They turned left again and walked onto the golf course. It was in very good condition. Once they had arrived after a storm, and large boulders had been thrown up onto the course by a fierce angry sea.

They strolled hand-in-hand along the shore for 20 minutes, and finally, as it became cooler, made their way back to the hotel. The door to the hotel was made of wood with an old-fashioned brass latch, which led into a porch where there was an old umbrella stand holding an array of umbrellas. They entered the lobby which in fact is a sitting room with wooden floors and colourful rugs. On either side of the room there are two beautiful fireplaces and of course, as usual, the turf burned brightly in the hearths and the smell of smouldering peat wafted through the air. Straight in front of the entrance was the wooden stairs, on the right the bar and on the left the dining room. Everything was just as it ever was. Nothing ever changed in Loughfarraig House.

Monique walked up to the reception area and pressed the button on the call bell. Immediately, a young woman with long red hair appeared and greeted Monique with a lovely soft Mayo accent. Having filled in the check-in form she returned to her husband who was sitting on one of the comfortable couches in front of the turf fire. They sat there quietly for a few moments and then a young waiter appeared with their tea and scones, which had recently come out of the oven, as the butter melted on them.

The Kings arrived two hours later. The two couples spent the afternoon and evening together enjoying each other's company and avoiding any talk of murders and poisonings.

The following morning, as arranged, the two ladies went to the tennis courts and the two gentlemen picked up their fishing rods, lifejackets and tackle from the cupboard in the hallway and headed towards the lake. They arrived at the jetty, turned the boat right side up and pushed it into the lake. While Robert held one side, Alexander climbed in, placed the rods and tackle to one side, and put one oar in the oar lock. As Robert jumped in, Alexander pushed off with the other oar, allowed the boat to slide out into the lake a little, before putting the second oar in the oar lock and then began rowing the boat towards the middle of the lake.

When they reached their destination, Alexander took in the oars. The two men put on their spools and bait and cast their lines into the water. They really didn't care if they caught anything. They just loved the peace and tranquility of sitting in a boat in the middle of the lake, bobbing up and down gently. It also gave them a chance to be completely on their own for a few hours. They both knew that while Monique quite enjoyed discussing murder and mayhem, Alison was different – they had to avoid the subject in her company, as she was completely fed up of hearing about it. She found it fascinating at first, but now had enough and Robert promised her that they would not discuss it during their break.

"Well, no one can overhear us or disturb our conversation here," laughed Robert.

"Apart from the swans and ducks who inhabit the shores of the lake," replied Alexander.

"Kindly give me an update," said Robert, as he slowly reeled in his line.

"John Galdstone is in jail, accused of both murders. Muldoon received a message, where letters cut from a newspaper or magazine were used – glued onto a sheet of paper. It was anonymous and of course no fingerprints. It claimed that he or she saw John Galdstone driving his mother's car the night that Mrs. Hannigan was knocked down. The car was found on the farm, all banged up with Mrs. Hannigan's blood on it and a pair of gloves under the seat, belonging to John Galdstone with his blood on them. The rest of the car inside was wiped clean. John Galdstone insists that he never drove his mother's car and that the gloves were kept in the haybarn for lifting bales. Then Muldoon questioned his wife again, and it transpired that John did not have a solid alibi for the morning of his mother's murder, as he and his wife Heather were sleeping in separate rooms, and she didn't actually see him until 8 am. So, he doesn't have an alibi for either murder. Muldoon and I then sort of came to the conclusion that the "they weren't there" conundrum – you know what I'm talking about – the conversation between Mrs. Hannigan and Monique – referred to the steak knives being missing. Mrs. Hannigan had given a set of steak knives to all the families she cleaned for, as a Christmas present. The set that she gave to Jinny Galdstone is missing, and the murder weapon, which was found in my ditch, is a knife from that set.

So, everything seemed to be pointing to John Galdstone. Muldoon and I aren't totally convinced, but a lot of pressure came from Garda Headquarters to charge him and therefore, Muldoon had little choice. So, you're up-to-date and I would really value your opinion. Oh, one more thing – Adam and Clara Galdstone tried to eject Heather and her children from Briar's Cottage. They didn't realise that John had signed a legal document making Heather joint owner. Following this altercation, the family dog was poisoned but didn't die. We don't know whether the two are linked or not. So, I need you to give me some sort of an insight into the psychology of all this."

Colonel Robert King sat quietly, reeling in his fishing line. He cast out again and then answered.

"It's the false flags that I find intriguing, the murder weapon thrown in your ditch to cast suspicion onto you, then the phone call accusing Pippa McHugh. That's someone whom we could call a cerebral narcissist – someone who thinks they're smarter than everyone else – they certainly think that they're cleverer than the guards. Of course, in my humble opinion, I believe that the message received by Muldoon claiming to have seen John Galdstone, driving his mother's car is another false flag, and most likely from the same person. I presume that Muldoon and yourself are veering towards one of the Galdstones."

"Yes, we certainly are, but although the circumstantial evidence points towards John, he certainly didn't send Muldoon the anonymous message. We are also working on the presumption, that there is only one killer."

"Let's take a look at John Galdstone's personality," continued Robert. "He was bullied by his mother – but it would appear that she ran roughshod over everyone, and from previous discussions, we came to the conclusion that Jinny Galdstone was a sociopath – which left you and Muldoon with a long list of people with motives. Whoever committed these two murders must also be a sociopath. We must ask ourselves the question, does John Galdstone fall into this category? He seems to have just gone along with whatever his mother wanted and she rewarded him with Briar's Cottage. It would appear that he knew what his mother was and so protected his wife and children by making Heather co-owner of all his property. Of course he must have felt some resentment towards his mother because of her interference in his marriage, which caused a rift between the couple. I think that John Galdstone has a compliant personality which makes him unassertive, particularly in the presence of a "dominant" personality like his mother.

People like him often seem reticent and aloof and can appear cold and disinterested. But much of this cautious style stems from their controlled side. John was reluctant to become involved in confrontations with his mother – so by behaving as he did, he managed to stay on her side and so got exactly as he wished – Briar's cottage. Perhaps the rift in his marriage had something to do with Heather's belief that he would not confront his mother about her interference – but the last point is mere speculation.

The husband Adam appears also to be compliant, but sometimes, with husbands or wives, they just become worn down, and crack finally. They did argue about Clara being thrown out of the house, but he still complied and allowed it to happen. Love in a marriage can turn to hatred and resentment over the years. But these killings are less likely to be planned and covered up. Whoever killed Jinny left no evidence for the guards, except what he or she wanted to be found.

Then there's Clara, a young woman who paid a very high price for her indiscretion. She appears to be more dominant and determined. She and her father showed very little empathy towards Heather when they asked her to leave her home. She does appear to harbour resentment, but claims that she and her mother were on the best of terms. She's a bit of an enigma.

I suppose, Alexander, the only speculation that I can add to your quandary is that I believe that John Galdstone is the least likely of the three to have committed the two murders."

Alexander had listened very carefully to what Robert had to say. He was of a similar opinion, but wanted to get Robert's input, because of his work in the field of psychology.

The two men sat in silence, casting off their lines and reeling them back in – a kind of soothing rhythm as the swans and ducks floated aimlessly around the shore of the lake. It became cooler and finally the two men decided that it was time to row back to shore. They hadn't caught any fish but that really hadn't been the aim of the exercise.

Having returned the boat to its original position and the fishing rods, tackle and lifejackets to the cupboard in the hallway, Alexander and Robert sat down in front of the turf fire and ordered two brandies to warm themselves. They held the brandy snifters in the palm of their hands and swirled the topaz coloured liquid around in the glass. They sipped their drinks slowly and felt a warm sensation in their throat as they swallowed. They remained by the fireplace for about 20 minutes and then retired to their rooms to dress for dinner.

The following morning, the two couples packed the cars and began their journey back to Briarstown.

"I suppose you had a great chat with Robert while you were out fishing?" asked Monique inquisitively.

"We sure did," answered Alexander, as he drove the car through the countryside towards Westport.

"He's of the same opinion as I am regarding John Galdstone, and of course, Muldoon also thinks that they made an arrest too quickly."

"Did he say anything about who might have poisoned the dog?"

"I told him about it, but we actually didn't get around to discussing it. We don't need a psychiatrist to tell us that whoever did it, is a nasty piece of work. We know from history that cruelty to animals is a sign of a major personality fault. Remember Albert de Salvo, the Boston strangler, who killed 13 women between 1962 and 1964 – well, he shot dogs and cats with arrows."

"Yes, indeed, anyone who causes suffering to animals or people is a sociopath, in my opinion," added Monique with emotion.

Four hours later they drove through the entrance gate to The Lodge . They were happy to be home after a long journey back from the west. Alexander was keen to collect the dogs from the Brownes. He strolled across the field and reached the front garden where he was seen through the bay window by Damien. Suddenly the front door opened and the two Bernese mountain dogs bolted through, and ran at top speed towards Alexander, barking with all their might , their tails wagging. They jumped all over him, licking his hands and then nuzzling into his thighs. He petted and hugged them and after a few moments of utter madness, they quietened down and he was able to greet Damien.

"Well, Damien, everything okay?"

"Yes, nothing to report at all. We loved having the dogs. They're great company. Horses all fine. I noticed the pony's abscess is all but gone. I had no problems at all in your absence. What about yourselves? Did you have a good time?"

"Absolutely great. Time just stands still in that part of Mayo. The ladies really enjoyed the trip as well. The food was wonderful as usual. We were lucky with the weather as well. Did a spot of fishing but caught nothing. I hope there were no more poisoning incidences in the last two days?"

"No, all quiet on the western front," replied Damien. "Lydia called up to see Heather. She seems a bit stronger and the poor dog continues to recover. Other than that – no news at all."

CHAPTER 31

DELIVERANCE

Inspector Muldoon arrived at The Lodge early on Monday morning with interesting news for Commandant de Bruin. He had with him his trusty briefcase, containing all the relevant documents and witness statements. The two men sat at de Bruin's mahogany desk in the office.

"The DPP has decided that there is not enough evidence to bring the case to trial, so John Galdstone will be released this afternoon," said Muldoon.

"I am not at all surprised. No more than yourself, I thought the arrest was premature."

"First of all, the DPP said that the anonymous tip we got would not be admissible. If we were to use that, we would have to locate that witness and he or she would have to testify. Secondly, without that witness, there is no proof that John ever drove the blue sports car. His fingerprints are not in the car. Although we found his work gloves under the seat with spots of blood, the blood group is his and interestingly enough he is a different blood group than his mother. Jinny Galdstone's blood type is AO whilst John's is A. I must also say that he looked quite shocked, when I showed him the gloves and told him where they were found. He insisted that they were kept in the haybarn. The DPP also said that your lack of alibi does not make you guilty. He has no alibi for either murder. Although his wife admitted that they slept in different rooms and that she didn't see him until nearly 8 o'clock, she still insists that he was ill and unable to go to the farm as usual."

"Of course he may have been ill after committing such an horrendous murder," added de Bruin. "It may all have been playacting."

"Although we believe that Mrs. Hannigan was speaking about the missing knives, in her conversation with your wife, the DPP just thinks this is conjecture. One of our officers asked "Newbridge Cutlery" to do a stock take and they found that there were 200 sets for sale before that Christmas of which 186 were sold. The remaining sets are supposedly in their warehouse. You can see how a defence attorney could poke holes in that assertion. The long and the short of it is that we need to find more solid evidence, before we charge anyone with this crime. The DPP was most insistent that we find some bloodied clothes with Jinny's blood on them. We have searched both of the Galdstone houses with a fine tooth comb – no bloodied clothes or boots or shoes. We have also meticulously searched the farms including barns and outhouses. We even did another search after we found the car."

"Does the DPP concur with us that it's the same murderer?" asked Alexander.

"Yes, he does. Otherwise it would be too much of a coincidence. So, when we solve either murder, we solve both. We need to find the bloodied clothes or we need to find a witness who saw whoever was driving the blue sports car on the night of Mrs. Hannigan's death, or preferably both."

The two men spent the next hour checking and perusing all their notes and witness statements, just in case they had missed a small important detail. Alexander also recounted his discussions with Robert King while they were fishing on the lake in Mayo.

"These false flags are very interesting. I presume neither of us believe that it's some idiot playing silly buggers with the guards any more," began Muldoon.

"No, I'm convinced that it's the murderer, trying to divert attention away from themselves and also believing that they are smarter than we are. So, that begs the question, why would John Galdstone point the finger at himself?"

At 8o'clock the same morning, Heather Galdstone had received a phone call from Mountjoy prison. It was her husband on the line who informed her that he was being released. It would take a while to deal with the paperwork. She left Rory to mind the children and she departed in her car to travel the 25 miles from Briar's cottage to the jail.

She parked the car as near to the prison as possible, on a road called Royal Canal Bank. She waited patiently, looking at the high wall, with a green in front of it. After 14 minutes, she saw her husband walking towards her, a small rucksack slung over his left shoulder, holding the meagre possessions he had with him in prison. She got out of the car, walked slowly over to him and hugged him. John took her hand and squeezed it, then led her back to the passenger side of the car and opened the door for her. He then got into the driver's seat, put the car in gear and headed towards home. They arrived back to Briar's

Cottage 50 minutes later, where they were greeted by a grinning Rory and delighted children, who jumped all over their father and chatted and screamed excitedly.

After a few minutes, when all the enthusiasm had subsided, Rory took the children outside to play, leaving Heather and John alone in the sitting room. John looked towards the fireplace in front of which lay Rover who was wagging his tail, still not strong enough to jump up to greet his master.

"Poor old thing," said John, as he knelt down beside the dog and patted his head.

"He's getting better every day," said Heather. "He's eating a bit, but still not strong enough to run around. He's getting there."

"Any idea who did this?" asked John.

"Nobody saw anything," answered Heather.

"Someone tried to set me up Heather," continued John, as he walked over towards his wife, took her in his arms and hugged her.

"I've never driven that stupid car in my life. Someone took my gloves from the haybarn and put them under the seat and sent an anonymous letter to the guards saying that they saw me driving that car the night Mrs. Hannigan was run over. Why on earth would I kill Mrs. Hannigan? Who on earth would want to do this to me?"

"I know you couldn't have done any of this," replied Heather. "I don't think the guards or Commandant de Bruin were convinced either. Mrs. de Bruin has been very kind to me when you were inside, as has Mrs. Browne. Commandant de Bruin, as you know drove Rory and the dog up to the Veterinary College – he wouldn't be alive only for him."

"I know you don't like him because of the business over the land between himself and your mother but maybe he could help you prove your innocence."

"To tell you the truth Heather, I never had any ill feelings towards him – we all know what my mother was like – I just went along with Dad and Clara, as usual. I'll think about it."

They were both exhausted now, so sat down on the couch in front of the fireplace. Rover looked up at them with his big brown eyes, wagged his tail, put his head back down on his front paws, closed his eyes and fell asleep. When Rory returned with the children, the couple were fast asleep on the couch.

Heather and John put the children to bed at 8 o'clock. Rory had headed back to Dublin earlier. The couple sat down in the sitting room with a cup of tea.

"I've something else to tell you," said Heather. "I know that you have enough on your plate but I just need to tell you about what happened when you were in jail."

"Go on, what's the matter?"

"The day after you were sent to Mountjoy, your father and Clara called down. To be honest, I thought that they were coming down to show me some support and ask if they could help. But no, they told me to leave the house. Clara said that this was Galdstone property and now that you were going away for a long time, that I had no business being here."

John was extremely shocked at this news. He sat on the couch inhaling and exhaling deeply. "What did you say to them?" he asked.

"I told them to leave the house – that this was my home as well. Clara told me that she'd see about that. I was extremely upset and I hope you don't mind but I explained it all to Mrs. de Bruin. I told her about the document that you had signed and she checked and then reassured me that I was safe."

"You did the right thing, Heather. They had absolutely no business coming here and frightening you like that. Don't worry about anything. I'll sort everything out."

Heather could sense a change in her husband. He appeared stronger and more confident in himself as if all the dreadful experiences he had endured had made him a better man. His demeanour had changed, being more determined and not as beaten down and broken as before his incarceration.

"What doesn't kill you, makes you stronger," thought Heather to herself.

For the first time in a long while, she felt that there was hope for their marriage – John was on her side, and she could depend on him. She made up her mind to ask Mrs. de Bruin to intervene on their behalf – to ask Commandant de Bruin to prove John's innocence. Now that she had her husband back, she didn't want to lose him to prison again.

Later that evening John Galdstone made his way up to the main house. He wanted to confront his father and Clara about the way they had treated Heather. When he entered the kitchen they were both watching television. Jack was already in bed.

"Great to see you son," greeted Adam." I knew they had it wrong. They had to let you go."

Clara looked up at John but didn't look quite as pleased to see him. "Hi, John, glad you're back," she said unconvincingly.

"I wonder, are you really?" answered John. "Heather told me all about your little visit to our house whilst I was away."

"I'm sure she got the wrong end of the stick, John," replied Adam. "We were only trying to protect all our assets if something were to happen to you. You know, it wasn't looking good there for awhile. We all thought you might be sent down for years."

"Briar's cottage and the lands are not your assets to protect. They legally belong to Heather and me – I've seen to that."

John looked closely and intently at his father and sister.

"Your mother wouldn't have wanted that," said Adam sheepishly.

"It doesn't matter what she wanted anymore – She's gone," replied John with conviction.

"I thought that she jointly owned that place," interjected Clara.

"No, you've got it wrong. The bank only allowed her to guarantee the loan and insisted that she take out an insurance policy in case anything happened to her – it was always mine and mine alone and now it's ours – it's mine and Heather's – nothing to do with you two."

John had remained very calm and collected during the interchange. Both Adam and Clara were quite taken aback by what he had said. This was a different John Galdstone, standing in front of them. Adam seemed somewhat deflated but Clara looked defiant.

"Don't give me that look, Clara, it's all legal and above board. So we seem to all have done well out of dear Mummy's death. Although, perhaps you, not as well as you thought Clara. Oh, and by the way, Rover is making a very good recovery, thanks for asking."

This last comment was directed straight at Clara who showed no reaction – she just glared at John as he left the kitchen.
Adam followed his son into the hallway.

"John, wait up, please!" he said." We need to get through this. We have to put all that behind us, and get back to working the farm again. You need to take over your mother's job in the milking parlour. Clara and I have been doing our best, but it's been really difficult. She has Jack as well. We need you here in the morning."

"Oh, for God sake Dad, you haven't asked me anything about my case – why I was released – is there a chance that I'll be rearrested – neither did Clara. What kind of people are you? You're only interested in getting me back to work, milking the cows in the morning. I don't think you really care what happens to me except in how it's going to affect you. I'm disgusted with you both – the way you treated Heather – your attitude to me. Well, if I can hold onto my freedom, things are going to change around here. Milk your own bloody cows tomorrow morning."

Monique had risen earlier than usual so that she could bake a sponge cake to take with her to welcome home John Galdstone, and check how Heather was coping. She allowed the cake to cool on a rack, cut it in half, lathered one side with home-made jam and cream, put the other side on top and placed it in an old biscuit tin.

She threw on a light Mac, as it was quite warm outside, picked up her offering and headed off towards Briar's Cottage. On arrival at the front door, she was greeted by a smiling Heather, who looked 10 years younger, as if the weight of the world had been lifted from her shoulders.

"Good morning Heather," said Monique. "You're looking so much better. How is John?" she asked as she handed Heather the biscuit tin.

"Come in, come in," she said excitedly. "He's out playing with the children. He should be back in about 20 minutes. We'll have a cuppa and a slice of your lovely cake."

The two ladies headed for the kitchen. Heather turned to Monique.

"I need to ask for your help. Will your husband take on our case? I want him to prove John's innocence. We need deliverance from this agony."

"Alexander is already working with Inspector Muldoon on the two murder cases. I can promise you that they will get to the truth," answered Monique, as she placed her hand on Heather's arm reassuringly.

CHAPTER 32

— ❖ —

A WEDDING

Two more weeks had passed and there were no more developments in the murder cases. The de Bruins were concentrating on their accountancy work and Inspector Muldoon had taken a week's leave to visit his elderly mother in Galway with his wife and child. No one quite knew what to make of John Galdstone's release from prison. The people in the area were suspicious of him – had he killed his mother and Mrs. Hannigan? Perhaps the guards just didn't have enough evidence or was he innocent and there was someone else around the neighbourhood who was the murderer?

Alexander and Monique visited Liam Hannigan regularly to check up on how he was coping. During one of these visits, he gave them some good news. Jean wanted to get married as soon as possible. She just wanted a very small, low-key wedding with only about 30 guests.

"That's wonderful, congratulations," said Monique on hearing the news. "Where does she want to have the ceremony?"

"She wants to have it in the church in the Curragh. Her mother loved that church and she has wonderful memories of her childhood there. It's small enough as well, not like the Newbridge Church – anyway she doesn't want her wedding to be in the same church as her mother's funeral. She wants me to organise the church and the catering. I wonder could you both help me? I don't know where to begin."

"I'll speak to the chaplain," answered Alexander. "I'm sure there won't be any problem at all. There won't be any difficulty either I'm sure, organising the catering in one of the messes – leave that to me."
"I'll speak to the ladies in the flower club about arrangements for the church and the tables in the mess. They were so fond of Joan. I'm sure that they would only be delighted to help out. Jean will only have to turn up," said Monique with a warm smile.

Three weeks later, the guests arrived at the military church in the Curragh Camp. The ladies from the flower club had done Joan and Jean proud. At the entrance to the church, on either side of the old oak door, stood two milk churns, teeming with flowers – ferns, eucalyptus and succulents, intermingled with white giant aelium, chrysanthemums, lisianthus and hydrange – a splendid spectacle. On every second pew in the church was placed a small spray - Baby's Breath with a single pink rose tied together with a pretty cream ribbon. And finally, on either side of the altar, they had prepared a beautiful arrangement of eucalyptus, Antirrhinum Magus or Royal Bride with white roses and Ranunculus in the foreground. The church was fit for any bride. A friend of Mrs. Hannigan's played the organ while a local soprano sang her heart out. The de Bruins and the Brownes were the only invited guests from Briarstown. There were some family members from the bride's and groom's side, the ladies from the flower club, including Mary Edwards, the vicar's wife who was blooming herself and some of Liam Hannigan's army buddies.

There were mixed emotions in the church – a very happy day tinged with sorrow as they watched Liam walk towards the altar with his daughter. There was one very important person missing in the front seat.

Jean was a beautiful bride. She wore an elegant, classic lace dress, stunning in its simplicity with an elbow length soft tulle veil with lace edging to complement the dress.

"She really does look like her mother when she was young," thought Monique. "How poor Joan would have loved this day. Some evil person has deprived her of one of the happiest days of her life."

At the wedding breakfast, there were only short speeches, but nobody objected. The catering staff produced a delicious buffet. Jean had decided that there would not be a band or a disco. Instead there was a harpist who played a wide ranging repertoire, including some of Mrs. Hannigan's favourite tunes. The guests mingled and chatted and all agreed that it was a beautiful wedding. Liam and Jean were delighted at how everything had gone.

At 7 o'clock the reception was coming to an end and all the guests were taking their leave and wishing the newly-weds every happiness. The Brownes and the de Bruins left the reception together and started the short journey back to Briarstown.

As the two cars were turning off the main road towards their lands, they noticed flashing lights at the end of the road. There was an ambulance, a firetruck and two Garda patrol cars. An incident had occurred near the cul-de-sac where the Lavelles lived. They couldn't see what had actually happened, as there was a roadblock just past the Old Rectory. The Brownes decided to drive into The Lodge after the de Bruins.

"Did you see anything Alexander?" asked Damien as he alighted from the driver's side of his car.

"No, I couldn't get a good look," replied Alexander. "Let's all go inside. I'm sure we'll hear soon enough. Bad news travels fast."

The two couples made their way into the house and down the hall towards the sitting room. Alexander poured out two sherries for the ladies and brandies for the men. They all sat around the fireplace waiting for news.

"There is a very large oak tree down there," said Damien, breaking the silence. "Maybe someone ran into it."

"People aren't normally speeding there, it's just leading to the cul-de-sac with a few houses. It's not a dangerous part of the road," interjected Alexander.

"Let's hope that nobody is badly injured," added Lydia. "But it's not looking great with the fire engine there."

The four friends sat back in their chairs and became silent again, deep in their thoughts. Their reveries were disturbed by the ringing of the telephone. Alexander jumped up and quickly moved to the desk to lift the receiver.

"Alexander de Bruin speaking. How can I help you?"

It was Inspector Muldoon on the other end of the line.

"John Muldoon here. I presume you know that there has been an accident at the end of your road. Just thought that you'd want to know that it was Heather Galdstone driving the car. One of the people who lives in the cul-de-sac where the Lavelles live came across it at 7.15 pm and rang for the emergency services. She's in a bad way and has been taken to Naas General Hospital. She hit the tree head on. She must have been going at an awful speed to have caused such damage, and had to be cut out of the vehicle by the fire services."

"Was she alone in the car?" asked Alexander.

"Yes, fortunately. The man who came across the accident recognised her, so one of our officers informed John Galdstone. He followed the ambulance into the hospital."

"Thanks for letting me know John."

"I'll ring you when I know more," replied John Muldoon.

Alexander returned the handset and looked over at the expectant faces.

"It's Heather Galdstone. She hit that tree and is very badly injured. They've taken her to Naas hospital. John has followed the ambulance over in his car."

"Oh my God, that's dreadful," said Lydia. "What can we do?"

"Nothing, at present," replied Alexander. "Muldoon will ring again as soon as he has more news."

And hour later Muldoon rang back.

"She's in surgery at the moment. There are a lot of injuries, including head injuries and broken bones. It's going to be touch and go according to the doctors. The surgery is going to last several hours. There is nothing any of us can do tonight, except wait and hope for the best. The car has been removed and I'll get our lads to go over it first thing in the morning, in case there's anything suspicious about the accident. As soon as I know anything I'll be in touch."

Alexander relayed what Muldoon had told him to the others.

"That's it, we'll just have to wait until tomorrow."

Damien and Lydia finished their drinks, headed out into the night and drove the short distance to the Old Rectory. None of them would get much sleep tonight.

Monique and Lydia had determined the night before, that they would call to Briar's Cottage first thing in the morning, to check on Heather's condition, and see if there was anything they could do to help. At precisely 9 am they knocked on the door. It was answered by Rory who looked completely exhausted.

"Hello Rory," said Monique.

"Mrs. de Bruin, please come in," he replied.

"I suppose you know Mrs. Browne from the Old Rectory?"

"Yes, I do, it's kind of you to call."

They all walked into the kitchen.

"My mother is looking after the children again."

"Is there any news of Heather?" asked Monique.

"She's still alive," answered Rory, tears welling up in his eyes. "She survived the operation. Her poor body is badly messed up – lots of broken bones. The main problem was the head injury. The doctors had to relieve a blood clot in her brain. They said that it was a near thing, as she crashed once during the procedure and had to be revived. She hasn't regained consciousness yet, so we won't know if there is brain damage until she comes around. I think they have her in an induced coma. John is still over in the hospital with her. He just rang about an hour and a half ago. I don't know why all of this is happening to them. It's just a dreadful nightmare."

"Thank heavens that she got through the night and that there's hope," said Lydia. "You look as if you haven't slept at all Rory."

"No, I couldn't," replied Rory "I was waiting for a phone call. I really feared the worst."

"Best if you had a lie down now," suggested Monique. "You need some sleep and John is going to need a lot of support when he gets home. We'll leave you in peace and don't hesitate to ring me or call up to us if you need anything at all. Stay where you are. We'll see ourselves out."

The two ladies walked down the hallway and out the front door, closing it gently behind them. They stood outside the house for a moment, and took in deep breaths. Then they made their way towards the gate. Monique stopped suddenly in her tracks.

"Look at that, on the ground," she said, pointing at a large dark stain on the driveway. "That looks like an oil leak."

"Yes, it does indeed," replied Lydia, taking a closer look, "it's not the usual one you'd see. There is a dry patch in the middle of it and a lot of spatters around as well."

"That's something that Inspector Muldoon needs to know about. Let's get back to The Lodge as quickly as possible and tell Alexander."

A phone call was made to the Garda Station in Naas and within a half an hour, there were forensic officers examining the driveway at Briar's Cottage.

Alexander and Monique were eagerly awaiting a phone call from John Muldoon all day.

"Did you think it was an oil leak or brake fluid?" Alexander had asked.

"How on earth would I know the difference!" answered Monique, slightly bewildered.

"Just thinking out loud my love," smiled Alexander." If it were brake fluid, that could have been the cause of Heather's crash."

"So now, do you think that someone tried to cause Heather's death? – the dog was just the start of it."

"Maybe it was John that they were after. There are a lot of people around here who believe that he killed Mrs. Hannigan and that he had to be released, only, because of lack of evidence. There is also a lot of ill feeling towards the Galdstones, following everything that came out about them during the enquiry."

"Does Liam think that John Galdstone killed Joan?" Monique asked, panic in her voice.

"He was extremely upset when the DPP decided not to proceed until more evidence was found, but I told him that Muldoon and I had reservations about John Galdstone's guilt, and I reassured him that we would get to the truth. I really don't believe that Liam did this. It happened yesterday, the day of his daughter's wedding. Let's not dwell on that. Let's wait for Muldoon to get back to us."

Although Alexander had tried to put Monique's mind at rest, he wasn't completely convinced himself, that Liam, a grieving husband, who is about to walk his daughter down the aisle, might not want to seek revenge on the person he believed to be responsible for his wife's death. Perhaps Alexander had misread Liam's reaction to his reassurances. He would discuss this with Inspector Muldoon .

In the ICU of Naas Hospital, Heather Galdstone lay in a coma in a bed in the corner of the ward, tubes coming out of her mouth, a bandage wrapped around her head and drips attached to both arms. There were monitors making beeping noises beside her bed. John Goldstone sat in an armchair, staring blankly at his wife. He had been there since she had come from the operating theatre. The doctors had told him that she was lucky to be alive – time would tell if she would recover completely. Their way of telling him that she might have brain damage.

As he sat there, someone came up behind him and he felt a hand on his shoulder. He turned to see Clara standing there, holding a bunch of flowers.

"Poor Heather, will she be OK?" she asked.

"We'll have to wait and see," he replied.

"Why don't you go home, have a shower and get some rest. I'll stay with her. There is nothing you can do at the moment."

"Thanks, Clara. I think I'll do that. I'm really exhausted. I'll be back in a few hours."

Clara watched as her brother left the ward. She sat down in the armchair and began her vigil, keeping watch on her sister-in-law. The monitors continued to beep and with her eyes firmly shut, Heather's chest rose and fell as she breathed laboriously. The nurses came to Heather's bed to check on her vitals every 10 minutes, diligently. Clara had brought a book with her to read. After an hour and a half a nurse offered Clara a cup of tea which she accepted gratefully.

"Is there much hope for her?" Clara asked the nurse, when she arrived with the tray of tea and biscuits.

"We really aren't sure. She's really lucky to be alive and to have come through the surgery. The surgeon will be around in half an hour to check on her. She's in very good hands."

Exactly a half an hour later, a distinguished looking man in a white coat carrying a clipboard made his way into the ward and towards Heather's bed. He was accompanied by a group of young, eager looking doctors and the matron. Clara was asked to leave as the matron pulled the curtains around the bed. Clara could only hear the odd word as she stood in the doorway of the ICU.

It was partly a checkup by the surgeon and partly a teaching class as he explained what the procedures had entailed and asked and answered questions. Five minutes later the curtains were pulled back and the entourage moved on to the next bed where the same ritual ensued.

Clara returned to the armchair, stared at Heather who hadn't moved an inch, and opened her book.

CHAPTER 33

━ ◆ ━

ACCIDENT OR ATTEMPTED MURDER?

It took another 24 hours before forensics had the report ready for Muldoon's perusal. He studied it carefully and then headed to Briarstown to examine the driveway in Briar's Cottage. He had already telephoned The Lodge to arrange a meeting with Alexander de Bruin. The two men sat in Alexander's office, studying the report.

"The brake lines were tampered with," said Muldoon . "Whoever did this knew what they were doing. They just didn't cut one line – the brakes wouldn't have failed completely if it had been only one line.

"So, it was brake fluid that Monique saw in the driveway."

"Yes, the lines were obviously cut there. It appears that someone crept under the car and did the damage. There is a clean spot in the middle – as you can see from the diagram – where the culprit was lying and then there is brake fluid on both sides."

"So, whatever clothes he or she was wearing will be spattered with fluid?"

"Looks that way," replied Muldoon." When Mrs. Galdstone applied the brakes to turn into her driveway, nothing happened, so she careered down the road and hit the tree."

"That poor woman – but why her? I really can't see Heather with any enemies."

"It's more likely that whoever the culprit is, was after John Gald-stone," remarked Muldoon. "There is a theory coming from head office that it could be John Galdstone himself who wanted to rid himself of his wife. They weren't very happy that the DPP did not proceed with the murder charges."

Alexander thought very carefully about this theory and said.

"I'm not so sure about that. There was the dog poisoning incident while John was in jail. Who else is on your suspect list? First of all, we have to find out who was the intended victim – Heather or John? There are still a lot of people around these parts who believe that John Galdstone killed Mrs. Hannigan and his mother," added de Bruin." They believe that he may get away with it. There's also very bad feeling towards the Galdstones in general, over their treatment of the Hobans and others.

"Well, our list of suspects is quite long then," continued Muldoon. "The list includes your friend Liam Hannigan unfortunately. By the way, I've decided to place guards in the ward with Heather Galdstone, just in case she was the intended target – she would be a sitting duck in the hospital."

"What about opportunity?" asked de Bruin. "When was the car tampered with?"

"I haven't had the chance yet to question John Galdstone. He's in the house at the moment. The two of us may as well head up there now to see him."

Muldoon placed his notes and reports back into his briefcase and both men headed out the door. They drove the short distance to Briar's Cottage. Young Rory answered the door and invited them in. John Galdstone was standing in the kitchen, just having had a shower and change of clothes.

"How are you John?" asked de Bruin.

"Coping," answered John Galdstone.

"I wonder are you up to answering a few questions?" asked Muldoon.

"Fire ahead."

"Could you tell me when was the last time your wife's car was driven, before the time of the accident?"

"The day before, she had gone down to Carlow to see her sister. She arrived back at about 5.30 pm. The car was parked there in the driveway until the next day, when she had to go into Naas to pick up a few things, and then call to a friend. I wasn't expecting her back until about 7.30 or 8 o'clock. Why do you ask?"

"The brakes were tampered with, John," replied Muldoon. "It wasn't just an accident."

John Goldstone went very pale and his eyes looked shocked. He became slightly unsteady on his feet, and had to sit down.

"What on earth is going on? Why would anyone want to hurt Heather, of all people?

"We need to know when the car could have been tampered with," said Muldoon.

"I suppose, during the night," replied John, his voice shaking. "Couldn't have been during the day – we were in and out all day – we would have seen something."

He stood up suddenly and went over to the counter, to pick up his car keys.

"I need to get back to Heather. Clara is with her at the moment. She stayed with her while I came home for a rest, a shower and change of clothes. Please! I need to go."

"Just another few questions," said de Bruin calmly. "Inspector Muldoon has sent some officers to be in the ward with her as well."

John Galdstone took a few deep breaths and sat down once more.

"We are not sure that your wife was the intended victim," continued Muldoon. "It may have been you. Do you ever drive Heather's car?"

"Not unless I'm really stuck, I don't like driving it."

"Have either of you had any threats recently?" Alexander asked.

"No, but someone tried to kill our dog, Rover when I was away. He was poisoned as you know."

"I think we can allow you to get back to the hospital now. Please check your car before you drive it, and be vigilant. It might be a good idea if your children were to stay somewhere else, until we've cleared this up," concluded Muldoon.

"They can stay with Heather's mother."

John Galdstone picked up his keys once more and went out the door, leaving Muldoon and de Bruin standing in the kitchen. As the front door closed, Rory made an appearance. Muldoon explained the situation to the young man, who promised to be on the lookout for anything out of the ordinary, and to be mindful of his own safety.

Ten minutes later the two men were back at The Lodge, comparing notes once again.

"It would appear that the brake lines were cut that evening or night, when the perpetrator couldn't be seen. John Galdstone could have done it himself of course," said Muldoon.

"Or someone else who had it in for them," replied de Bruin. "Do you think that this is linked to the murders? Could it be the same person who committed all these crimes or is this one separate?"

"Well, if it's John Galdstone, he could have committed all three crimes. He certainly had means and opportunity but what about the motive for killing his wife."

"Monique is adamant that they were getting along much better. Heather had told her that John had changed since his time in prison – that he had stood up for her when his father and sister had tried to bully her. Heather had also asked Monique if I could help to prove John's innocence. If John Galdstone is the perpetrator of all these heinous crimes, who on earth poisoned the poor dog?"

Next port of call for the two men was the Hannigan home in Clonee village. Alexander knew that the newly married couple and John, the son, had intended to spend a week with Liam Hannigan after the wedding, before returning back to England. Jean and her husband were not going on honeymoon until later on in the year.

De Bruin and Muldoon were greeted very warmly by Liam Hannigan. All three walked into the kitchen where the rest of the household were standing around chatting.

"How lovely to see you again, so soon, Commandant de Bruin," said Jean smiling.

"Lovely to see you all too, after such a beautiful wedding. We are so sorry to disturb you and please be aware, that the questions we have to ask you, are routine and hope that you don't find it too upsetting."

"What are you talking about, Commandant?" Liam Hannigan asked.

"You know that Heather Galdstone was found injured in her car the evening of the wedding."

"Yes, we know about that, but I don't know how we can help you," said Liam Hannigan.

"It transpires that it wasn't an accident, Liam, the brake lines were cut. Someone meant her harm or perhaps meant her husband harm," added de Bruin.

The atmosphere changed in the room. Liam looked quite annoyed and the other members of the family appeared shocked.

"Are you accusing one of us of tampering with the brakes?" Jean asked angrily. "It was the day of our wedding."

"I know that these questions seem inappropriate at this time, but, Inspector Muldoon and I are in a bit of a quandary. We have to look at anyone who may have a motive to hurt the Galdstones . John Galdstone's arrest for your mother's murder and then release must have been very upsetting for you all, to put it mildly. I know that I explained to you, Liam, that inspector Muldoon and I had our doubts, and that we would find the truth. However, on paper, it looks like you have a motive. I assure you that we only want to rule you all out."

"I must tell you Commandant de Bruin, that I took you at your word," said Liam Hannigan. "I promise you, that none of us did this dreadful thing. When could the brakes have been cut?"

"The evening or night before the wedding," said Muldoon.

"Oh, that's easy," said Jean. "We were all here all evening. We had dinner, we opened a bottle of champagne and toasted Mam . We sat around and chatted for hours. I suppose we went to bed at around 12 o'clock. I didn't sleep well at all, neither did David. We got up a few times for water. We were just restless and nervous I suppose. Dad was snoring all night."

"I can attest to that," added John Hannigan.

"That's all we needed to know," said Muldoon.

"We are so sorry for the disturbance," said de Bruin. "I hope you can forgive us for the intrusion."

"It had to be done," interjected Liam Hannigan. "We have every faith in you that you'll find Joan's killer. We have no intention of taking the law into our own hands."

They all shook hands and Inspector Muldoon and Commandant de Bruin walked back to the car.

"That was really unfortunate and extremely awkward," said Alexander de Bruin.

"I know," answered John Muldoon. "It's a shame that we had to question them like that, but at least now they are completely ruled out. I certainly believe that Liam Hannigan knew that we were only doing our job."

"What next?" Alexander asked.

"Sergeant Dunne is going to Baroda to check on Jerry Hoban's alibi. I think this is just going to be a formality as well. Can't really see that man trying to murder John or Heather Galdstone because of Jinny Galdstone's sins."

"Although the young Galdstones are now living in Briar's cottage where the Hobans were hoping to be. Still, it's a very long shot!"

John Muldoon dropped off his passenger at the front entrance to The Lodge . Alexander hurried into the house to relate all the news to Monique, who was waiting patiently for him in the sitting room.

"Well," she said. "Is Liam in the clear?"

"Yes he is. The conversation was very awkward to begin with, but they gave each other very strong alibis, so you can stop worrying about him now."

"Thank goodness for that," replied Monique, very relieved. "I never really believed that he would do such a thing, but then you wonder what grief might drive you too."

"I wonder was it some vigilante in the area who believes that John is a murderer and got away with his crimes, and decided to take matters into his own hands. Didn't realise that it was Heather's car and she paid the price."

"It's all fraught with confusion. We have two murders that we believe were committed by the same person, and an attempted murder which may or may not be directly linked to the other two. What does Muldoon think?"

"He's as bewildered as we are, and he's under a huge amount of pressure to solve the murders and now this, on top of it all."
"Any more news about Heather's condition?"

"No, she's still in a coma. Clara is with her and Muldoon has placed a guard to watch over her – just in case she was the actual target."

"Hard to believe that Heather was the intended victim. She really is an innocent in all this. Her only sin was to marry into that family. Can't imagine she had any idea of what she was letting herself in for."

When John Galdstone arrived back into his wife's ward in Naas hospital, he noticed the young female constable sitting at the nurses station, looking intently in the direction of Heather's bed. On his way in, he had seen another young Bean Garda sipping coffee in the hallway.
He made his way over to Heather's bed. Clara was still sitting in the chair, reading her book.

"Any change?" he asked his sister.

"No, none at all," she answered. "The nurses have been in and out a lot. They didn't say anything to me. What's the guard doing here?"

"They are keeping an eye on Heather, just in case someone wants to kill her, I suppose. But they really think that I'm the one that needs protecting. Listen, thanks for being here."

"No problem, I've got to get back to the farm and to Jack. I'll see you later. Ring me when you want me to take over again."

Clara rose from the chair, gathered up her handbag and left the ward. John sat down on the same chair and stared at Heather, lying in the bed, helpless. She was in exactly the same prone position as when he left her earlier that day. He thought her breathing was shallower. The monitors were making exactly the same noises as before. He took her hand, which had a line in her vein, leading to a bag of some sort of liquid. He looked at her face. A big tube coming from her mouth, her eyes firmly closed and bandage wrapped around her head and forehead. He squeezed her hand gently but her hand was limp. As he glanced across to the nurses station, he realised that the young officer was keeping a very close eye on him, as per her orders.

He became acutely aware that he was now a suspect in Heather's attempted murder, as well as the other two murders.

The nurses came and went, checking Heather's vitals. They changed the bags that hung on hooks. John Galdstone sat in that chair, hour after hour until finally the matron arrived.

"Mr Galdstone, I think you need to go home and rest. We will phone you if there is any change in your wife's condition. She is receiving the best of care, as you can see. We believe that she is completely stable. It will just take time. We don't know when she will wake up, but the consultant is very hopeful that she will wake up. You'll need your strength later. So, my advice to you is to go home and get some sleep."

John Goldstone reluctantly agreed, squeezed his wife's hand once more, kissed her on the forehead and walked out of the ward slowly, down the long corridor, which smelled of bleach, out the front door and towards the car park.

He sat quietly in his car, lit a cigarette and inhaled deeply. He stared out the window and wondered whether Heather would ever be the same again. Would she ever open her eyes again? He thought about the unending beep beep of the monitors.

CHAPTER 34

A REASSESSMENT

Alexander de Bruin was up very early that morning as per usual. The sun had risen at 5.30am and by the time he walked out of the house at 6.30am, the haze was clearing. He always found it easier to think while walking in the fields in the clear, morning air, with his two Bernese mountain dogs. Since Rover, the Galdstone's dog had been poisoned, everyone in the area was very careful, when bringing their dogs outside. It was much harder of course, to keep an eye on the cats.

Before leaving the house, Alexander had tied on muzzles around their mouths, so that it would make it very difficult for them to pick up any bait. The two dogs were not one bit happy with this, but needs must, and at least they could run around freely, when they were muzzled. The morning was cool and the air was fresh. The birds were singing in the trees. It was a very peaceful, idyllic setting. Alexander and the two dogs walked into the paddock where Cailin was chewing grass. She looked up and trotted over to them. The two dogs never chased the ponies and horses – there was a mutual respect. Alexander rubbed her nose and ears. He could see that her hoof had recovered completely. The other ponies and horses ignored him as he checked the fences. The two dogs chased each other around the paddock

He looked at his two dogs, muzzled, because there was some lunatic around who had tried to kill an innocent dog, and just might try to poison others. The dew was still on the grass, he could see a hare on the brow of the hill.

"What are beautiful place to live," he thought – "how wonderful nature was."

But then, there were the shadows surrounding the whole area – the feelings of unease permeating the community. People felt unsafe, they even had to protect their animals. Muldoon and he really had to solve these crimes very soon, so that the whole area could go back to some semblance of normality.

He knew that they must go back to the first murder – everything stemmed from that. Alexander thought again about the evidence that had been gathered – the murder weapon – the steak knife found in his own ditch. There were no fingerprints – just a few drops of Jinny Galdstone's blood found under the handle, which the perpetrator couldn't clean. There were no bloodied clothes found. The murderer's clothes must have been covered with Jinny's blood, as must the shoes or boots that he or she was wearing. Where were these items? All the cars of the suspects were checked for blood stains – nothing. The Galdstone's property was examined with a fine tooth comb. The land and the outhouses were finally searched. Her blood wasn't in the blue sports car that had killed Mrs. Hannigan. The likelihood was that they had disposed of the bloodied clothes before they got into their car or walked wherever they were going. In this scenario, the clothes and footwear must have been disposed of quite near the murder scene, but not on the Galdstone property. The murderer had disposed of the knife in Alexander's own ditch – he couldn't think of anywhere handy on his own property to hide the items – in any case he would have found them in the intervening months. Briar's Cottage had been searched as well, as had the lands and outhouses. The only other place close enough to the milking parlour was the Old Rectory and lands. Alexander was sure that Damien Browne would have located anything suspicious on his property, since the murder. Nevertheless he decided to double check with the Brownes when he next saw them. If anyone could think of a hidey-hole in the area, it would be Damien Browne.

The death of Mrs. Hannigan just has to be linked to Jinny Galdstone's murder. The poor woman noticed that something or someone was missing. Alexander was still convinced that it was the set of knives. The only set of knives missing from the sets that Mrs. Hannigan had given as Christmas presents, was the one she had given to Jinny Galdstone. So, whoever took that set, is probably the murderer – this, needless to say, points back to one of the Galdstones. Of course, the powers that be weren't too convinced by the "set of knives" theory, and the DPP certainly wasn't going to base his case on that.

Alexander then thought about how unlikely it actually was, that no one had seen the blue sports car, the night of Mrs. Hannigan's death. There must be a witness who saw something suspicious – maybe someone whom the guards haven't interviewed, or perhaps someone who just doesn't want to get involved, for whatever reason. He was determined to ask Muldoon to get his men to do another trawl through the village and surrounding area – maybe to put out another appeal on radio and television – just in case someone was just driving through the area on their way from A to B, who has no connection at all with Clonee and Briarstown and doesn't even realise that they have relevant information.

Finally, he thought about poor Heather and her dog, Rover. Were these happenings linked to the two murders or was the perpetrator someone who believed that John Galdstone was guilty? He really had no clear thoughts on this. Whatever way you looked at it, Heather appeared to be an innocent in all of this. He made up his mind that the Heather Galdstone affair would be solved once he and Muldoon had figured out the first murder.

Alexander was very glad that he had taken this time to figure out his thoughts and organise a plan of action. He and Muldoon were at a standstill and must start again, recheck everything. As he was walking back towards the house, the two dogs ran off towards the ditch. They stopped just inside the ditch and began sniffing and pawing excitedly, at something on the ground. As Alexander approached them to investigate, he realised that they were trying to chew something in the grass. His heart missed a beat as he saw two pieces of fresh liver lying among the blades of grass. He grabbed hold of the dogs' collars and pulled them away. He clipped the lead reins that he had been carrying onto the collars, and led the dogs quickly back to the house. On reaching the back kitchen he unceremoniously pulled the dogs in behind him, took off the lead ropes and searched for a plastic bag. He then quickly ran back to where he had seen the pieces of liver. He retrieved them and placed them in the plastic bag.

Monique had heard some sort of commotion, coming from the back of the house. Then the dogs began to whine. She ran into the back kitchen to find the two dogs, still muzzled, scraping at the back door. She took the muzzles off and petted the two dogs, to calm them down. Less than five minutes later, Alexander came in the back door, holding the plastic bag.

"What on earth is going on?" Monique asked.

"The dogs found what I believe is poisoned bait just this side of the ditch in the paddock," answered Alexander. "I got to it before they managed to get any of it into their mouth. Luckily they were muzzled which made it very difficult for them."

"Oh my God," said Monique, kneeling down and hugging the two dogs." What kind of bloody lunatic is on the loose?"

"I'm heading straight up to the Veterinary College to get this analysed. On my way back I'm going to call into Muldoon in Naas. Will you start ringing round to warn the neighbours – start with Damien – he'll help you. Might be a good idea to get onto the local radio as well, so that they can let people know to watch out again for bait."

Monique watched her husband walk swiftly to the car and drive down the avenue. She had seen that look of determination many times before. She closed the door and made her way into her office to make the first of many phone calls.

Alexander de Bruin arrived at Naas Garda Station, report in hand, parked his car in front of the building, before climbing up the stairs to Inspector Muldoon's office. He knocked on the door and waited for a response.

"Come in," said Muldoon. He stood up to greet his friend. John Muldoon looked very tired, black rings under his eyes.

"What can I do for you Alexander?"

"I've just come from the Veterinary College. Someone threw poisoned bait onto my land, obviously to poison the dogs. I have the report here – exactly the same type of poison injected into the pieces of liver as with Heather Galdstone's dog. There's an evil presence around the place. I don't believe that this is a one off. I don't believe in coincidences. I've been giving this a lot of thought. Could we start again? We need to find the bloodied clothes that the murderer wore, and I believe that there is a witness out there somewhere, who can help us."

"I agree completely. I've already arranged for my men to go back to Clonee Village and Briarstown to question everyone again. By the way, the Hobans were away the night that Heather Galdstone's car was tampered with. That's them out of the picture for that anyway," continued John Muldoon.

"I wonder if the dog poisonings is another false flag – trying to get us investigating events that don't appear linked to the original murder. What would poisoning my dogs have to do with Jinny Galdstone's murder? – apart from, of course, upsetting the whole family and so, I'd take my eye off the ball. If the same person has done all of this, then our prime suspect, John Galdstone is out of the picture, as he was in jail when his own dog was poisoned. I presume that there has been no further contact from the anonymous witness, who claims to have seen him driving his mother's sports car the night of Mrs. Hannigan's death."

"No, nothing at all," answered Muldoon.

"I know that you and your men have searched high and low for any evidence, both at Galdstone's farm and Briar's Cottage. I have searched my place but I intend having a chat with Damien Browne, regarding any hiding places in the vicinity that he's aware of. As you know his family has lived in Briarstown for generations. He just might be able to come up with something to help us."

"Go ahead – we need all the help we can get."

Just at that moment, the telephone rang in Muldoon's office. He picked up the receiver.

"Yes, inspector Muldoon – yes – I see – great news – will she be able to see me... Okay... I'll be there in 15 minutes."

John Muldoon replaced the receiver and looked at de Bruin.

"That was the hospital. Heather Galdstone has regained consciousness and is lucid and able to speak to us. I'm going over to see her now. Do you fancy tagging along?"

"Yes, absolutely. I'll drive – the car is just parked outside the station. I can drive you back afterwards."

Ten minutes later, the two men were walking down the corridors of the hospital in the direction of Heather Galdstone's ward. As they arrived, Alexander noticed the young female Bean Garda, sitting at the nurses station, keeping a very keen eye on proceedings. Heather was propped up in the bed – tubes no longer protruding from her mouth, but the drips were still in her arms. John and Clara were sitting either side of the bed – John holding onto Heather's hand.

"We are very sorry to bother you," began Muldoon, "but I've been informed that you are up to answering a few questions."

"I'm so happy to see that you are recovering," added Alexander. "How are you feeling?"

"Well, I'm alive and according to the doctors I'm very lucky to be alive – it was touch and go for a while. They don't believe that I have any brain damage."

"Do you remember anything about the accident?" Muldoon asked.

"Not a thing, I don't even remember getting into the car. I vaguely remember having lunch, but that was a good while before I drove off." Heather winced and put her hand up to her head. "I still have a very bad headache, but that's to be expected. Seemingly my bones will heal in time, but I won't be up and about for a long while."

"We'll take very good care of her," added Clara.

This was the first time that she had spoken. Alexander noticed a look that Heather gave Clara – a look that demonstrated some ill will, and who would blame Heather following the altercation she had had with Adam and Clara over Briar's Cottage, when John was in jail. It seems that Heather wasn't convinced about Clara's ability to turn into Florence Nightingale.

"We'll leave you in peace," said Muldoon. "If you do remember anything, will you let the Bean Garda know. I'm going to leave someone here to look after your well-being for the foreseeable future," continued Muldoon.

"I know that Monique would love to visit you – do you know when might be the best time?"

"I'd love to see her – any time that suits her."

The two men took their leave and walked back down the corridors. Alexander dropped Muldoon back to the station.

As he alighted from the car, Muldoon said "I'm going to put all my manpower into solving this. We don't want any more so-called accidents."

"Ditto," replied Alexander. "I am going to search every piece of ground and building till I locate those clothes. They have to be somewhere. There's someone out there who thinks they're very smart, diverting our attention – smoke and mirrors all around. Hopefully, they're not as smart as they think they are. We have to find them, John, before someone else gets hurt."

Alexander drove back to The Lodge, where Monique was waiting for news from the Veterinary College. She opened the front door as her husband walked towards it – she had been looking out the window in expectation of his arrival.

"Well, was it the same poison?" she asked.

"Yes, exactly the same – same method as well – injected into the liver."

"Nasty person, whoever did this," she added.

"But, I have good news. While I was with Muldoon in his office, he got a phone call from the hospital – Heather Galdstone is conscious. We went to see her and while she's in some pain, she is improving and in time, hopes to make a full recovery. John and Clara were with her. I got the impression that she wasn't too keen on having Clara around. I also asked if she would like you to visit, and she said that she would be delighted. Of course, she has no memory at all of the accident. Maybe it's just as well."

An hour later, Monique was on her way into the hospital to visit Heather. She had decided to bite the bullet and go in that day – she could give John a break, so that he could go home. She would volunteer to stay with Heather until he returned. She purchased a bouquet of flowers en route. Flowers always made a hospital ward look more cheerful and she knew that Heather loved flowers.

When she arrived in the ward, Heather looked delighted to see her. She smiled broadly. Monique thought how fragile she looked, lying helplessly in the bed. Alexander had asked Monique to explain to the Bean Garda on duty, who she was, so as not to cause any undue worry.

Having checked in at the nurses' station, she walked slowly over to the bed.

"Heather, it's so good to see that you are getting better. You gave us all a dreadful fright," said Monique.

"Yes, I'm very lucky," replied Heather.

"You must both be so relieved to see such an improvement," said Monique, directing her comment towards John and Clara.

"You can say that again," said John.

"Why don't you both go home and take a break," suggested Heather to her husband and sister-in-law.

" Monique will keep me company for a while."

"Are you sure?" Clara asked.

"Absolutely, off you go – there is no need to come back until tomorrow. When Monique leaves, I'm going to get some sleep."

John and Clara both kissed Heather on the forehead and left the ward. Heather took a deep breath and seemed to relax a little.

"They are beautiful flowers, thank you so much Monique. The nurse will come around and put them in a vase in a few minutes."

"Are you in much pain, Heather? Alexander tells me that you can't remember anything."

"I'm not too bad. They've given me loads of painkillers. My head still hurts, but I'll survive. I'm so glad that you've come. I thought Clara would never leave. She's here nearly all the time. She's an awful hypocrite – pretending to care, after trying to kick me out of my own home when John was in jail. Adam hasn't even come to see me – he's probably ashamed of himself. I wish Clara would just piss off and leave me alone."

"Don't worry about her or Adam, just concentrate on getting better. If she's annoying you, I could have a word with the matron to restrict her access to you. You certainly don't need any more annoyance with a concussion. I can have a word with John as well."

"That would be swell," said Heather, as she laid her head back on the pillow and closed her eyes.

CHAPTER 35

— ◆ —

NEW APPEALS

Alexander de Bruin was delighted to see a hive of activity in
Clonee village, where Mrs. Hannigan was run over by the blue
sports car. There were about 10 young gardai with their clipboards
going from house to house, hoping to get some piece of new information.

Inspector Muldoon had made an appeal on radio and television for
any information no matter how unimportant it might seem. Monique
and Alexander had watched the Garda programme. They showed a
photo of the blue sports car and a map of where the incident had
occurred. It was a very well put together appeal. Muldoon himself
came across as very efficient and capable. The only thing to do now,
was to wait patiently, and see if there were any phone calls made to the
emergency confidential number, given out by the gardai. Although
the gardai would have preferred not to receive anonymous calls, they
insisted that they would accept them – it was amazing the number of
people who just didn't want to get involved.

Alexander made his way over to the Old Rectory to ask Damien
Browne if he had any idea where there might be a space where the

bloodied clothes could be hidden. Both men decided to do a thorough search of their own lands and outhouses once again.

"There is an old cemetery as you know up the road, maybe we should go there first," suggested Damien.

The two men made their way up the hill to Briarstown Cemetery where some patriots of the revolution were buried. The gravestones were all very old and there were very few visitors. Alexander and Damien walked among the graves searching every crevice meticulously. Despite the fact that there were very few visitors, the council kept the grass cut and the graves in very good nick, probably because there was a republican plot in the middle of it. After about two hours, Alexander and Damien were satisfied – there was nothing to be found. As they made their way back, they scrutinised the ditches. The guards had done a very thorough job originally of searching the ditches, looking for the murder weapon, which of course they had found in the ditch at The Lodge.

"If whoever did this, wanted to get rid of their clothes quickly, they must have dumped them nearby. They didn't sit into their car covered in blood – anyway, all the cars of the suspects were checked for blood stains, and not a speck of Jinny Galdstone's blood was found – so, we can only conclude that they changed their clothes after the murder and dumped the ones covered in blood."

"I wonder why they didn't dump the murder weapon in the same place?" Damien asked.

"They wanted to divert attention away from themselves and on to me," answered Alexander.

"Let's walk right around the edge of our land that's nearest the road. They certainly wouldn't have run into the field and dumped the clothes in the open," suggested Damien.

"We may as well do that now," said Alexander.

The two men walked slowly around the edge of the fields.

"Did you check your copse?" Damien asked.

The de Bruins had a beautiful copse full of native trees and hedging, where small animals lived and birds nested. In Spring, the beautiful dawn chorus can be heard at daybreak.

"Yes, I checked it thoroughly but we may as well walk through it. I even checked the stumps of dead trees."

The two men spent a half an hour rummaging through the dead-wood, nooks and crannies, doing their best not to disturb any wildlife. They were satisfied that there was nothing hidden there.

"Did you check your own little copse?" Alexander asked.

" Well, I strolled through it, but I certainly didn't search it with such thoroughness. Sure, let's do that now, and get it done."

"I didn't realise that this borders onto the Galdstone farm," added Alexander, as they moved between the trees. "It would be very handy to throw or toss something in here. It's only a stones throw from the milking parlour."

They picked up two sticks and searched carefully among the foliage – not a sign of anything.

"What's that over there? "asked Alexander, pointing to a small round wall of stones covered in ivy.

"Oh, that's the old well," answered Damien. "It was dug about a century ago. It's extremcly deep. My father said it was about 350 feet down, but it never produced water – it's a dry well, so it was covered over years ago."

"Who would know that it was here?" Alexander asked.

"I suppose any of the families who've lived here for generations. It was a source of ridicule when it was dug, because it was such a failure, and my grandfather kept digging down, hoping to find water.

He eventually had to give up and another well was dug at the other end of the farm."

The two men walked over to the well. The opening was covered with planks of wood. When they looked closely, they could see that one plank had been moved, as the ivy was disturbed. When they tried to shift the plank they realised that it was loose.

"Someone has moved this recently," said Alexander. "No one would have noticed, it's so well hidden with the ivy covering it. How deep did you say the well was?"

"About 350 feet," replied Damien. "If anything was thrown in there, it's right at the bottom. Are you going to call Muldoon?"

"There might be nothing to it. I don't want to waste the man's time. We could check ourselves."

"How do you suggest we do that?" asked Damien cynically. "We'd need ropes and harnesses and all that. I suppose you're going to tell me that you know a mountain climber."

"Well, when we were in France, we trained with the Chasseurs Alpins which is the elite mountain infantry force of the French Army – so both Robert King and I are capable of doing this and I believe Robert would be able to get hold of the necessary equipment."

"Well, well, you never cease to amaze me. So the plan is to check this out ourselves and not tell Muldoon. Do you think that he'll be pleased?"

"I suppose he'd be less pleased, if he were to use up a load of manpower and equipment, and it was a false alarm. My plan is to check if there is anything there. If we see something, of course we won't touch it. We can then inform him. However, if there is nothing there, Muldoon won't have wasted police time and we'll say nothing."

Damien wasn't at all sure that this was a good idea, but decided to go along with it. Alexander was the experienced one in these matters.

He wondered would he tell Lydia and made up his mind fairly quickly that keeping secrets from her would not go down well. Anyway, he knew that Monique would be informed. The two men walked back to The Lodge where Alexander made a phone call to the Curragh Camp and asked to be put through to Colonel Robert King.

Sometime later, Damien and Lydia were discussing the plans to check the well. Despite Damien's initial reluctance, having discussed the legalities of it all, they concluded that they were well within their rights to examine their own property. So, it was decided that Colonel King would locate all the equipment necessary, and make the descent into the well the following morning.

At ten a.m. the three men were standing beside the well. Alexander had brought along a strong post, which he hammered into the ground, where they would place a carabiner through which they were able to thread the rope, which would strengthen their hold on the rope as Robert King made his descent, and later ascent. Colonel King was wearing his harness and a helmet which held a torch. They checked all the equipment. Robert King placed the Polaroid instant camera in his chest pocket. They had all decided that it would be best to take photographic evidence, and to use the Polaroid, as they needed to peruse any evidence found immediately.

Robert King climbed over the top of the well. Alexander and Damien had a firm grip of the rope. They slowly allowed the rope to slacken slightly, as Robert began to abseil down the side of the well. The whole manoeuvre did not take very long and was extremely easy compared to other operations in which he had been involved. He did not want to land on the bottom, in case he disturbed whatever evidence was there. The diameter of the well was about 4 feet, so he was able to balance himself about 2 feet from the bottom. He shouted up to the two men to hold the rope steady as he began to take photos. He took the photos one at a time, allowed them the few minutes to develop and then placed them carefully in his pocket. This took patience. Finally, he shouted up to the two men above ground to start pulling him up. He helped them by using his own legs against the wall of the well, to heave himself up. When he arrived at the top, Alexander and Damien grabbed the back of his halter and unceremoniously dragged him over the top and onto the ground.

"Well, was there anything there?" Damien asked with excitement.

"There certainly was – a pair of wellies, gloves, two work overalls – both covered in something, – couldn't see if it was blood, and a number of knives and a wooden knife holder."

Robert King removed his helmet and gloves, took the Polaroids from his pocket and handed them to Alexander, who examined them very carefully.

"I made sure that I didn't step on anything," said Robert.

"That's great work," added Alexander.

The three men inspected the photos, then Alexander produced an envelope from his pocket, in which he placed the evidence.

"Let's get back to The Lodge," he added. "I have to ring Muldoon immediately, so that he can get his forensics team out to the well."

Having made their way through the fields, they reached The Lodge. Damien and Robert went into the kitchen to put on the kettle, as Alexander walked into his office, to make the phone call. He was patched into Muldoons's office immediately.

"Hello, John, Alexander de Bruin here. I have news for you. As you know, I had intended searching every nook and cranny on the properties near to the Galdstone farm. To cut a long story short, we located a dry well on Damien Browne's land. With Damien's permission, Robert King climbed down and located, clothes, knives and wellingtons. He didn't disturb anything but took Polaroids. It really looks like we've located the bloodied clothes."

"I'll be there in half an hour. I want to see those photos."

He hung up the receiver. Alexander returned to the kitchen.

"Well, gents, Muldoon is on his way as well as the forensics team. I think we deserve something stronger than tea after our find. Let's go into the sitting room."

Robert and Damien happily followed their host into the sitting room and threw themselves onto the couch. Alexander poured three glasses of brandy.

"Congratulations on a job well done," he toasted. "We might solve this yet."

The three glasses clinked and the three men sipped their brandy contentedly.

Half an hour later on the dot, there was a loud knock on the front door. Alexander opened it to Muldoon who walked straight past him and into the sitting room.

"This could be the breakthrough we needed," he said. "Where are the photos?"

Muldoon hadn't even greeted the others, such was his enthusiasm. Alexander picked up the Polaroids from the table and handed them to Muldoon.

"Nothing was disturbed, I trust," he added, examining each Polaroid painstakingly.

"No, we took great care not to. Robert went down, stayed about 2 feet above the bottom, took the photos and then we hauled him up," added Damien, keen to get in on the conversation.

"Well, I must say that this is great work, gentlemen. I'm a little confused as to why I wasn't brought in on it immediately."

"We thought about it and just decided to check ourselves first. If there wasn't anything there, it would have been a complete waste of your time."

"It worked out well in the end, I suppose," concluded Muldoon. "And there is no doubt that you can be trusted not to make a mess of things. The forensics team is going straight to your place, Damien, so if you wouldn't mind showing them where to find the well."

Damien took the last swig of his brandy and headed out the front door. He was very much looking forward to telling Lydia all about their find, and watching the forensics team at work.

Back in the sitting room, Muldoon was still looking at the photos.

"I presume you noticed that there are two work overalls in the photos and that there are stains on both, and two pairs of gloves, but only one pair of wellingtons."

"Yes, we noticed that," replied Alexander. "It's impossible to say what these stains are, from the photos."

"I suppose we need not speculate, as the forensics team will ascertain all the facts as soon as they retrieve the evidence from the bottom of the well," answered Muldoon.

"I have to leave you gentlemen," interjected Robert King. "I need to get back to the Curragh Camp, unless I'm required for anything else, Inspector Muldoon."

"No, no," said Muldoon. "And thanks for all your assistance."

"By the way, Alexander," added Muldoon. "We are going to go about our business very discreetly. I don't want to alert our culprit to our find – that is, if it is what we think it is. I've told the forensics team to arrive in an unmarked car and not to draw attention to themselves. The plan is for the young climber to descend the well, extract the evidence as quickly as possible, making sure that the top of the well looks as it did before, and take everything back to the lab for analysis."

"Sounds like a very good plan, John. Whoever is committing these crimes is very dangerous and we certainly don't want to spook them."

The two men walked across the fields to where both Lydia and Damien were waiting. A few minutes later, an unmarked car drove in the driveway of the Old Rectory. Damien led them to the site of the well. Very quickly a young man performed the same manoeuvre as had been performed by Colonel King, a few hours earlier. He emerged from the black hole carrying several evidence bags containing everything that was relevant. They were done and dusted in less than half an hour.

"I'm going back to the station," said Muldoon. "I'll let you know as soon as I hear anything."

Alexander, Lydia and Damien watched as the car drove down the avenue and turned onto the road.

"Well, that was some find," said Damien.

"I'm not sure that it would ever have been found without your knowledge," added Alexander.

Muldoon arrived back in his office 20 minutes later. He sat down at his desk and looked over at his blackboard with all his suspects names.

He was hoping that he would be able to eliminate many of them later on in the week, when all the tests came back.

Sergeant Michael Dunne knocked at his door.

"Come in."

"Good afternoon, Sir, I was just reading through all the questionnaires and reports from the young lads who made a second sweep of Clonee village and Briarstown. There's nothing new – still the couple of houses that are vacant, but there is an explanation for it. We are still hoping that we get some bites from the appeal that you made on radio and television, but nothing yet."

"Is it possible that nobody saw a banged up blue sports car – it's not as if it's a run-of-the-mill car – you'd notice it."

There was a great deal of irritation in his voice. Alexander had said to him that someone always sees something. It may take a while for it to appear, but evidence will pop up to the surface. Well, he was getting a little impatient. He took a deep breath and counted to 50 quietly in his head. When he looked up Michael Dunne was still standing there.

CHAPTER 36

— ✦ —

"KEEP THE FAITH!"

There was a Christening due to be held at the Church of Ireland in Briarstown on Sunday afternoon, so the ladies of the flower club were helping the vicar's wife Mary with the arrangements. The ladies thought that Mrs. Edwards looked very tired, being heavily pregnant at this stage. There were three ladies with Mary, Mrs. Henry, Mrs. Wall and Mrs. Young, all in their early 60s and full of chat.

"How are you feeling, Mary?" asked Mrs. Henry as she moved the flowers around a vase.

"I'm quite well," answered Mary, "but a little tired. It's hard to get any rest with the other children and Jonathan needing my attention as well."

"Take a pew Mary, and just supervise," added Mrs. Henry.

Mary did as she was told and watched the other ladies prepare the vases.

"I hear that poor Heather Galdstone is out of her coma," said Mrs. Young. "She was very lucky to survive that crash. It wasn't an accident you know. It would appear that someone cut the brake lines and tried to kill her."

"I don't know what's happened to our lovely quiet parish," added Mrs. Wall – not to be left out.

"Has the vicar been to see Heather?" Mrs. Young asked.

"No, not yet," answered Mary. "We were planning to go in this evening, Jonathan and I. I have to ring the hospital after this, to check if she's up to having visitors."

"It's an awful business, someone trying to kill a young mother like that," added Mrs. Wall.

"Does anyone else think that it's the husband, John, who did all this?" asked Mrs. Young.

"It's looking very suspicious indeed," interjected Mrs. Henry. "We were all very surprised when they released him. Imagine if he killed his mother, then Mrs. Hannigan and then tried to kill his wife. That makes him a raving lunatic and he's loose in our parish."

"Ladies, please! The police must not have had enough evidence to hold him. Why would he try to kill his wife?" added Mary. "There were enough people who might have wanted Jinny Galdstone out of the way – the amount of hurt she caused so many people, but not poor Mrs. Hannigan and Heather."

The three ladies became silent, knowing full well why Mary Edwards might have liked to have seen an end to Jinny Galdstone. The silence was broken as the vicar entered the church.

"Hello, ladies! You're doing a wonderful job. The church looks absolutely splendid."

"We were just discussing all the mayhem and murder around here and the ladies were espousing their theories," said Mary, wearily.

"Now, now, we should leave all that to the police. Idle speculation doesn't help," added Jonathan. "I need to borrow my wife for a while, as I need her help with something."

Mary pushed herself up off the pew, followed her husband down the aisle and out the door.

"He's a very nice man, but he can be so patronising sometimes," said Mrs. Young.

"Mary is the one who holds everything together there," added Mrs. Wall. "When you think about what that witch Jinny Galdstone tried to do to that family, and muggins didn't even know what was happening to him."

"Mary certainly knew, as did the rest of us," said Mrs. Henry.

Mary and Jonathan Edwards sat at the kitchen table. Mary was reading through a sermon that her husband had written, as she always did.

"This is very good Jonathan. I can't think of any changes that I would like to make. It's empathetic, caring and just the right length."

"Thanks Mary, I really value your opinion. Are you okay? You look very tired. Did the other women annoy you with all their talk of murder?"

"No, not really. I just wish it was all behind us, and that we could forget about Jinny Galdstone and all her poison. I want to get on with our lives."

"Are you up to visiting Heather Galdstone this evening? I can go on my own if you like."

"No, I'd better go with you. Let's just get it over and done with, and remember that Heather is a victim too."

At eight o'clock that evening, Mary and Jonathan drove into the car park of the hospital. They were fortunate to find a parking spot near the entrance. Jonathan helped Mary out of the car and they walked slowly towards the entrance door which automatically opened as they approached. The hospital seemed quiet despite the fact that it was visiting hours. They walked slowly along the white corridor, Mary carrying a lovely bouquet of flowers which she had prepared herself. Suddenly, coming towards them, they saw Clara Galdstone walking at pace, followed closely by her father Adam. As they passed each other, the Edwards stopped to greet them, but Clara stormed past them, looking extremely angry. Adam nodded at them, but kept moving, following his daughter down the corridor and out of sight.

"I wonder what on earth is going on there?" Mary said. "She looks as if she's about to explode."

"God only knows," replied Jonathan.

The couple reached the nurses station where they noticed a young Bean Garda keeping watch. They introduced themselves to the nurse in charge who told them that they were expected and showed them to Heather Galdstone's bed.

Heather was propped up in the bed, two pillows behind her head. There was a drip attached to her arm and a cage underneath the blankets to protect her broken leg. She had black and brown bruising under both eyes, and was holding a tissue in one of her hands.

"Hello!" She said as she saw Mary and Jonathan approaching the bed. "It's good of you to come in to see me."

Her voice was stronger than was expected, given the state of the rest of her body.

"Are you feeling any better?" Mary asked, not knowing really how to begin the conversation.

"You know, Mary, I am feeling a good bit better. I have a lot of injuries, but I'm lucky to be alive. The painkillers are working a treat – so just waiting for the old body to heal," she smiled. "The nurses are fantastic and there's always a guardian angel looking after me, in case someone comes in to finish off the job."

She was looking straight over at the young Bean Garda who in turn smiled back at Heather.

"How are John and the children coping?" Jonathan asked, in his "vicarly" tone of voice.

"The children are fine – they are with my mother for the foreseeable. John isn't too bad, considering he's been in jail, is probably still the prime suspect in two murders and someone has just tried to kill his wife, as well as the dog."

The couple were a little taken aback by Heather's sardonic tone but who could blame her, with everything that had happened to her.

"How are your own children and how are you feeling these days, Mary? You only have a few months left," said Heather, changing her tone of voice to a more kindly one.

"We are all well, thank you Heather. I'm just very tired but as you know it goes with the territory. The ladies from the flower club sent their best wishes. We prepared the church today for a christening which will take place in a few days time."

"We saw Adam and Clara leaving the hospital as we were entering – they didn't stop to chat," added Jonathan.

"I was too tired to see them," answered Heather. "The flowers you brought me are lovely Mary. I adore getting flowers. Monique de Bruin also brought flowers – they really brighten the place up."

Suddenly, Heather winced with pain and put her hand up to the side of her head.

"Are you okay?" Mary asked, "should I call a nurse?"

"No," replied Heather. "I get these waves of pain in my head every so often. They are very severe but pass very quickly. The painkillers don't work for that."

After about a minute, Heather once again relaxed in the bed – the pain had subsided. Mary handed her a glass of water which she sipped slowly.

"Thank you – all better now," she smiled. "You know, I can't remember the accident. I can't even remember getting into the car. The doctors don't know if I'll ever get that part of my memory back – maybe I'm better off. I'm going to be here for weeks, you know. I realise that I should be grateful to be alive, but why should this have happened to me in the first place. It's like there is some sort of a curse on us. Can you explain, Vicar , why all this should happen to one family?"

"I'm sorry Heather, but I have no explanation. I could give you all the clichés, but I know you wouldn't believe them. Bad things happen to good people."

"As has happened to Mrs. Hannigan and yourself," added Mary, cradling her tummy." I'm certain that this will all stop soon. I'm sure that they are going to find whoever is responsible, sooner rather than later. Try not to dwell on this, too much. You need to get better, not just for yourself but for your family."

Mary held Heather's hand and squeezed it gently.

"Keep the faith," she whispered.

Heather closed her eyes and lay back on the pillows. Her breathing became shallower and Mary knew that she was drifting off to sleep. She gave her a few moments, then gently removed her hand from Heather's, mouthed silently "she's asleep", to her husband and both moved quietly away from the bed and towards the nurses station.

"We'll be off now, Heather has dozed off. "She seems exhausted," said Mary to the nurse, sitting behind the desk.

The young Bean Garda nodded and smiled at them.

The Edwards left the ward and strolled slowly and quietly, as if still not wanting to wake Heather, down the corridor towards the exit. The hospital doors opened automatically in front of them and they headed towards their car.

"That was very difficult," said Jonathan.

"Yes, these things are," replied Mary, slowly guiding herself and her bump into the passenger seat. She clipped on her seatbelt, putting the lap part underneath her bump – she found wearing a seatbelt so uncomfortable during pregnancy.

Jonathan jumped into the driver seat, looked at Mary and said, "All set to go home?"

"Yes, Jonathan, let's go home and count our blessings."

CHAPTER 37

—— ✦ ——

THE MISSING WITNESS

Sergeant Michael Dunne entered Muldoon's office with a smile on his face. Inspector Muldoon heard him come in and raised his head from the notes he had been reading.

"You look like the cat that got the cream," said Muldoon.

"You could say that Sir," replied Dunne ."There's been a bit of a development in the case."

"Forensics aren't back, so it can't be that," replied Muldoon. "Put me out of my misery – what have you found out, Michael?"

"As you may recall, when all the reports and questionnaires came back re the night of the hit-and-run, there were a number that couldn't be done, as the officers couldn't gain entry to a few houses. Well, one of the houses belonged to an elderly woman who had passed away a few weeks earlier. The neighbours told our officers that it was unoccupied so we thought no more of it. It seems that the son had spent a few days clearing out the house around the time of the incident, and was in his car that night and may have seen something. He rang the station from Larne in Northern Ireland. He should be here in about three and a half hours."

"Why has it taken him so long to come forward?" Muldoon asked.

"I don't know, Sir, he was calling from a payphone at the ferry terminal so the line wasn't great. He mentioned something about work, and going to drive here to the Garda station straight from Larne, and that he'll explain everything when he arrives."

It took Jimmy Staunton three and a half hours to drive from Larne Ferry Port to Naas Garda Station. When he arrived at reception and introduced himself, he was shown immediately up the stairs and into Inspector Muldoon's office. Muldoon and Dunne were awaiting his arrival with anticipation. They greeted him warmly as he entered the office.

"I'm Inspector Muldoon, this is Sergeant Dunne with whom you spoke on the phone." They shook hands.

"Jimmy Staunton, Sir."

"Please take a seat Mr. Staunton. Sergeant Dunne has informed me that you may have vital evidence regarding the hit-and-run in Clonee Village."

Jimmy Staunton sat down and took a sip of water from the glass which had been placed on the table in front of his chair.

"Perhaps if you could give us a bit of background, leading up to and including what you witnessed that night," said Muldoon encouragingly. "And perhaps explain to us why it has taken you so long to come forward with your statement."

"I work on the oil rigs off the coast of Scotland, Inspector Muldoon," replied Jimmy Staunton. "My family lived in Clonee Village for years. I moved away about 15 years ago to find work. I usually came home about twice a year. My mother died in January, but I had to go back to work after the funeral. We do shift work on the rig. We could be there for six weeks or more if the weather is bad. When I have time off, I usually spend it with my girlfriend in Glasgow."

"So, were you in Clonee the night that Mrs. Hannigan was run over?" asked Muldoon.

"Yes Sir, I had come back to clean out the house a bit. I never met up with any of my old friends or anything. It was a flying visit. Everyone was watching a match that night anyway. I had just locked up the house. I was driving towards the main road when Mrs. Galdstone's MGBGT drove past me. I was a bit surprised to see it, as I had heard that she had been murdered, and everyone in the village knew that she was the only one who drove it. I hadn't really any time to think about it because I had a long drive ahead of me, up to Belfast, you know, to catch the ferry. I was on the rig a day later, and thought no more about it. As I said, I spent my time off with my girlfriend in Glasgow. Then a new fella started on the rig from Dublin, and one night we were on a break in the canteen when he started talking about all the fuss around the two murders in Kildare. I didn't know anything at all about poor Mrs. Hannigan. You get very isolated out on those rigs. He told me that they were looking for witnesses and it dawned on me, that I had seen the car on the night. I had to wait 'til I got off the rig to make the phone call, and that's what I did. I rang as quickly as I could and then came back here as soon as I could get a ferry."

"We are very grateful that you did, Mr. Staunton," said Muldoon.

"I got an awful fright when I saw that car being driven around Clonee – I knew she was dead like – but I was in such a hurry to get to Belfast."

Sergeant Dunne continued to take notes. Inspector Muldoon sat patiently behind his desk, waiting to ask the very pertinent and most important question.

"Did you see who was driving the car Jimmy?"

Muldoon sat upright in his chair, Sergeant Dunne stopped writing for a moment. Both men stared expectantly at their witness.

"Yes, I did indeed Sir," replied Jimmy Staunton.

Later that day the reports from the lab arrived in Muldoon's office. One of the overalls was splattered with Jinny Galdstone's blood. There were also some specks from a different blood group – the murderer must have nicked himself or herself with the blade during the frenzied attack . There was also blood on one of the pairs of gloves. On the second pair of overalls and gloves the technicians found brake fluid. The wellingtons had blood and muck on them as well. But the piece de resistance was the discovery of two fingerprints on the set of steak knives, that had been recovered from the well.

Inspector Muldoon was very pleased with himself as he read through the report again. It was all coming together. Alexander had been right all along – things tend to work out – murderers rarely get away with their crimes. They make a slip up. A witness comes forward who hadn't realised that they had seen something important.
It was time to call out to The Lodge, so that Alexander and he could plan their next move.

CHAPTER 38

THE DENOUEMENT

Alexander and Monique were working in their office at The Lodge, when the telephone rang. It was Inspector Muldoon on the other end, informing Alexander that there had been a major breakthrough in the case. He suggested that he, Muldoon, would call to the de Bruins and give Alexander all the details in person.

"Who was on the phone?" Monique asked, as Alexander replaced the receiver.

"That was John Muldoon. He's on his way here. I believe the case is solved. The treasure trove we found in the well seemingly yielded quite a bit of solid evidence. A witness has also come forward. He's going to explain it all when he arrives."

"Damien will be delighted that he played some part in solving it," smiled Monique. "Has Mrs. Hannigan's murder been solved as well?"

"It appears that the new witness relates to the hit-and-run," replied Alexander.

"Let's hope it's all solved, including whoever tried to kill Heather," continued Monique.

"I always believed that they were all linked," said Alexander.

Monique rose from her desk, and headed towards the kitchen. "I'm going to prepare a few sandwiches for when John Muldoon arrives.

I'm sure you'll have a long meeting to discuss the findings."

Forty minutes later, Inspector Muldoon arrived at The Lodge. Monique showed him into the front office, where she had laid out tea, coffee, sandwiches and cake. Alexander was waiting for him at his desk.

"I'll leave you two gentleman to work," said Monique, as she took her leave.

"Please sit down John," said Alexander. "Help yourself to the refreshments before we begin."

John Muldoon gladly accepted, and poured himself a cup of strong coffee. He hadn't realised how hungry he was, until he saw the array of sandwiches and cake.

"It's all coming together," Muldoon said, as he finished his last bite of cake. "I can't believe it's nearly over. This has been a very difficult case – two murders and an attempted murder in North Kildare. But you were right. The murderer made mistakes and a witness came forward."

Alexander watched John Muldoon as he spoke, and thought that he had aged ten years since all this began. This had taken its toll on his health.

"Well, John, tell me everything that you know now," said Alexander.

Inspector Muldoon explained in detail the findings of the forensics team – the blood stains, the fingerprints – the brake fluid stains. He then related everything that Jimmy Staunton had witnessed, including and most importantly, the fact that he had seen the driver.

"That's it then, we have the culprit," added Alexander.

"I suppose you're not surprised?" Muldoon asked.

"Not really, I've had my suspicions for a long time, but it was finding the proof, and now we have it."

"None of the suspects are aware of what we found in the well and only Michael Dunne and I know anything about the witness. How do you suggest we proceed? Under normal circumstances I would just appear at the door with my warrant and a few men, and make the arrest, but this feels different, there are so many people involved, so many suspects and so many innocents, who deserve an explanation."

"I agree completely," added Alexander. "Perhaps we should gather all the suspects together under the pretext that there has been a development, and we need clarification on certain aspects from them."

"I don't think that we need to bring the Healeys up from Roscommon, but I'll ask if they want to be present," added Muldoon.

"There is a meeting house that's used in the village of Clonee that is probably suitable for what we want. I can organise that," said Alexander.

Muldoon returned to his office in Naas and began to make the phone calls, inviting all those involved to the meeting house at 4pm the following day. Nobody objected, as everyone appeared very keen to put the whole dreadful saga behind them. James Healey, surprisingly, was very enthusiastic to attend, stating that if Muldoon was going to tell people who killed Jinny Galdstone, that he wanted to shake the person's hand. Jimmy Staunton had also agreed to attend as he wished to make a formal identification of the driver he had seen, the night of Mrs. Hannigan's death. Muldoon had left it to de Bruin to ring Liam Hannigan to see if he wished to be present.

The following afternoon, the scene was set. Chairs were arranged in a type of semicircle but a little haphazardly, as this allowed people to sit where they wished, and move chairs around if they preferred. Muldoon had organised for his officers to be discreetly positioned at all the exits and in the hall. Jimmy Stanton was seated at the side of the hall and there was a table with three chairs at the top of the hall, for Muldoon, de Bruin and Sergeant Dunne. People began arriving at 3.50pm. Adam and Clara Galdstone arrived together and sat in the middle. John Galdstone arrived a few minutes later and took a chair at the side of the hall. The rest filed in, each nodding at the others. The vicar and his wife greeted everyone warmly. Liam Hannigan acknowledged Alexander as he took his seat.

"Thank you all for attending this meeting at such short notice," began Muldoon. "As I intimated in my phone calls to you all, there have been some major developments in both murder cases. All of you are directly involved in these cases, in that you are either a victim, a relative of one of the deceased or a suspect. This is a very small community, so everyone became aware of who was being questioned, so we thought it only fair that you be given an explanation about what has transpired. When Jinny Galdstone was murdered in her milking parlour, we were led to believe by her family that she was an upstanding member of the community, was popular and had no enemies. The finger was pointed at Commandant de Bruin, whom you all know by now, as a suspect, because of words between Jinny Galdstone and him, about land leasing. The murder weapon, a steak knife, was located in a ditch outside his property. The murderer obviously knew of the row and decided to divert attention away from themselves and onto Commandant de Bruin. It really didn't take us long to realise that de Bruin had no legitimate motive. Because of his past experience as an intelligence officer in the army, we also enlisted his help in the case. Very quickly, we became aware of the fact that Jinny Goldstone had made many enemies throughout the years. She was involved in very shady dealings which had dreadful consequences for innocent people. Not alone were her business dealings dishonest and caused her victims great hardship, but her personal dealings also caused pain to others. As you know, Commandant de Bruin and I questioned you all. There is no doubt, but you all had motive.

This was a well planned murder. Whoever did this knew that Jinny Galdstone would be in the parlour from around 6.30 am to 8 am. It was a very personal murder, full of revenge and frenzy. However, there were no bloodied clothes to be found during our searches which led us to believe that the murderer had a change of clothes ready, and had a place to dispose of the garments, which had to be covered in Jinny Galdstone's blood. It was convenient that there now was a scapegoat, so the murder weapon was thrown into the ditch near de Bruin's land. We are dealing with a murderer who believes that they are more clever than the police. When Alexander de Bruin was ruled out, we received an anonymous phone call which pointed the finger towards Pippa McHugh. Unfortunately for the murderer Miss McHugh wasn't even in the country at the time and had an airtight alibi. This second attempt at diversion only led us to the conclusion that whoever committed the murder had a great deal of local knowledge and was probably very close to home. Unfortunately, we did not find the evidence to charge the murderer in time before they committed another murder. It was poor Mrs. Hannigan who noticed something amiss. She was on the phone with Mrs. de Bruin when she realised that she knew something of significance. Regrettably she only said "they aren't there," and then rushed away to catch her bingo bus. She never got a chance to explain her suspicions to Mrs. de Bruin, as she was knocked down and killed on her walk to the bus. The murderer obviously knew that she suspected something and had to silence her. Once again, our investigations were stymied – we couldn't find any witnesses. Then low and behold, we received an anonymous letter pointing to John Galdstone and the blue sports car. Both Alexander de Bruin and I found it just rather too convenient. However, because John's gloves were found in the car, the powers that be insisted that he be arrested. He was held in Mountjoy prison until the DPP decided that we did not have enough evidence to charge him. In the intervening time, as you all know, there was an attempt on Heather Galdstone's life. The brake lines were cut and she was nearly killed and is now recovering in hospital. Also, while John was in jail, someone tried to poison Heather's dog. We now know that the same person committed all these crimes. The murderer probably still believes that we haven't found the incriminating clothes and that there still isn't any witness to the hit-and-run in Clonee village. Wrong on both accounts."

Inspector Muldoon took a breath and looked at all the faces that were staring back at him. The innocent were looking at him in anticipation and the guilty party sat upright in her seat, her hands clenched tightly in her lap, her icy blue eyes glaring at him.

"We have found the bloody garments, gloves, wellingtons, and a second set of overalls with brake fluid on them," Muldoon continued." There were two blood types on the clothes – Jinny Galdstone's type AO and the murderer's type O. We know that John Galdstone's blood group is A, so it's not him. Not alone do we have the murderer's blood group but we also found the set of steak knives with two fingerprints. The set of steak knives is very significant in the death of Mrs. Hannigan. She had purchased a set from Newbridge Cutlery the Christmas before last, to give to each of the families that she cleaned for. Mrs Hannigan knew where each of the sets was displayed in each house. She was very proud of her purchase, and noticed when one of the sets was missing. This is what she wanted to relate to Mrs. de Bruin on that fateful night. We can only presume that the murderer noticed Mrs. Hannigan, looking for the set. Isn't that correct Miss Galdstone?"

Clara Galdstone sat very still in her chair. Everyone else stared at her in disbelief.

"I don't know what you're looking at me for, I didn't kill anyone," she said.

"We have your fingerprints, your blood group, and we have a witness to the hit-and-run," answered Muldoon.

"What witness?" she asked, her voice hardening.

"Please stand up, Mr. Staunton," asked Muldoon.

Jimmy Staunton stood up slowly. Everyone's gaze turned towards him.

"Do you see the person who was driving the blue MGBGT the night of the hit-and-run?"

"Yes, I do, it's Clara Galdstone," said Staunton, pointing in the direction of the killer." I got an awful fright when I saw her. I thought it was Jinny Galdstone driving at first, but then I realised that she was dead and that it was the daughter who looks very like her."

"This is ridiculous," Clara screamed, as she stood up and looked around. "I'm out of here."

"There's nowhere for you to go. My men are at the exit - best if you just sit down."

Clara sat down beside her father who was staring at her in confusion and disbelief.

"Why would you do that to your mother? I thought everything was okay between you," whispered Adam.

"Okay?, Nothing was okay. You are a stupid, weak man, who let her rule your life. She ruined my life. She threw me out when I got pregnant. I had no money. I had to leave college. I was going to be an architect. I had a future – but no, I was left in a dingy flat, working as a waitress, with nothing. My mother was a bitch of the highest order. She deserved to be knifed in the heart."

There was an audible gasp from all those present. There was a look of shock on all the faces. Clara glared at her father and then across the room at her brother.

"Why did you set me up?" John Galdstone asked in disbelief.

"You and that stupid wife of yours got everything. Why should you get Briar's Cottage and the land and me and Jack get a renovated shed – how fair is that?" Clara screamed.

"You wanted me to go to prison for life for something I didn't do, and throw Heather and the kids out of their home. You even tried to drive them out by poisoning the poor dog. You really are quite mad. Then you try to kill Heather by cutting the brake lines." John Galdstone shook his head in disbelief and sat back into the chair.

Alexander de Bruin looked over at Liam Hannigan whose eyes were filling with tears. His mouth opened and closed again. He was unable to speak. Alexander knew the question he wanted to ask, so Alexander decided to ask it for him.

"Miss Galdstone, why did you have to murder Mrs. Hannigan?"

Clara Galdstone's features had hardened completely, her lips had tightened, there was a crazed look in her icy blue eyes.

"That interfering busybody was looking for the bloody knives that she had given to my mother. She knew where they were kept and started asking me about them. She wouldn't leave it alone – she kept searching the presses. I knew she was getting suspicious and was going to point the finger at me. I knew then that I'd have to get rid of her. She was always wittering on about her silly bingo nights. The way she left the house at exactly 7.20 pm, a few minutes after her husband left the house for the pub. I knew exactly where to park – where I wouldn't be seen. If only she'd minded her own business."

Liam Hannigan put his head in his hands and wept. Mary Edwards rose from her seat to walk over towards him, to comfort him.

"Think it's time she was removed from here," Alexander whispered to Muldoon.

"Sergeant Dunne, will you please take Miss Galdstone to the police car and drive her to the station. Miss Galdstone, please go with the Sergeant."

Clara Galdstone stood up as Michael Dunne walked in her direction. Her eyes darted from side to side and her breathing became heavy. Muldoon feared that she might try to make a run for it, but she didn't. She was led out quietly and without fuss by Sergeant Dunne. Everyone else still sat silently in their seats, not knowing what to do or say. Alexander made his way over to Liam Hannigan.

"Let's go outside Liam."

Liam stood up slowly and followed Alexander outside, where they breathed in the fresh air. Alexander put his hand on Liam's shoulder and they walked together around the garden behind the meeting house.

"What a wicked girl!" said Liam. "Just like her mother."

An hour later, John Muldoon and Alexander de Bruin were sitting in the living room at The Lodge, sipping a brandy. They were both exhausted but relieved that the case was closed.

"Why do you think she wanted to kill Heather, especially after she found out that John had signed over half the place to his wife?" Muldoon asked.

"For that exact reason, I suppose. She thought if she could get rid of Heather, John would be back on side and she would be able to take over where her mother left off."

"I'm really glad that it wasn't any of those poor people, who were so badly treated by Jinny Goldstone. I would have hated to have had to arrest any of them."

"I don't think that it was in any of their natures to commit such a cold blooded, vicious murder. None of those people are sociopaths. Anyway, when poor Mrs. Hannigan was murdered, there only really remained the Galdstones."

"She must have planned her mother's murder meticulously. The timing was perfect. She had to leave the house when both her son Jack and her father were still sleeping. She brought a change of clothes with her and the whole set of knives. She donned the overalls, gloves and wellingtons, went into the parlour and viciously stabbed her mother. Afterwards, she calmly went out to the barn, changed her clothes, wrapped up the bloody overalls, knives, gloves and wellingtons, made her way to the well, threw the offending items into the well, covered it over, then ran up the road and left the murder weapon, which she had wiped clean, in your ditch to throw suspicion onto you. Back home then, before she was missed, to play her part as the shocked, grieving daughter."

The door to the living room opened. Monique entered. She walked over to the drinks cabinet and poured herself a large sherry.

"Thought I'd join you for a drink. Thank heavens this whole ordeal is over. You must both be so relieved." She sat down on the couch beside her husband.

"I suppose everyone was shocked when the murderer was revealed," she said.

"I think a lot of people thought that it was either John or Adam," replied Muldoon. "It's just difficult to think of a daughter stabbing her mother in that fashion."

"How was poor Liam?" Monique asked.

"As you can imagine, he was in a dreadful state," replied Alexander. "I had a long chat with him afterwards. He's going to need a lot of support."

"She didn't need to kill poor Joan," continued Monique. "I think the missing set of knives could have been dismissed. Clara could have just said that her mother didn't like them, if she had been questioned about them. There were so many sets around."

"Killers become paranoid, seeing and hearing things amplified," suggested Alexander.

"She started covering things up. I also believe that she thought that she was smarter than us all. First of all, she was convinced that we would never look in Damien's well. It wasn't on the Galdstone property. The murder weapon had been found. The second diversion didn't work out for her at all, but she nearly got away with framing John."

"To be fair," added Monique, "you two never fell for that, and luckily neither did the DPP."

"In any case, our witness would have come forward eventually," said Muldoon.

"Talking about our witness, I thought what he said about thinking that it was Jinny Galdstone driving the car – the daughter looking so much like her – was very weird," said Alexander.

"To tell you the truth, it gave me the shivers. When I first went into the parlour, that Tuesday morning, and viewed the body, it was a frightful sight – the long blond hair splayed behind her head, the strands matted with blood – actually blood everywhere and those icy blue eyes staring at the ceiling. I thought of Medusa with writhing snakes for hair. I remember shivering that morning, as if evil was everywhere. I got exactly the same feeling today, as I looked at Clara Galdstone with her long blond hair and blue eyes when she realised that she had been caught."

"You know your Greek mythology, Alexander," said Monique. "Did Medusa have any children?"

"First of all," replied Alexander, "Medusa was the only Gorgon who was mortal and those who gazed into her eyes turned to stone. Fortunately, we haven't turned to stone. The slayer of monsters, Perseus, was able to kill her by cutting off her head. From the blood that spurted from her neck sprung Chrysaor and Pegasus, her sons by Poseidon. She doesn't appear to have had any daughters."

"Well, that's a lovely tale!" added Monique, "but it really doesn't work here as a metaphor. Clara is more like a baby Medusa, she's no Perseus."

"Okay, Okay," added Muldoon, "let's move on from the weird! I'm just grateful that we have the culprit."

"No one told me why she tried to poison our dogs," said Monique.

"That didn't actually come up. She didn't deny poisoning Heather's dog," replied Alexander. "It was probably just badness. Maybe just because she could. Perhaps an attempt to frighten us all."

"I wonder will she just plead guilty and give everyone a break?" Monique asked.

"We have enough evidence to put her away for a very long time," answered Muldoon. "I've told Jimmy Staunton that he can return to Scotland and that I'll contact him if I need him to give evidence in court. It would be better for her own family and certainly for Liam Hannigan and his family, if she did plead guilty."

Two months later, Briarstown has returned to some sort of normality. The hedges and trees are heavy with green lush leaves .The summer flowers are blooming in all the gardens. The children and teenagers are on holidays from school.

The de Bruin children are riding out their ponies every day, and it's once again safe to allow the dogs to chase around the fields.

Mary Edwards has given birth to a healthy baby girl. Heather Galdstone has been released from hospital. Her mother is staying in Briar's Cottage to help out with the children. Jack Galdstone has also moved into Briar's Cottage to be with his cousins. Adam Galdstone is not seen around much and when he is, he portrays a very lonely, fragile figure wracked with pain and guilt. According to Inspector John Muldoon, he is the only person who visits Clara Galdstone in prison.

One morning in late August, the telephone rang at The Lodge.

"Alexander de Bruin, how can I help you?"

"It's John Muldoon here. I have a bit of news from the DPP, regarding Clara Galdstone. It seems that she is now claiming to be not guilty by reason of insanity. She was going to plead guilty but then changed her mind. She is going to have to be assessed by a few psychiatrists. That's disappointing news for everyone concerned. Our psychiatrist is going to see her today and then get back to me," continued Muldoon.

"I can't imagine that this will fly," added Alexander.

"Let's hope not," replied Muldoon. "I'll ring you as soon as I hear anything."

Both men hung up and immediately. Alexander de Bruin headed over to the Old Rectory to discuss the matter with the Brownes. Alexander located Damien in the front paddock.

"Hello there neighbour," greeted Damien, who was repairing one of the fences.

"Hello, Damien, have you a few minutes to chat? I've just had some news from John Muldoon, about Clara's case and I'd like to put some points by you and Lydia, if she's around."

"Lydia is in court today, so I'll have to do you," laughed Damien. "I'll just finish this off and then we'll head inside."

Ten minutes later the two men were seated at the kitchen table.

"How can I help you?" Damien asked.

"Got a phone call, from John Muldoon, as I said. Seemingly Clara Galdstone is going to play the "I'm not guilty, I'm insane" card. Is there any chance that she'll get away with it?"

"A person will be considered legally insane if they were suffering from a mental disorder at the time of the offence and, as a result (a) Did not understand what he or she was doing or (b) Did not know what he or she was doing was wrong or (c) Was unable to not commit the crime. In my humble opinion, Clara Galdstone does not fit into any of these categories. Her solicitor is just going for a "hail Mary". It's a waste of everyone's time."

"I was just thinking about the anguish that poor Liam Hannigan will have to go through if it goes to court," added Alexander.

"I would be very surprised if any psychiatrist goes along with this. The murder of her mother was planned meticulously, down to where she would hide the bloodstained clothes. There were two murders and one attempted murder. Trying to set other people up for the crimes, including her own brother. This wasn't insanity according to the law anyway – it was sheer evil. She's just a sociopath or psychopath – whatever the right word is. I'll eat my hat if she gets away with this, Alexander."

"Let's hope you're right, and I'm sure you are. John Muldoon is ringing me later with news of the report, and I'll certainly let you know about the findings."

John Muldoon rang The Lodge that evening with good news.

"It was as expected," he said. "There is no way in hell that this insanity business will work. She knew well what she was doing. She shows no remorse at all, apart from sorry that she got caught. Our man doesn't believe that there is another psychiatrist in the country who would support her claims, so now we have just to wait for the judges ruling."

"Damien doesn't think that she has a legal leg to stand on," replied Alexander. "I wonder what kind of sentence she'll get?"

They didn't have long to wait for an answer. The following week, the judge in the case threw out the "insanity" plea and so Clara Galdstone pleaded guilty and was given a life sentence for her crimes.

The whole of Briarstown and Clonee Village breathed a sigh of relief, but especially thankful where John Muldoon and Alexander de Bruin. To celebrate the successful collaboration, the de Bruins invited John Muldoon and his wife to Sunday lunch at The Lodge. It was the first time that Alexander had met the long suffering, ever patient Lucy Muldoon, who turned out to be a petite, soft spoken, very intelligent woman. Monique and Lucy got along very well. It transpired that Lucy was a French teacher and so they were able to converse in Monique's native tongue . The two couples had a very enjoyable afternoon and finally the Muldoons left The Lodge at 4 pm. They got into their car and waved goodbye to their hosts.

Muldoon turned the car in the direction of the main road into Naas.

As they neared the Galdstone farm, there was a rope across the road. He brought the car to a halt and waited. The cows were slowly crossing, on their way to the milking parlour.

THE END.

Printed in Great Britain
by Amazon